I0616690

Pel and the Prowler

Also by Mark Hebden

★

PEL AND THE BOMBERS
PEL AND THE PREDATORS
PEL AND THE STAGHOUND
PEL UNDER PRESSURE
DEATH SET TO MUSIC
PEL AND THE FACELESS CORPSE

Pel and the Prowler

MARK HEBDEN

Walker and Company
New York

Copyright © 1985 by Mark Hebden
1986 by Mark Hebden

All rights reserved. No part of this book may be reproduced or transmitted in any
form or by any means, electronic or mechanical, including photocopying, recording
or by any information storage and retrieval system, without permission in writing from
the Publisher.

All the characters and events portrayed in this story are fictitious.

First published in the United States of America in 1986 by the Walker Publishing
Company, Inc.

Library of Congress Cataloging-in-Publication Data

Hebden, Mark, 1916–
    Pel and the prowler.

    I. Title.
PR6058.A6886P467 1986   823'.914   86-13242
ISBN 0-8027-5658-1

Printed in the United States of America

10 9 8 7 6 5 4 3 2 1

Though Burgundians will probably decide they have recognised it – and certainly many of its street names are the same – in fact the city in these pages is intended to be fictitious.

I

The first rays of light were touching the spires of the city's churches – Notre Dame, St. Michel, St. Jean, St. Philibert, Ste. Odile, Sacré Coeur, and all the others – catching the high roofs of the Palais des Ducs and filtering slowly towards the Porte Guillaume and the Place de la Libération. The first cars appeared and the first cyclists began to head towards the university or the Industrial Zone. In the Cimitière des Pejoces an old man in blue overalls hauled a barrow from a wooden shed and set off between the tombs. Under the trees down the Cours Génefal de Gaulle the mist began to disperse as a bus trudged slowly towards the city, trailing a cloud of blue smoke. In the narrow streets in the Rue de Rouen area north of the city centre, the first cafés and bars had opened and early workers were leaning on the zinc counters to take a coffee and rum to combat the chill. It wasn't yet winter but the mornings were already cool enough to demand warm clothing.

Finishing his roll and coffee, the small man in the Bar des Chevaux zipped up his windcheater and limped out of the fug of cigarette smoke. Heading for the small premises he maintained in a yard at the back of the Rue d'Enfer, he moved slowly along the narrow streets of tall narrow-gutted houses. He had been passing down these same streets for thirty years now, never making much money at his work but always managing to live.

As he limped along, people who had passed him at the same time and the same place every day nodded a greeting. Reaching his place of business, he turned into the narrow alley between the houses that led to the yard where his workshop was situated. The entrance to the alley contained a coca-cola bottle, a beer can and the crumpled sheets of an abandoned newspaper that had drifted in on the breeze during the night. He pushed them aside with his foot, irritated at the thoughtlessness of people who could live in what was one of the most beautiful cities in France yet could destroy it with their litter.

It was still dark in the alley and he stopped as he became aware of someone lying in the shadows at the far end. A drunk, he decided. Drunks often chose the alley for a night's sleep and, though they were usually quiet enough and simply heaved themselves to their feet in silence and shuffled off, sometimes they could be argumentative, and then he had to go back to the bar and telephone the police.

Then he realised the figure in the shadows was a woman's and finally it dawned on him that the clothes she was wearing were those of someone he met regularly on his way to and from his work. She must, he decided, have been seeking him, fainted and knocked herself unconscious.

Or been attacked!

His heart thumped suddenly and he looked about him for a sign of an assailant. But the yard at the end of the alley was empty and there was no sign of movement. Then, as he stepped closer and saw the woman's face, his breathing stopped. For a second or two he peered down at her in the increasing daylight, then he turned and bolted, his limp more pronounced than ever as he tried to hurry.

Stepping out of his kitchen door on to the lawn behind his house, Chief Inspector Evariste Clovis Désiré Pel drew a deep breath and decided that life was very good.

It was a thought that had occurred to him a lot lately and he couldn't remember any period in his life when he had felt such a sense of well-being. That sad specimen, Evariste Clovis Désiré Pel, of the Brigade Criminelle of the Police Judiciaire of the French Republic, was a new man. He was married.

It had happened unexpectedly, and just when – being inclined to pessimism by nature – he had begun to think he was entering on a gloomy old age. Now he had moved from the cramped little house he owned in the Rue Martin-de-Noinville into this new house his wife had acquired in the Avenue des Pins in Leu, just outside Fontaine, to the north of the city. Large and furnished with taste, it was expensive enough to give

Pel, who had never been known as a big spender, nightmares until he'd grown used to it.

It had, however, relieved him for ever of the bullying of Madame Routy, his housekeeper. Madame Routy, he had considered, was the only bad cook in a country which boasted of its culinary expertise and for years she had offered him little else but half-cooked casseroles. Addicted to television, she had never been able to tear herself away from it long enough to give her full attention to her duties, and when the new Madame Pel had insisted on taking her over with Pel he had been terrified of what might result. But, since Madame Pel ran a fashionable hairdressing salon in the Rue de la Liberté, which was noted for its ability to charge its customers vast sums of money for the privilege of its attention, he had submitted not unwillingly in the end, and on the very first occasion that Madame Routy had turned her hand to a meal for them, she had surprised him by what she had produced. These days she wore a white linen overall, something she had never done for Pel, and the television she had once watched so avidly was firmly established in the bed-sitting room she occupied at the back of the house, a move which reduced her watching time to off-duty hours only. Why, Pel wondered, had he never thought of that? There were some things, he was beginning to realise – though it troubled him to admit it – that women did better than men. Madame Pel appeared to be a gem beyond price.

He was just struggling – and it *was* a struggle! – to decide whether or not to light a cigarette when the lady herself appeared behind him to call him to breakfast. Studying her across the table, with Madame Routy bobbing subserviently in and out of the kitchen, completely under control, he wondered – because he personally had never been particularly impressed with Evariste Clovis Désiré Pel – just why she had agreed to spend the rest of her days with him. With his hair – what there was of it – lying limply across his skull like skid marks on a wet road, he considered that he resembled a rather bad-tempered terrier. Fortunately, Madame was inclined to be shortsighted without her spectacles and, preferring like many attractive women past their youth to go about half-blind rather than be caught at a disadvantage, she probably didn't always see him quite as clearly as she might. Perhaps, he thought, he could get

3

away with it and she might *never* see him at his worst.

After all she had plenty to put up with, without that. The names he bore were enough on their own to put any normal woman off. As a schoolboy he had always felt the burden of the labels his mother had bestowed on him. Evariste, Clovis or Désiré – none of them entirely un-noteworthy – might have been all right on their own; together they hung in the air like the flags of a battalion on the march. At the very least like blasts from the horn of Roland or a chorus from an opera. They could well, Pel had often thought, be sung on a high C by a soprano built like a rugby forward with a fifty-strong choir in the background. Perhaps his wife felt the same because lately she had taken to addressing her lord and master by his surname alone. At least, there wasn't enough of that to cause problems.

As they finished breakfast, the telephone went. Unlike the one he had used in the Rue Martin-de-Noinville before his marriage, which was black and old and ugly, it went with the furnishings. He made no attempt to answer it. He had just returned after two weeks in Amiens investigating complaints of corruption against a senior police officer there, and was not due in the office until the following day. It had been a pretty clear-cut case but there had been a lot of documentation to go through and Pel had never found Northern France exciting. It was too cold for a start and Pel's blood was like water (since Madame Pel liked a cool room and Pel liked to live parboiled, he could already see cracks in his marriage). It was also barbaric, too near the sea, too near to Belgium and Holland, and finally too far from Burgundy. Anywhere outside the borders of his native province, he felt, left him in danger of falling off the edge of the world into the abyss. It was the attitude of a bigot, he knew, but he had long since accepted he *was* a bigot of the first water and, for his own pleasure, had even founded the Society of Bigots with himself as president, secretary and only member.

Madame Routy put her head round the door. 'It's for you,' she said sharply and Pel knew at once she meant him because when she addressed Madame her tones were full of honey and weighed down with admiration and deference.

It was Darcy, Pel's second-in-command. 'Thought I'd ring, Patron,' he said. 'Have a good break?'

'Yes. Anything happen while I've been away?'

4

'There was a strangling. Day after you left.'

'I read about it in the papers. Any progress?'

'Not at the moment.'

'I'll have a look at it when I come in tomorrow.'

There was a long pause and Pel was suspicious at once. Inspector Daniel Darcy was as modern as the space age and knew exactly what life was about. Normally he sat by the telephone smoking like a chimney – superbly indifferent to the ills it could cause – and smiling with his large even white teeth which enchanted girls wherever he met them. Now, however, his voice was strangely humble – almost pleading.

'Patron, I'd be grateful if you could manage to come in today. The Chief also asked if you'd consider it.'

It was with a smug feeling that the department couldn't get on without him that Pel announced the request to Madame. She didn't complain. She had already learned that Pel concerned with police business was a very different man from the Pel who had nervously wooed and married her. It was something which had curiously endeared him to her. Pel was a split personality, brusque and confident in his professional life but a mass of uncertainties in his private affairs. He had long been in need of someone to manage him and, because she had a feeling she could do it very well, she sensed that the best way to hold him was to give him his freedom when he needed it.

'To tell you the truth,' she said, 'I've been itching to get down to the office to see what sort of mess they've been making of my affairs.'

The way she always put him before her business left Pel surrounded by a warm glow. Affection, love, he could understand; indifference to the making of money took his breath away.

He was in no hurry to put on his saddle but, as if she were eager to be shot of him, Madame Routy appeared, with his hat and briefcase, giving him as she did so the sour look she reserved only for him.

Madame Pel stood on the doorstep as he climbed into his car. The ancient Peugeot, with which he had wooed her, had gone, together with its stinking exhaust, its failing gears, its always dubious petrol pump and the oily doors which had deposited

5

smears of black on everything he wore. It had caused him a great deal of pain to draw out from his bank account the savings he had been putting away for his old age, but since, with a wealthy wife, the prospect of a poverty-stricken old age no longer terrified him, he had felt he could just manage to bear the parting. He had turned the old Peugeot over to Madame and hadn't been in the slightest surprised when she'd promptly changed it for a new one.

The road into town was full of people going to work. One day, he decided, he would have to get to know them. He had always fought shy of friendships, chiefly because he had never felt anyone would want to be friendly with anyone like him, but he was unselfish enough – just! – to accept that Madame might have different ideas.

The sun had got up and he drove with the window open, light of heart for a change and willing to enjoy the day – provided nothing happened to make him change his mind. Burgundy was a generous region. Totally ambiguous, it had no coastline, mountains or rivers to form its boundaries. Even its history – like its art – was an amorphous one and was made up from slices from other regions. Even the Burgundians' favourite description of Burgundians – 'sympathetic, fresh, smiling, colourful, frank' – had been written by a Burgundian, so it couldn't really be trusted. But Burgundy *was* different from the rest of France without any doubt, and had produced men of the spirit of Charles the Bold. It had produced the *'On ne passe pas'* defiance of Verdun, the gallantry of the cadets of Saumur, the courage of Vercengetorix at Alesia, a spirit he felt that Evariste Clovis Désiré Pel possessed in large measure.

As he passed the Ducal Palace, he was as always caught by its magnificence. Rebuilt after the passing of the Valois dukes, it had been finished in 1692. Then the great bronze statue of the King, waiting in Paris for that very day, had set off for its place of honour in front. Unfortunately, after travelling as far as Auxerre, it had stuck there for thirty-three years until the difficulties of establishing it – which included demolishing houses and widening streets – had been overcome, and they had got it erected just in time for the demagogues of the Revolution to use its plinth for their tirades against the monarchy. That, Pel thought cynically, was life all over. Something always

6

happened when you least expected it.

As he breezed into the Hôtel de Police, the man at the desk inside the door looked up and nodded. But he made no comment. Like everybody else in the Hôtel de Police, he had often drawn a great deal of merriment from the disasters of Pel's private life, but he was also wary of the cutting edge of his temper and, having seen Madame Pel, was also like everyone else beginning grudgingly to admit that there must be more to Pel than met the eye.

As he passed the sergeants' room, Pel noticed it was empty except for Sergeants Misset and De Troquereau. Misset appeared to be deeply engrossed in work and didn't look up, but that didn't fool Pel. Behind the file Misset was reading – he probably had a pornographic book. De Troq' was openly reading a newspaper with his feet on his desk and, apart from a glance in Pel's direction, made no concessions whatsoever to his arrival. But that again was completely in character. Expensively educated and an expert in at least three languages, De Troq' was a baron – even if a baron with no estates – and it showed. When he accompanied Pel on a job, his title, in fact, was inclined to produce a drop-on-one-knee attitude that was often useful, because it wasn't a Second Empire creation, which wouldn't have impressed even the servants, but belonged to the Old Régime. The fact that his father had spent everything he possessed didn't alter De Troq's marble imperturbability.

The Chief seemed pleased to have Pel back. He was a big man with a slow manner that hid a quick diplomatic brain. Pel, he felt, was sometimes a pain in the neck with his bad temper and the sharp comments that were always causing complaints to drop on the Chief's desk – chiefly from Judge Brisard, one of the juges d'instruction, who constantly felt that Pel was leaving him out of the investigations he was supposed to be involved in. The Chief had no doubt they were well justified because Brisard was a pain in the neck, too. What was more, Brisard detested Pel but since Pel detested Brisard, it meant everything remained well-balanced and the Chief didn't have to take sides. However, Pel's methods of doing things not only didn't always suit Judge Brisard, they didn't always suit the Chief. But, unlike Judge Brisard, the Chief was shrewd enough to be aware that in Pel he had someone to be cherished because his successes had a habit of reflecting on him, too, and he was careful to ignore the complaints and even at times bite back his own objections.

'You've heard what it's all about?' he asked, as he poured a brandy to go with the coffee he had ordered.

Pel looked up. 'All what's about?' he said.

'There's been a strangling.'

'So I read. When I was in Amiens.'

The Chief frowned. 'Haven't they told you? There's been another. Last night or early this morning. It's just come in. And it's exactly the same as the one twelve days ago. I think we've got a nutter loose in the city. It has all the hallmarks. I'm glad you're back.'

2

As Pel entered his office, Cadet Martin, who helped with the mail, ran errands and fetched beer from the Bar Transvaal when it was needed, stood up. 'I've got the papers, Patron,' he said. Martin went through the newspapers like an editor looking for follow-up stories, ringing in blue anything he thought might be of interest and in red anything he felt Pel ought not to miss. It tended to spoil Pel's enjoyment of his newspaper but there were also occasions when it saved time.

Claudie Darel was going through a file. Neat, dark-haired and looking like Mireille Mathieu, she gave Pel a small uncertain smile that had a suggestion of nervousness about it and he guessed it was because of the murders. Two murders at such a close interval worried everybody.

'Inspector Darcy?' he asked.

'Out of the office, Patron.'

'Scene of this murder that was reported?'

'Yes, Patron.'

'And Misset's been left behind to hang on to the telephone while De Troq's here to drive me to the scene and fill in the details as we go?'

Claudie smiled. 'That's about it, Patron.'

De Troq' was standing in the doorway as Pel finished glancing at the few papers on his desk. As they drove through the city, he handed out what facts he possessed.

'Both the same, Patron,' he said. 'Both girls and both in their early twenties. We think they're the work of the same person.'

'Got the names?'

'Only the first one, Patron. Second one's not yet identified.'

'I left here on the first of the month. If I remember rightly,

9

Number One happened two days later. Right?'

'Right, Patron. Name of Marguerite de Wibaux, aged twenty-one. Student at the University–Faculté des Médecins. Wealthy family. Father of Belgian origin living at Mezières near the Belgian border. Going steady with another student. Good reports on her. Keen worker. Friendly. Moral. Doc Minet said she was a virgin. No political interests. Never involved with demos. The new one came in only a couple of hours ago.'

'Right, let's keep them in order, with the first one first. Where was it?'

'She was found in the entrance of that block of student flats in the Rue Devoin. We've checked it. Including the ground floor, it has three floors, each with two flats – bedroom, living-room, kitchen, bathroom, you know the sort. They're all occupied. She lived on the ground floor and, from the marks that were found, she seems to have been killed within a metre or two of the door of her room. As she entered from the street, the Lab. boys think.'

'And this morning's?'

'In a passage in the Rue d'Enfer. Rue de Rouen area.'

Pel nodded. The Rue de Rouen area was the oldest part of the city, a district of sagging walls, sway-backed roofs and streets noted for their sharp turns, twists and unbelievable narrowness. American tourists in vast American cars, unaware of the perils of parked vans, were constantly getting stuck there as they tried to about-turn, and the owner of one vast Cadillac had even managed to get the nose of his car in a butcher's shop doorway and the stern halfway up a flight of stairs so that it had taken the Police three hours to clear the blockage.

'Who found this one?' he asked.

'Carpenter who has a workshop there. The passage runs between some old apartments to a yard at the back where there are one or two small workshops. The carpenter's shop. A plumber's premises. A small metal foundry. That sort of thing. He was going to work. He's an early starter and he's usually the first one down the passage.'

'Dates?'

'Marguerite de Wibaux on the 3rd. This other one this morning. Twelve days between them.'

'Sexual?'

'No, Patron. Their clothing hadn't been disarranged.'

'Robbery?'

'Apparently not. Handbags appear to be untouched and there was pleny of money. In both cases.'

'Method?'

'Strangled. They'd been garrotted. Doc Minet said De Wibaux was attacked from behind and a loop of rope, probably strong clothes line, thrown over her head. She never knew what happened. I gather the new one's the same.'

Darcy was standing alongside his car in the Rue d'Enfer, speaking on the radio to headquarters. As he saw De Troq's car swing into the curb, he immediately switched off. He offered a packet of Gauloises.

Pel shook his head. 'I'm giving them up.'

'I don't believe it.'

'Well – ' Pel hesitated and finally took one of the cigarettes ' – let's say I'm cutting them down. I've got them down from half a million a day to a hundred thousand. I'm trying now to get them down to fifty thousand.'

'What brought on this rush of blood to the head?'

'Being married,' Pel explained. 'Kissing me must be like kissing an ashtray.'

Darcy managed a laugh but it was strained. 'How did the trip go?'

'He was guilty as hell.' Pel leaned forward. 'Alors,' he said. 'We've been through the formalities. Now let's get down to brass tacks. Out with it. You're worried.'

Darcy shrugged. 'Well, Patron,' he admitted, 'two murders in twelve days aren't enough to panic about these days. In some cities they have them in droves. The way things go, it's a wonder the streets aren't littered with dead. But even though it's a bit unusual here, it still wouldn't have worried me if one had been a strangling and one a stabbing, if one had been a middle-aged shrew who nagged her husband and the other had been in the drugs game. But it wasn't that way, Patron. They were both killed in exactly the same way and both were decent girls. The people who knew them seem to have nothing but good to say about them.'

'Anybody seen near them?'

'Nobody, Patron. You know this area. It's full of old yards

and alleyways. He could disappear down one of them easily.'

'De Wibaux. Have we still got her?'

'In the morgue, Patron.'

'And the new one?'

Darcy nodded his head towards a passage across the road. 'Down there.'

Above the girl's head, scrawled crudely on the crumbling brick of the old wall, as if by a sharp stone, was the date, 1940.

'What's that?' Pel asked.

'I don't know, Patron,' Darcy admitted. He jerked his head at the girl. 'I can't see what it has to do with her. She can't be old enough to know much about that date. Perhaps some kids were in here fooling about.'

'So why 1940?'

'Some date they'd heard perhaps. You know what kids are when they're talking together. It might not mean anything at all. In fact, it's crude enough to be 1840 – or even 1949. The figures look pretty scratchy.'

'Or,' Pel suggested, 'as if they were done by a murderer in a hurry.'

He turned to the girl. Her hair was curving about her face in a wide sweep along the grubby paving stones. She was quite small and was wearing a uniform under her coat. She must once have been pretty, though her face was now the suffused puce of someone who had died for want of air. The eyes were bulging and on her cheek was a livid mark, not deep, but deep enough for the blood to well up and congeal in small hard blobs.

'What's that?'

'I wish I knew,' Darcy said. 'It didn't get there by accident – when she fell to the ground or anything like that. It was done deliberately with a sharp, pointed instrument – probably a knife – after she was dead. That's what worries me. That's why I think we have a nutter. It seems to be a trade mark. There was one like it on the other girl, too.'

'What is it?'

They bent together and peered at the dead girl's face. There were what appeared to be three shallow cuts, two upright ones joined by a third across the middle.

'It looks like an H,' Pel said.

'Or a W.'

'Signature?'

'That's what it looks like.'

'Know anything about her yet?'

'She's Bernadette Hamon. Nurse. She's a widow. Aged twenty-six. Address, Apartment 2, 41 Rue Philomêne. It's just round the corner.'

'Hamon.' Pel frowned. 'Might it be the initial letter of her name?'

At the back of the yard the wall had partly collapsed, with a gap in it which left an opening two metres wide which fell almost to the brick surface of the yard. Putting his head through, Pel found he was looking into a yard in the next street.

'Escape route,' he said. 'He left that way, I'll bet.'

The place was swarming with policemen, both uniformed and plain clothes. In the yard, in the alley, and in the street men were on their hands and knees, going over every square centimetre for anything that might give a clue to the identity of the killer. A policeman was marking the dead girl's position. Another was making drawings and two more were manoeuvring cameras and lights to get pictures. Doctor Minet, who was bending over the body, looked up as he saw Pel.

'Same as the last one,' he said. He indicated the livid weal round the throat. 'Rope. You can see the pattern quite clearly on the neck. There are also bruises behind the neck to show where his fists gripped it and pulled it tight.' He shook his head and sighed. He was a small, plump, kindly man who loved his fellow human beings, so that death – especially the death of someone young – always upset him a little.

'When did it happen?' Pel asked.

'Last night,' Darcy said. 'She worked at the Children's Hospital and was on duty there yesterday afternoon and evening. She finished later than usual because there was an emergency, then she stayed behind to take a cup of coffee and a sandwich at the canteen. She chatted for about an hour then collected her things and drove home.'

'That would be about right,' Minet agreed. 'Some time just before midnight.'

As they talked, Sergeant Nosjean approached. Jean-Luc

Nosjean had arrived on Pel's squad some years before, more worried about his expenses than his duties, but, because he was keen, shrewd and imaginative, he was now running the sergeants' room and taking precedence over more senior men like Lagé and Misset. With his dark, intelligent eyes and thin face, he looked a little like Napoleon on the bridge at Lodi. He offered a sheet of paper. 'List of what we found on her, Patron,' he said.

Pel glanced at it. Driver's licence. Banker's card. Bank book showing that she had two thousand francs to her account. Packet of *Weekend* cigarettes. Book of matches. Comb. Forty-five francs, twenty centimes in notes and coins. Small plastic packet of paper handkerchieves. Ball-point pen. Holiday brochure with the price for two persons at a hotel in Corsica circled in ink.

'We think she drove home and parked her car round the corner there,' Darcy said. 'There's no space where she lives and there's a type round the corner who lets her leave it behind his house.'

'Got his name?'

'Robert Josset. We'll check him. She paid him, of course. She seems to have been walking along here towards her apartment when it happened.'

'Anything to connect this with the De Wibaux girl, apart from the mark on the cheek?'

'Same method, Patron. Roughly same area, too. Within a couple of kilometres of each other.'

'Got the type who found her?'

Darcy gestured to the passage. 'Through there. Name of Jacques Charier. He's in his workshop.'

Charier was a small man with a crippled foot. His clothes were engrained with sawdust, and he was sitting on a stool alongside a bench carrying a vise and carpenter's tools. He stood up nervously as they entered.

'I didn't do it,' he said. 'I swear I didn't.'

It had always been Pel's firm belief that noisy protestations of innocence usually meant guilt. 'I swear on my mother's grave' meant a fear of being found out, and 'On the life of my unborn child' meant not only a fear of being found out but of being found out at once. This one was different.

'Nobody's said you did,' he said gently, gesturing to the carpenter to sit down. As he did so, Darcy pushed forward another stool and Pel lowered himself on to it. 'Just tell us what happened.'

Charier gestured helplessly. 'I knew her,' he said. 'I often saw her when she'd been on night duty. I even met her once or twice in the Bar des Chevaux round the corner. Sometimes she stopped there on the way home in the morning to have a cup of coffee and a croissant. To save preparing it, she said. So she could roll straight into bed. Everybody in there knew her. She's at the Children's Hospital. I've known her ever since she came to live here. I live in the Rue Manatour, three streets away, and I usually stop in the bar on my way to work. My wife's dead, and I can't be bothered to make coffee at that time in the morning either.'

After a few more questions, they took him back into the alleyway. He kept his eyes averted from the corpse. Pel indicated the number on the wall.

'Seen that before?' he asked.

Charier shook his head. 'No. At least, I've never noticed it.'

'Was it there yesterday, do you think?'

'I don't think so. But I'm not certain. I think I'd have noticed it, but I'm not sure. It's only scratched on, isn't it, and it's not very clear.'

His eyes finally fell on the dead girl and, as he stopped, Pel waved him on.

'She was a nice girl,' he said in a choking voice. 'Always smiled at me. Full of life but not pushing. Nothing like that. She was just – well, nice. We said good morning. Sometimes we talked.'

'What about?'

'Well, *I* hadn't much to talk about but she told me she was going to Corsica for her holidays.'

'Who with?'

'Her boyfriend, I suppose.'

'She'd got one?'

'Oh, yes. It was quite recent. She was knocked over when her husband died. It was leukaemia. Six months after she married. But she was brave. She didn't let go and gradually she came round. Lately, she'd begun to come to life again and she told me she'd met someone. I was glad for her.'

'Know his name?'

'Yes. She told me. Bréhard. René Bréhard. He's a doctor at the Hospital. I think she was hoping to get married again.'

'What sort of relationship was it?'

Charier looked blank and Darcy enlightened him. 'Were they living together?'

'Oh, no!' Charier seemed shocked.

'Did she bring him home?'

'I shouldn't think so but I don't know. She didn't seem the type.'

'And when you found her?'

'I just turned into the passage as I usually did. It'd be about seven-thirty. That sort of time. I leave home at seven, have a coffee and a roll and a glance at the paper at the bar, then come on here. It takes about half an hour. I almost trod on her. She was right there, lying on the ground. She could have been sleeping. Her coat was open a bit so that I could see she was in uniform and I guessed she must have been coming off duty when it happened.'

'Did you touch her?'

'No. I thought at first she'd fainted or something – you know these young girls; they slim a lot. But then I saw her face and went straight back to the bar to telephone. Did I do it right?'

'You did it exactly right,' Pel said. 'We might not have to bother you again.'

Charier shook his head. 'It'll not be the same without her,' he said.

No, Pel thought. It never was.

3

The plumber and the metalworker who occupied the other two small premises in the yard were being interviewed by Nosjean, and Darcy had got his men enquiring in shops, houses and offices in the neighbouring streets and around Bernadette Hamon's flat, and acquiring a list of the regulars at the Bar des Chevaux who knew her. She had been seen by three different people going to work the day before but by none on her way home.

Standing by the car as the reports came in, Pel was fighting not to light a cigarette.

'You'll never do it, Patron,' Darcy said.

'I might.'

'You'll get fat.'

'I'll do exercises.'

Darcy couldn't see it happening. Pel's idea of exercise wouldn't have made a centenarian pant.

Some time in the early afternoon they realised they'd had nothing to eat and headed for the nearest bar for a beer and sandwich. They were joined there by Judge Polverari, the juge d'instruction, who was paying a visit to the scene of the crime. He was a small stout man who had married a wealthy wife and liked occasionally to invite Pel to lunch to hear his observations on their common enemy, Judge Brisard. It pleased Pel that now he was married himself he might be able to return the compliment.

Later they headed for the Hospital to see the dead girl's fiancé, Doctor Bréhard. Someone had just informed him what had happened and he was sitting in the doctors' room, a glass of brandy in front of him, staring at the floor.

'How did it happen?' he asked as Pel appeared with Darcy.

When they told him, Bréhard, who looked about sixteen, thin, hatchet-faced and dark, put his face in his hands and sobbed.

'Has she any relations in the city?' Darcy managed to put the question, but all he got was a shake of the head.

It seemed Bréhard wasn't going to be much help for a while and they left him in the hands of one of the other doctors. Outside, they were met by a third doctor, a brisk young man called Padiou who led them down the corridor to answer their questions. As far as he knew, Bernadette Hamon had no relations. She came from Arles but her parents were dead and her only other relation was a sister in America.

'Think he'll be able to identify her?' Darcy asked, jerking his head at the door of the doctors' room where they could still hear Bréhard's sobs.

Padiou shook his head. 'I think he'll take some time to get over it.' He held up two fingers alongside each other. 'They were like that. Would you like me to do it?'

'It would be a help.'

From Padiou they learned that Doctor Bréhard had been in his room asleep at the time of the crime. Or at least, that was what Padiou supposed. 'Like all housemen in hospitals,' he said, 'we work overlong hours. When he finished he staggered off to his room and, I suppose, went straight to sleep. It's the sort of thing that happens. I can vouch for that. It's the sort of thing I do – regularly.'

'The date 1940 mean anything to him, do you think?'

Padiou looked puzzled. 'Shouldn't think so. He wasn't even a gleam in his mother's eye at that time. In fact, I'd imagine even she was still at school. Is it significant?'

'It might be.' Pel looked about him. 'They were thinking of getting married, I understand. Had they lived together?'

'No.'

'Slept together?'

Padiou hesitated. 'Well, you know how it is.'

'No, I don't. Inform me.'

'Well, since the Pill, nobody worries much about that sort of thing. A lot of girls sleep around. Some sleep with their boyfriends when they feel like it. Some couples don't really sleep together, but occasionally they slip. There aren't many who never do.'

'And these two?'

'Occasionally they slipped.'

'How do you know about this? Did Bréhard boast about it?'

'Name of God, no! As a matter of fact, I don't really know. I'm just assuming from the way they occasionally disappeared at parties. The way they went off together. That sort of thing. I may be quite wrong, of course.'

'Why might you be quite wrong?'

Padiou shrugged. 'Well, Bernadette always had plenty of spirit.'

'What sort of spirit?'

'Well, she wasn't cheap. Don't get me wrong. But she liked to laugh, and why not? If there was a party, you could rely on her to make it go. But that's all. She enjoyed company.'

'Men's company?'

'Of course. And again, why not? But after she met René Bréhard, she belonged to him. It was clear to everybody. It didn't change her but it was obvious she wasn't interested in any other man.'

'Before this meeting of her and Bréhard, had *you* ever – ?'

'With Bernadette?' Padiou looked shocked. 'Never.'

'Did you try?'

Padiou smiled. 'You're not accusing me, are you?'

'I'm merely trying to find out.'

'Then, yes, I tried. A long time ago. But she wasn't having any and I didn't push the matter. If I'm given a firm no, that's it. Most men are the same.'

Returning to the office, Darcy produced the report on the De Wibaux killing.

'She was found by a German student who has a room in the same house. Name of Wolfgang Schwendermann. He's here on some sort of scholarship. He got up early to go jogging and when he came back he went to the broom cupboard because it was his day to sweep the stairs – they take turns, it seems – and found her there. We decided she'd been placed there after she'd been killed. Schwendermann called the Police straight away.'

'Time?'

'Doc Minet thinks she was killed somewhere between 11.p.m. and 1.a.m. but he can't be more exact. The girl who shared a flat with her says she hadn't arrived home when she herself fell asleep and the next morning she was awakened by the noise in the hall when the body was found.' Darcy frowned. 'There's one curious thing, Patron. It isn't in the report because it doesn't seem to have any connection, but you ought to know. At five minutes after midnight someone rang the Hôtel de Police. The man on the switchboard logged the message so the time's exact. There was some muttering he couldn't distinguish, then the words "*Les Français maudits*". Then he rang off.'

'"The cursed French?" That all?'

'That's all, Patron. It might not mean a damn' thing, of course, because there are always nutters ringing up and abusing us. Types we've sent down. Types we've leaned on. Relations of types we've sent down or leaned on. It happens all the time. But it seemed curious that it should happen around the time when the De Wibaux girl was killed, so I haven't forgotten it.'

'Nothing to identify the caller?'

'Nothing. The words were just distinguishable. But it was from a callbox, the man on the board said. We can't tell which, of course, but he did hear a church bell chime just before the call ended. The clock must have been wrong, though, because he had the time exactly. Midnight plus five minutes.'

Darcy laid an extra folder down – 'It's all in there, Patron, just in case' – and produced the belongings of the dead girl. They seemed almost identical to those of Bernadette Hamon. A little make-up. A few paper handkerchieves. A crumpled pack of cigarettes and a lighter. A paperback. Rather more money – two hundred and twenty francs, fifty-seven centimes. The rest might almost have come from Bernadette Hamon's handbag. The only difference was that this time there was a letter. It was addressed to Marguerite de Wibaux and was clearly a love letter. Or at least, it was a suggestive letter masquerading as a love letter. It was signed with a single initial, F.

'Who's this F?' Pel asked.

'Guy who claims to be her fiancé,' Darcy said. 'Name of Frédéric Hélin. Another student. Post-graduate this time. Big guy. Studying European languages. Penniless and on a grant like the rest of them.'

'Seen him?'

'Yes.'

'What do you think?'

'Wouldn't trust him as far as I could throw a grand piano.'

'Could he have done it?'

'He has an alibi. He was out drinking with his pals. All post graduates. All on grants. There are three of them to swear for him. Names: Aloïs Hayn, Jean-Pierre Jenet, Hubert Detoc.'

'Can we believe them?'

'I think we've got to believe *three* of them, Patron.'

'We'd better go and see him. But first let's have a look at the girl herself.'

On the dead cheek were the same deep cuts, though this time the uprights were not parallel but drew together at the bottom and the cross stroke was uneven.

'What's he up to?' Pel asked.

'Branding them? Showing his mark? Didn't the Ripper in London at the end of the last century do that?'

'*His* brand mark was more grisly than this. And *they* were all prostitutes. This one looks like a W and her name's De Wibaux.'

'If he was indicating her name,' Darcy pointed out, 'then he must have known her. And if the other was an H then it means he knew the Hamon girl too.'

'We'd better look for mutual acquaintances. Has she been formally identified?'

'Yes. The parents are asking for the body. She seems to have been popular but that might be because she had a car and more money than most students. Father's a successful doctor, which was why *she* was studying medicine, I suppose. I gather she was also due to inherit money from an aunt. She shared a flat with another girl. In that house in the Rue Devoin with the mansard roof that looks a bit like a Chinese pagoda. The rooms have been made into bed-sitters. She was surrounded by students. They had occasional parties and drinks. I expect they slipped into bed together occasionally – but no worse and no better than any others. If anything, better because I gather this one didn't. Hélin – a Belgian from Chimay, just over the border from Mezières, by the way, which is probably how they came together – admits he was keen but she wouldn't hear of it. I think it annoyed him.'

'Is he available?'

Darcy looked at his watch. 'He'll be in the Sputnik Bar near the Faculté des Langues about now. He seems to go there most days.'

'How about this type who found her? Wolfgang Schwendermann, the German. Is it possible to speak to him?'

'Oh, yes. He speaks French quite well. I've seen him twice already. Seems straightforward. Doesn't drink. Very earnest. Hard worker. Doesn't go around with other students much. Prefers to study. Locks himself in so he can't be disturbed. He has a flat on the top floor of 69, Rue Devoin. The De Wibaux girl shared one on the ground floor.'

'Right.' Pel tossed away his cigarette and tried to fight off the need to light a fresh one. 'While everybody's busy here, let's have a look at this place in the Rue Devoin. If the two murders are connected – and it seems they might be – we'll tackle the De Wibaux one first. It might produce pointers leading to this new one.'

As Darcy had said, Number 69, Rue Devoin *did* look a little like a Chinese pagoda. It had a mansard roof into which windows had been set, and the ground floor was wider than the rest of the building so that a small slate roof jutted out above it on either side. The first floor windows lay just above them and the whole building had the look of a rather battered two-tiered wedding cake. It had been built at the turn of the century when the district had been more genteel, but now it had a shabby cramped look with a narrow driveway leading to a yard at the back where what had probably been a coach-house and stable alongside a low rear wall had been changed into a garage and a shelter for two or three mopeds.

'The De Wibaux girl kept her car there,' Darcy said. 'Yellow Dyane. We've got it down at the back of headquarters. The Fingerprint and Lab. boys have been over it. We have their report.'

There was also a lock-up brick-built shed which, judging by the pots of colour wash, paint, step ladders and the drum of white spirit that they could see through the window, had been let to a painter and decorator for the storage of his equipment.

'Who does this stuff belong to?' Pel asked.

'Type called Roussel,' Darcy said. 'Self-employed. Does odd jobs. Pays rent to the owner of the house.'

'And *his* name?'

'Normand. Lucien Normand. The students pay for their rooms through the university and the university pays Normand. The university's responsible for damage, repairs and so on. We checked both Normand and Roussel and we've had a man watching the place ever since De Wibaux was killed.'

Wolfgang Schwendermann's rooms were on the top floor. There was no concierge and the stairs had an unswept neglected look. Schwendermann was out and they found themselves enquiring at the room directly below. The door carried a chalked sign '*Save the franc. Burn a bank for Christmas*', and the occupant was a dark-skinned strong-looking youngster whom they found clad in track suit trousers and a blue T-shirt bearing the deathless phrase, *Le Jogging*. He was sweating to a blaring radio over a set of weight-lifter's weights and seemed to have recovered remarkably well from having a flat-mate murdered on his doorstep.

'Just getting a bit trimmed up,' he explained. 'Have to keep in shape. It's every man's duty to keep himself looking his best for the girls. It's worth it, too, I find. I don't have much trouble.'

Darcy and Pel exchanged glances.

'Moussia's the name,' the boy went on. 'Nöel Moussia. Expect you'll want to know all about me in view of what happened to Marguerite. Father's an Algerian. Mother born there, too. The Old Man had to bolt from Algiers when De Gaulle and the army made a mess of things there and we became settlers here. *Pieds noirs*. Second-class citizens. After the Old Man served with the North African troops in Italy in 1944, too. He and my mother separated soon after I arrived on the scene. Makes you bitter.' He grinned to indicate how little bitter he was. 'I visited Algeria once to see what I was missing. I decided it wasn't much.'

'Wolfgang Schwendermann,' Pel prompted.

'Wolfi? Never in at this time of day. Have to come at night to catch him. Great worker, Wolfi. Doing European languages. Attends all lectures. Never misses one. Always got his head in a book. If it's not languages, it's architecture. He's nuts about

23

architecture. Wants to be a diplomat. He ought to get a girlfriend, I reckon. They always say you learn a language best in bed.'

'Did you know Marguerite de Wibaux?'

'Of course. We all did.' Moussia was on the floor now, face-down, doing press-ups in a way that made Pel feel ill at the amount of energy they used. 'She was all right. Father has plenty of money. Makes a difference, because most of *us* haven't.'

'How many of you live here?'

'Eight most of the time. Two of the rooms are doubles and shared. The other four are singles. Two boys on each of the two top floors. Four girls on the ground floor. We all have kitchens – at least that's what they're called but they're more like cupboards – and there's a big kitchen at the back of the ground floor we can use if we have a party. Mostly we stack things we don't want in there. Bathroom on each floor, and usually the boys' bathrooms are full of girl because it's obvious one bathroom between four dames isn't half enough. Not bad rooms, though. Some better, but plenty worse. Fireplaces on the first two floors and stoves in the rooms up top. Sometimes we share for studying to save fuel bills.'

'What about the other occupants? Exactly which rooms do they occupy?'

Moussia was now resting on his right hand, his arm and body stiff, and was lifting his left leg up and down. 'Up top, above me,' he said, 'Wolfi Schwendermann. Other side, Louis Sergent. This floor, me and Antonio Aduraz – known as Tonino. He's Spanish. Ground floor, four girls. Below me, Marguerite and the girl she shared with, Annie Joulier, who's Swiss. Across the landing, under Aduraz, Teresa Sangalli, who's Italian, and Marina Lorans. That's the lot.'

'There are a lot of foreigners.'

'This is a good university for languages. Easy to get by train to Germany, Switzerland, Italy, Luxembourg and the Low Countries and with cheap student travel we take full advantage of it. They call this house the United Nations. We like it and we get on.'

Pel had listened quietly without interrupting. Finally he spoke.

'Marguerite de Wibaux was killed in the entrance hall of this house at around 11.30 on the night of the 3rd. Were you in your room at the time?'

'Yes, I was. I hadn't any money so I had to be.'

'Any proof?'

'You can ask Schwendermann. He banged on the floor around that time. He complains about the noise I make exercising.'

'So he was in his room, too.'

'Upstairs the whole time. Heard him moving about and heard his record player belting out. He likes to play Beethoven while he's studying. We all have our methods. I do press-ups with the radio going and the book under my nose.'

'Did you hear anyone come in?'

'No. Though sometimes this place's like the Place de la Concorde with the traffic. People visiting. That sort of thing. We have parties from time to time.'

'At which everybody in the building appears?'

'Not Wolfi.'

'Why not him?'

'Always too busy. Came once but it got a bit lively and one of the girls got sloshed and started taking off her clothes and making a set at him. Some type had spiked her glass of wine. It was a riot. Talk about laugh. Old Wolfi left in a hurry. Embarrassed. An innocent, that one. Told me next day he had too much to do to get involved with that sort of thing. No father. Mother starving. Has to get a good job to support her. Always telling us. You know the song and dance. Mother always telling him never to bring trouble home so he tries not to.'

'How about you?'

Moussia stopped dead. He looked surprised. 'How about me what?'

'Have *you* ever brought trouble home?'

Moussia turned on to his back and tried to touch the floor beyond his head with his toes. His face red, he looked up at Pel from beneath his knees.

'No, I haven't. I'm a good boy. Like Wolfi. Only more intelligent. *We* didn't do it. He heard me and I heard him. Moving about. Radio going. Besides, if he'd gone out I'd have

25

heard him on the stairs. This is an old house and, like the floorboards, they squeak like banshees. No secrets from each other here.' Moussia grinned. 'For instance, I know – and I expect everybody else does – that Annie Joulier sneaks occasionally up to Tonino Aduraz's room. We can tell from the stairs. Mind, they creak less for a girl. He also sometimes slipped down to share her bed when Marguerite was away, and she often was because she could afford it.' The grin came again. 'Some of us are living in sin, though most of us are too tired with studying to get much fun out of it.'

With a last contortion, he climbed to his feet and, looking at his watch, began to fish into a drawer for the blouse of his track suit.

'Ever heard the name Bernadette Hamon?' Pel asked.

Moussia stopped dead and his head jerked up quickly. 'Who's she?'

'A girl.'

'Student?'

'A nurse.'

'Where does she come into it?'

Pel didn't answer and Moussia began struggling into the blouse. 'If you want Wolfi,' he said, 'you'll find him eating in the Amphitryon. Corner table by the door. Like clockwork. Same time, same place every day. Very organised. As for me, must dash. Due to play netball and I'm late.'

Shooting out of the room, he left them feeling as if they'd just come in out of a high wind.

Darcy looked at Pel. 'Think he was involved?' he asked.

Pel drew a deep breath. It felt like the first since they'd met Moussia. 'I shouldn't think he ever had time,' he said.

4

As they'd been told, they found Schwendermann in the Amphitryon, a small restaurant in the Rue Ecaries, frequented by students and university staff. Taking no chances, they had recruited De Troq', who spoke German fluently, but it turned out that he wasn't needed because Schwendermann spoke reasonable French. As Moussia had said he would be, he was sitting at a corner table, a large fat boy with a volume of Racine propped up in front of him. He had finished his meal and was drinking coffee, and he looked up through thick glasses as they stopped at his table.

'Police,' Darcy said, showing his card.

Immediately, the boy rose. The movement was stiff and entirely German but it was awkward and he knocked his coffee flying.

'Mind if we join you?' Pel asked.

Schwendermann was bobbing about, flustered and red-faced, dabbing with his napkin at the cloth. 'Bitte – please – sit down.' The waitress arrived to whip off the cloth and Schwendermann was sweating with embarrassment and confusion as they took their places. 'I expect you have come about that poor girl,' he said. 'Iss very unpleasant.'

'How did you come to find her?'

'I get up most early each morning to go jogging. I am too fat and must lose weight. But iss difficult because running makes me hungry and then I eat more. As I return I bring in the brot – bread – for my breakfast. When I find her iss a good morning. The sun shines. Alles ist in ordnung, I decide. When I come back I go to the broom cupboard to sweep the stairs. But there iss a body. It iss Marguerite.'

27

'Go on.'

'She iss lying in the shadows. I know her at vunce, of course. I see her often on the stairs. I have meet her at parties, you understand. Everyone here in this city iss most friendly.'

'Do you like parties?'

'Yes, sir. Parties are good when you are alone.'

'Go to many?'

'Not now. I am at a party and a girl takes off her clothes. Iss most embarrassing. I think my mother will not approve. So now I stay away.'

'What are you studying?'

'The French language. I become good at it, I think. I wish to know all European languages. But I also read a lot about architecture. There iss much here in this city. Roman. Renaissance. It iss called here the "ville aux beaux clochers". It has many fine buildings, and there are in the libraries drawings and prints from the Middle Ages showing the skyline. Much iss destroyed in the Revolution, of course, but there are maps of the city through the ages. I go next year to Valencia and then perhaps to England. Then I see Spanish architecture and English architecture and much Roman remains.'

'Where do you come from?'

'Siegen in Westphalia. There is not much architecture there. My father was a Lutheran pastor. Iss now dead, though, and the pension my mother receives iss small and I must work hard because she iss poor and I must look after her.'

'These parties you were invited to? Where you met people. Did you ever go with anybody in particular?'

'Please?'

'Marguerite de Wibaux. Did you ever go with her?'

'Oh! No, sir! Never. I don't think she likes me like that. Perhaps because I am fat and wear spectacles. Also it iss Marguerite who takes off her clothes at the party. She apologises the next day but I am much embarrassed.'

'Did you quarrel about it?'

'Oh, no! Afterwards she iss always kind. She speaks nice words when we pass on the stairs.'

'Nice words?'

'Goot morning. Goot evening. That sort of words. Always she iss polite und friendly. Sometimes we talk. But not much.

Just about the weather. Once at a party before this I talked much mit her. About many things.'

'About sex, for instance?'

Schwendermann looked shocked. 'No, sir! Never!'

'Did you ever go to her room?'

'To borrow a cupful of sugar for coffee iss all.'

'Never late at night?'

'Never, sir.'

'Did anybody else?'

'I never see anybody. But I do not look. I am not a spion – how you say? A spy? I am not a spy. I stay in my room and work.'

'Ever see a type called Hélin?'

Schwendermann's eyes narrowed behind his glasses. 'Often I see him in the hall mit Fräulein de Wibaux.'

'In her room?'

Schwendermann shrugged. 'I cannot say I have when I have not.'

Schwendermann led the way towards his flat, wrinkling his nose at the dust on the stairs. 'We take it in turns to sweep them,' he said. 'Sometimes it iss done. Sometimes it iss not. Always I do it when iss my turn. We Germans are very thorough. Unhappily – ' he shrugged ' – others have not been so well brought up, I think. Perhaps that iss why Marguerite is put in the cupboard. So she will not be very quickly found.'

They stopped in the entrance hall. It was wide and dark with a deep recess near the stairs.

'What about the light?'

'Iss one which you must press. A minutière, which shines for a liddle time. Unfortunately, I think it does not work. Iss usually dark. Iss a liddle light comes from the street lamps at night, but I think not much.'

'Where were you when it happened?'

'In my room, Noël Moussia will tell you. He always knows when I am in. He teases me much because I don't run after girls as he does.'

'Did you hear anything?'

'No. But Marguerite's flat is on the ground floor. She iss killed on the ground floor, I think.'

29

'No sound of a struggle? No scream?'

'No, sir. Nothing at all.'

'And you saw no sign of any assailant?'

'No, sir. I think when I find her that he has long since run away. There is nothing to stop him, iss there?'

'What do you know of Moussia?'

'He is sad, I think.'

'Sad?' It seemed a strange description. 'Why?'

'I think it iss because he iss part-Algerian. He has a – how do you say? – an obsession. Nobody else worries about it but it makes him aggressive and silly. I think he iss lonely.' Schwendermann obviously considered himself something of a psychologist. 'This iss why he does exercises all the time. It iss a sort of refuge. Somewhere to hide.'

A thorough search had been made of the hostel at the time of the murder, but Pel decided to have a look round for himself. The back kitchen contained an old cast-iron stove which had once been black-leaded but now showed streaks of rust. The room was filled with trunks, suitcases, two bicycles and numerous cardboard cartons. The kitchen door leading to the backyard was locked and secured by half a dozen screws. There was no chance that the murderer could have slipped in that way. Near the cupboard in the hall stood a bucket containing a floorcloth grey with dirt, a small shovel and a broom almost devoid of bristles.

'Iss for cleaning,' Schwendermann said.

'The Lab. boys went over it thoroughly, Patron,' Darcy said as he unlocked the cupboard. 'He could have hidden in here and waited for her.'

The students' rooms reflected their owners' tastes. Moussia's seemed to be filled entirely with apparatus for developing muscles, Schwendermann's with books, which even rested on top of the cold cast-iron stove whose chimney was pushed through the wall. Aduraz's was knee-deep in pop records. Sergent's interest seemed to be sport.

'We went through the flat the De Wibaux girl shared,' Darcy said. 'We found nothing. She was exactly what she appeared to be. Normal.'

The room was a typical student's room, spartan and devoid of good furniture but relieved by a large window looking out on to the narrow drive. Alongside it was a table carrying the photograph of a distinguished-looking man and woman.

'Parents,' Darcy said. 'He's well known at the Faculté des Médecins and the hospitals here. Gave lectures until recently.'

There was also a blurred picture of a girl with a long-haired man. He had his arm round her and both were smiling broadly.

'That her?'

'That's her. The guy's Hélin.'

Pel sniffed disapprovingly and began to open cupboard doors and drawers. The clothing they contained seemed rather better than the garments the average student wore. In one corner was a space where a single bed had once stood but now it was empty and bare-looking. An attempt had been made to cheer the place up with pictures of film and television stars, plants and piles of cushions. The other downstairs flat across the hall was similar but it had a cramped look, with a third bed jammed in where obviously there wasn't really room for it.

'Annie Joulier's,' Darcy said. 'She moved in with the other two girls after the murder.'

They met the student Sergent in the street as he arrived from the lecture halls and took him back inside to question him. He clearly didn't like the Police but he answered their questions. He had been at a meeting the night of the murder – apparently there were plenty of other students who could vouch for the fact – and had returned home around 11.p.m. and gone straight to his room.

Slowly, they worked through all the occupants of Number 69, asking questions. It wasn't easy because they all had their radios going and they all appeared to be deaf and had the volume turned well up. Like Sergent, they all claimed to be in their rooms. Antonio Aduraz and Annie Joulier, whom they found in Aduraz's room, vouched for each other. They had been in Aduraz's room, listening, they claimed, to jazz. The girl said they'd all been nervous since the murder and that she'd thought of moving to another building, but now she'd left the room she'd shared with Marguerite de Wibaux and moved in with Marina Lorans and Teresa Sangalli she felt safer. Aduraz, a slight boy with grey eyes and a shock of dark hair, clearly didn't like Moussia and he spoke rapidly to De Troq' in Spanish.

'He tried to muscle in with Annie,' he said. 'We're going to get married when we qualify. She's *my* girl.'

'What happened?'

'I punched him on the nose.'

'Wasn't that dangerous? He's bigger than you and does a lot of exercises.'

Aduraz sniffed. 'He's not tough,' he said. 'He just smells strong.'

The girls' attitude to the male students was enlightening. Moussia was a drip. Sergent was comme-ci-comme-ca because, although he was good-looking enough, he wasn't interested in much beyond sport. Aduraz, with those Spanish eyes of his, was a dream. Schwendermann – 'He's all right but not a type to rush into a dark corner with.' Marina Lorans and Teresa Sangalli vouched for each other and Marina confirmed Moussia's comment about the creaking stairs but admitted it *was* possible to sneak up and down if you were careful and kept to the outer edges of the treads. Especially for a girl, and especially if people had their radios on – which they usually had. She confirmed the fact that Annie Joulier sometimes sneaked up to join Aduraz.

'We all knew it,' she admitted.

She herself had heard nothing, though she'd heard Moussia banging about most of the evening. 'Sometimes it sounds as though he's fighting King Kong up there,' she said. 'Sometimes I think it's a pity he doesn't. It would be better than fighting everybody else.'

Pel's ears pricked. *'Does* he fight everybody else?'

'Well, he and Tonino had that fight.'

It seemed that the United Nations wasn't as united as Moussia had made out, because Moussia had also had a scuffle with Sergent.

'Why?' Pel asked.

'Because of Marguerite.'

'I thought she went around with a post-graduate student called Hélin.'

'Before that it was Louis Sergent. I think he liked the fact that she had a car.'

'Is Moussia a troublemaker?'

The girl frowned. 'Not really. Just silly. He does stupid

things.'

'What sort of stupid things?'

'Well, he got Marguerite drunk at a party we had, didn't he? She never drank much as a rule and he put vodka in her glass. Louis wanted to punch him on the nose for that, too, and we threatened to kick him out. He's pathetic really. He just pushes his nose in everywhere. He thinks because he's strong and fit all the girls are going to fling themselves at his feet. He followed me around for a while. Everywhere I went. It was like having a shadow. In the end I told him if he didn't stop it, I'd report him at the university.'

'Has he followed other girls like this?'

'Oh, yes. He followed Marguerite. That was what the fight with Louis Sergent was about. She didn't like him much. Perhaps that's why he fixed her wine. He also followed Teresa. *And* a few others. He just can't pluck up courage to do any more and when people tell him to push off, he says he's not wanted because he's not European. It's not that at all. It's because he's a creep.'

It was late in the day when they found Hélin. He was standing at the zinc in a bar near the Porte Guillaume. He was older than the other students they'd talked to and, as his photograph had shown, wore a great deal more hair than he needed, together with a grubby sweater over patched jeans, down-at-heel shoes and a greasy windcheater. Considering his fiancée had been murdered only a few days before, he didn't seem to be suffering too much. He showed no great willingness to talk.

A juke box was pounding out pop so they persuaded him to sit in Darcy's car where he looked with dislike at Pel. 'I told it all to him,' he said, nodding at Darcy.

Pel studied him coldly, wondering for the thousandth time why it was that decent young women fell for such useless pieces of humanity as Hélin appeared to be. He would never make a good husband. After years of studying people, of that Pel felt quite sure.

'Well,' Pel said. 'Now I'd like you to tell *me*. How long had you been engaged?'

'Too long,' Hélin said. 'It went on and on. She didn't want to get married until she'd finished her examinations. And with a medical student, that's a long time.'

'Didn't you fancy waiting?'

'Would you?'

'Did you argue about it?'

'Sometimes.'

'About anything else?'

'Such as what?'

'Sex.'

Hélin looked from Pel to Darcy and back again. 'I see he's been giving you the grimy details,' he said.

'Some of them. Did you?'

'Wouldn't you? She was an allumeuse, a cock teaser. That's all. She'd get you into a clinch then start fighting you off. You never got anywhere with her.'

'You *wanted* to get somewhere?'

'Of course.'

'I've heard she *wasn't* an allumeuse. That she just wanted to stay – '

'Pure?' Hélin laughed. 'That's old-fashioned these days.'

'She was a virgin,' Darcy said. 'It seems to indicate that her beliefs were very firm. Why didn't you break off the engagement?'

Hélin hedged and Darcy supplied the answer for him. 'Was it because her father had a lot of money and because she was due eventually to inherit more money from her aunt?'

Hélin gave him a sour look. 'It was nothing like that.'

'Where were you the night she was killed?'

'Here. Ask the boys.'

'We will.' Though there wasn't really much point since the boys were obviously prepared to back Hélin's word to the hilt. Just possibly they might be pushed a little later.

'Didn't you see her at all that night?'

'Well – ' Hélin held out his hand and tilted it one way then the other to indicate uncertainty ' – like that. For an hour. In the Bar du Traffic. Near the university.'

'About anything in particular?'

'The usual. She didn't think I paid her enough attention.'

'Perhaps if you had she might have been alive now. Do you know a woman called Bernadette Hamon?'

Hélin's reaction was the same as Moussia's had been. 'Who's

she?'

'A nurse.'

'Am I supposed to have done her in, too?'

'Do you know her?'

'I've never heard of her.'

Pel decided he disliked Hélin as much as Darcy did.

When he'd been returned to his friends, Pel sat back, took out a packet of cigarettes, remembered his decision to give them up, sighed and pushed it away again. 'It'll play hell with your temper, Patron,' Darcy warned.

Pel looked up. 'Could Hélin have done it?' he asked.

'He was with his friends, Patron.'

'Suppose – just suppose – he *weren't* with them. Would he have reason to kill her? It seems unlikely to be over money because he was benefitting from the fact that she had some. Could there have been some other reason?'

'In a temper or something?'

Pel frowned. 'Perhaps he'd been trying to give up smoking, too.'

Darcy frowned. 'Well, he could have gone with her to her flat, hoping to get her into bed and she made it plain that there was nothing doing and he killed her in a temper. It's been known, Patron.'

'And,' Pel ended, *'his* name – like Bernadette Hamon's – begins with an H and his first name is Frédéric. Could those strokes have been an H or a crude F on its side? I think, Daniel, that we should look more closely into Monsieur Frédéric Hélin.'

5

As they left the bar they remembered they hadn't eaten since lunchtime and then only a sandwich and a beer, so Darcy suggested the Hôtel Centrale.

'It's better than the Bar Transvaal,' he said. 'That's got no class. Always full of cops.'

The manager of the hotel, a man called Gau, came forward as they entered. He knew Pel well but he knew Madame Pel better because she attended business functions in the hotel and sometimes even ate luncheons there with clients. He was all for Madame Pel, in fact, because she gave tone to the place, but the Police, well, they were all right when they had to be called to attend to someone who wasn't all he claimed to be, but to have them sitting around drinking could get the place a bad name. Nevertheless, he stopped by their table with a smile, a tall man with a nice line in plump prosperity, and did his stuff with a bottle of wine to go with their food.

As they tucked into it, Darcy admitted his relief at having Pel back. 'It doesn't get any easier,' he admitted.

'It never did,' Pel agreed.

'It's the politicians in the end,' Darcy said. 'They're quick enough to give themselves a rise but when it comes to providing money for the Police they always complain that social services will be neglected. What in God's name are the Police but social services? We spend too much of our time struggling with bad equipment.'

'We always did.'

'When I read of the Americans it makes me spit. They have enough computers to choke them. *We* can't even get new typewriters for the sergeants' room and we're still having trouble with personal radios. The last batch from Electro-ménage just don't work as they should, and Traffic are going spare because they can never call in when there's an emergency.'

Darcy was only working off steam, Pel knew, because the faulty personal radios had been a thorn in their side for a long time now. 'And the Hamon case?' he asked gently.

Darcy sighed. 'Well,' he admitted, 'I've done it all before and I don't think I'm bad at it. But you're better, Patron. You bring it together somehow. I hope it won't keep you from home too much.'

'I suspect the situation's well under control there. What's your set-up?'

'Aimedieu's at the university, and Brochard's gone to Arles where the Hamon girl came from, in case there's anything there. Lagé's covering the bars near the Rue d'Enfer. He did the same job round the Rue Devoin after we found the De Wibaux girl. De Troq's spare man, and Nosjean will be clearing up the old stuff that's still in the book.'

'While Misset's sitting on his fat backside watching the telephone?'

'I don't trust him much, Patron.'

'Neither did I when I had your job.' Pel studied his glass for a moment. 'This Hélin. A likely prospect, do you think?'

'Yes, I do, Patron. But so, I think, is our Algerian friend, Moussia.'

'Only for Marguerite de Wibaux, Daniel. And both he and Hélin say they've never heard of Bernadette Hamon. So there's no connection there, yet it looks as though both jobs were done by the same man.'

They finished their wine and headed for the office where they found Misset in a panic. He looked, in fact, as if, having panicked, he was wondering what came next.

'I've been trying to get hold of you everywhere, Patron,' he panted.

'What's happened?' Darcy asked. 'World War III broken out?'

'Hit and run at Borgny. Old touch found at the side of the road by Uniformed Branch. They reported by telephone because their personal radio –'

'– wasn't working,' Darcy growled. 'Go on.'

'She hasn't been identified yet. De Troq' went out to it.' Misset's fat hands flapped. 'Then this other one came in. Nosjean's gone.'

'Why didn't *you* go?' Pel snapped.

'I was just about due off duty. I have a family, Patron.'

Pel snorted. Misset's family didn't mean a lot to him but they were always a good excuse for wanting to vanish.

'What was it?'

'Rape, Patron.'

Pel and Darcy looked at each other.

'Well, not rape exactly. This bell starts ringing in this house –'

'For the love of God, which house?' Pel rapped. 'Give your report properly. You know how to.'

'Number 15, Rue Charles-Borderay. Home of Louis Abrillard. He runs Plastiques de Bourgogne. I looked him up. He's worth a lot –'

'Get on with your report, man!'

'Yes, Patron. Of course. Well, the bell goes and, as it's the maid's night out, Abrillard himself answers it. He's careful, mind – he told me on the telephone – and he never lets anyone in unless he knows them. Not with all the muggers there are about. He's got one of those spyholes and when he looks through it he sees this girl on the doorstep. She's distressed and crying and her dress is torn. "Let me in," she says. "A man tried to rape me."'

'Another one?' Darcy's eyes flew to Pel's.

Misset's hands flapped. 'Well, he lets her in, full of sympathy and offering to call the police, and she promptly pulls a gun on him.'

'So it wasn't rape. It was armed robbery.'

'Well, yes, it was. Because she then lets in a guy with a suitcase who's waiting just outside out of sight, and they ransack the house. Hold the Abrillards at gunpoint and start to beat up the old lady until the husband tells them where the safe is and gives them the key. Then they hit him over the head with the gun and disappear with all the jewellery and a lot of silver. They must have had a car outside.'

'And you thought of going home?' Pel's voice was like broken

38

glass. 'Why in God's name didn't you go along there at once?'

Misset was full of excuses. 'Well, Nosjean came in. I said I'd been told to stay here.'

'Well, now you've been told to go and help Nosjean.' Darcy snapped. 'Beat it!'

As Misset vanished, Darcy looked at Pel. 'It looks as if it's going to be a busy night, Patron,' he said.

Nosjean's red Renault was outside the door of Number 15, Rue Charles-Borderay. Inside, a doctor was attending to Madame Abrillard's wounds, which, though they looked unpleasant, were only superficial. But there was blood down the front of her dress and she was white with shock and still giving hiccoughing sobs. Abrillard, a short, grey-haired man with a sticking plaster on his head, was talking with Nosjean.

'How can such a thing happen?' he said as Pel and Darcy arrived. 'In the middle of the city? Within reach of the public highway? With buses running past?'

'Unfortunately, Monsieur,' Pel said, 'this is a new trick we haven't struck before. Every time we counter the last one, they think of a new one. We shall counter this one, too, I'm sure, but I'm afraid there'll be another.'

He took Nosjean aside. 'Where was this silver?' he asked quietly.

Nosjean shrugged. 'Displayed in the dining-room and salon, Patron. In full view of the road. Open invitation to somebody to consider ways and means of nicking it. There are no photographs of it.'

'And the girl?'

'Young, Patron. Well-dressed. Medium height. Fair. Blue eyes. Slim with a good figure. The old boy was smart enough to keep his eyes open. She was heavily made up. Lots of eye-black and so on. As a disguise, Abrillard thinks.'

'Would he recognise her again?'

'He thinks so. His wife was too distressed and in some pain.'

'What about the man?'

'Stocking mask. He also had a gun. But I suspect both weapons were probably imitations because, although they hit the Abrillards with them, the wounds aren't the sort of wounds you get from being pistol-whipped. I've got cars scouring the

39

streets and Uniformed Branch's asking in the bars. I've told Misset he's to ask round the antique shops. But you know how that goes. The dishonest owners say nothing and the honest ones are indignant that we should ask.'

'You'd better get the old man down to headquarters and let him look at the files. He might recognise their faces. Though it doesn't sound to me like a professional job. More like someone who's just thought of a new idea. They probably saw it on television even. Still, we might be lucky.'

It was late when Pel arrived home and the house was in darkness. He stopped his car in front of the garage and stood for a moment sniffing the air and catching the smell of pines and grass. It smelled different from the Rue Martin-de-Noinville where he'd lived until recently. The smell there had been of the streets – wet or dusty according to the season – and the warm oil and hot machinery from the traffic and the railway that ran nearby. He wondered why he had never missed the country because he'd been born in a village and hadn't lived in a city until he'd joined the Police.

He tried to resist the urge to light a cigarette but he was tired and succumbed without much of a struggle, to stand by the door, drawing in the smoke and enjoying the silence. Finally, tossing the cigarette away, he went inside. There was no sound so he imagined Madame had gone to bed. As he climbed the stairs, he found his depression over the murders had been lifted a little by the silence of the night.

A light went on. Madame was sitting up in bed, small-framed and, without her spectacles, large-eyed in the subdued glow. 'You're late,' she pointed out. 'I heard you arrive. Why didn't you come straight in? What have you been doing?'

Pel smiled. 'Standing outside,' he said. 'Sniffing the air. It smelled like wine. When I lived in the city I never realised how much I liked living in the country.'

She studied him gravely. 'Was it a difficult day?' she asked softly.

'Yes.'

'Are you tired?'

Pel felt he ought always to be tired, the amount of work he got through, and this time he was. 'Yes,' he said in a pained voice.

'Exhausted.'

She eyed him with a warm affection. She had got to know her Evariste Clovis Désiré better than he realised and she was well aware that what he said wasn't entirely true because he had remarkable reserves of energy. He thrived on crises that put other men flat on their backs and could keep going long after everybody else had come to a full stop. Nevertheless, she was also aware that this time he must be more tired than normally but she also knew that he liked sympathy and even expected it when the occasion was right. She gave it in full measure.

'You must be worn out,' she said, touching his cheek. 'What happened?'

'Murder. Two murders. One the day after I left for Amiens. A new one this morning. They're connected. Both girls. Young girls. Pretty young girls.'

Madame's face twisted into a grimace of unhappiness. 'What a thing to come back to!'

He sat on the bed alongside her and with a sigh unfastened his collar. 'I'm going to be busy for a while, I think,' he said. 'There was also a hit and run and a robbery with violence.'

Her hand touched his and he turned towards her. As he did so the telephone went. In the silence it seemed to shriek at him.

'Holy Mother of God!' Exacerbated by his frustrations, Pel's always lurking temper leapt to the surface at once. 'Now what?' He picked up the telephone alongside the bed. It clattered in his ear for a while. When he replaced it, he was frowning. 'I'm going back,' he said.

'You've only just come home.'

'Doesn't change things. That was Darcy. They've called him in.'

'Can't he handle whatever it was?'

'Probably,' Pel said. 'But I don't think he should have to. They've found another one.'

6

The press were waiting in the hall of the Hôtel de Police when Pel arrived - Sarrazin, the freelance; Henriot, of *Le Bien Public*; Fiabon, of *France Dimanche*; Ducrot, of *Paris Soir*. How they had learned so quickly he couldn't imagine. He had often suspected that Misset, who was always short of money, was their contact, but he'd never been able to prove it.

Aimedieu had been on duty and had called everybody in, and the whole team were there – Nosjean; Misset; Aimedieu with his choirboy's face; Brochard and Debray, the Heavenly Twins, great friends but curiously anonymous with their light colouring; Lacocq and Morell, new recruits from Uniformed Branch; Bardolle, until recently a country cop at Mongy, big as a brewery dray with his enormous shoulders; even Claudie Darel and Cadet Martin. When something big broke, there was no such thing as time off.

'De Troq's out there already with Lagé,' Darcy said.

'Where is it this time?'

'Rue Constance. Cop in a car saw her lying on the pavement, half-in, half-out of a shop doorway near the Church of St. Josephe.'

The St. Josephe area contained many old blocks of houses left over from the last century with a multitude of narrow streets and dark courtyards. Like the Rue de Rouen area, it had a high crime rate, but it was a long way from the Rue d'Enfer and the Rue Devoin. A police car was waiting at the end of the Rue Constance and as they pulled up the man standing alongside it jerked a hand to give direction. A few seconds later they were halting with the squeak of brakes halfway along the street. A policeman was standing by the recessed doorway of an empty shop. The windows were dirty and notices had been pasted to the glass. Opposite was an open space where buildings had been demolished.

'Sous-Brigadier Boucher, sir. We spotted her from the car.'

As he stepped aside, Pel saw a pair of legs and the sheen of nylon stockings. The feet wore high-heeled red shoes, and round the knees was a froth of tawdry lace from an underslip. The woman lay on her back, her hips twisted sideways. She was older than the De Wibaux girl and Nurse Hamon, and her face was heavily made up, but like them she had been strangled with a cord, and on her cheeks, as they bent over, they saw the same hurried cuts.

'Know who she is?'

The policeman nodded. 'Yes, sir. Name of Alice Magueri. She's got an apartment in the Rue Mellier. Known as Alice the Alsatian.'

'Why?'

'She comes from Alsace. Maiden name was Hermann.'

'Respectable women don't get nicknames,' Pel said coldly.

'Oh! Well, she's one of them, sir. On the game.'

'Prostitute?'

Boucher shrugged. 'Not full time. She's married and has a couple of kids just entering their teens. But she's always picking up men. They pay her.'

Drawing Darcy to one side, Pel spoke quietly. 'Name begins with M,' he said. 'Could that mark be an M?'

'It *could*, Patron.'

'Then who in God's name's going round killing women and putting the initial letter of their name on their faces?'

Darcy frowned. 'He'd have to know who they were to do that, Patron, and I don't see how he could know them all. Their handbags are left untouched. Hers is there under the body.'

'Check all known sexual deviates. Rapists, sadists, clothes slashers, exhibitionists. The lot, Daniel. Let's have mental health institutions checked for escapees. Ask at dry cleaners for torn clothes. One of these girls might have grabbed hold of him and torn something before she died. And let's remember the usual one – if it's a psychopath, there'll be nothing odd about him. He'll look exactly like everybody else and won't be foaming at the mouth.' Pel glanced at the sky. 'He *could* be one of those. The moon's high and three-quarters full.'

They all knew of the belief that mentally deranged people

were affected by a full moon. Yet this wasn't a *full* moon and when Marguerite Wibaux had died there must have been almost no moon at all. Pel glanced along the street. He could see Sarrazin arguing furiously with a policeman who was refusing to let him approach. Behind him were the other newsmen.

'Have barriers put up, Daniel,' he said. 'We want nobody to see that mark on her cheek. If that lot get hold of it they'll blow it up into a scare – '

'Which it is, Patron.'

Pel acknowledged the fact. 'But let's not make it worse. We're going to have to tell them something, if only so they can put out a warning to women to watch what they're doing – but we don't want to start a panic, and any mention of mystic marks on the bodies will suggest strange practices – even the supernatural.' He gestured at the newspapermen. 'They'd love that. They'd play it big and use both hands. They'd scare everybody to death. Besides – ' he paused and gestured at the bloody marks ' – this is something we'll want to keep quiet so that anybody who mentions it will have some knowledge of what's happened. Any references in the report are to be only about scratches caused as they fell to the ground. Only *we* know they have some significance.'

'Right, Patron.'

'And, Daniel – as few as possible to see the reports. Understood? Claudie can type them. Above all, keep them from Misset. Just in case.'

Within minutes, the cameramen had arrived and begun setting up their lights, while other men started the usual processes of drawing pictures and marking the position of the body. Tapes were strung up to cover a large area round the doorway and Inspector Nadauld, of Uniformed Branch, arrived with barriers and a van load of men to keep away the spectators who would inevitably arrive in dozens. There were already a few with their heads out of windows, drinking it all in. Pomereu, of Traffic, started setting up diversions, and finally Goriot, who was supposed to co-ordinate all the different branches, appeared, sour-faced and fussy, to organise the paperwork. Leguyader, from the Lab., was directing men on their knees searching for anything that might be a clue. Pel didn't have much hope. There would be no weapon because all that had been used was a short length of something like a clothes line which, like the knife which had marked the woman's cheek, would go into a pocket.

Prélat, the fingerprint man busy on the glass of the window round the recessed doorway, turned. 'Patron. There's something here.'

'Fingerprint?'

'No, Patron. Looks like a message.'

Crudely written on the dusty glass were two words, or, to be exact, the parts of two words – 'Stras-St D Nov 9.'

Pel stared at the dirty glass. '"Stras-St D Nov 9."' He spoke the broken words aloud. 'What do they mean?'

Darcy stared at the smudged letters, too. 'What sort of nut have we got, Patron?' he asked. 'Who writes messages to us? "Nov 9" must be November 9th and that's in a week's time.'

'And "Stras-St D."?'

'A place. "Stras" is probably Strasbourg.'

'And "St D"?'

Darcy fished in the pocket of his car for the street map he always carried. 'Here you are, Patron. It'll be the Boulevard de Strasbourg. Right alongside it's the Ecole St. Dominique. That must be what he means by "Stras-St D". Boulevard Strasbourg-Ecole St. Dominique. It must be the corner there. And something's going to happen there on the 9th.'

'If it is,' Pel said grimly, 'we'll be there.'

As soon as the Medical Examiner, the photographer and other specialists had finished, Pel nodded and the body was removed. Underneath it was the red handbag of which they had been able to see only the corner. After Prélat, of Fingerprints, had dusted it for dabs and photographed it, they took it to the car and emptied the contents on the seat. It was as anonymous as the others. Cigarettes, matches, handkerchief, identity card, little else. Nothing unusual except a slip of paper bearing a name and address.

'Gaspar Magueri, Apart C, 113, Rue de l'Industrie.'

'That her husband?' Pel asked, showing it to Sous-Brigadier Boucher.

'That's him, sir.'

It was three hours before Pel agreed to speak to the newsmen and what he told them was precious little.

'This is three murders in fourteen days, Chief,' Sarrazin pointed out. 'Are they all by the same hand?'

'They might well be,' Pel said cautiously. 'And you people can help a lot by putting out a warning. If it is the same hand, then it'll be as well if women who have to be on the streets late at night have themselves escorted. Housewives shouldn't open their doors unless they know who's outside. And they should watch their children, especially teenage daughters.'

'You think he's a nut, Chief?' Henriot asked.

'I can't tell you that until we have more knowledge, so don't push it too much. We don't want a panic.'

By the time they returned to the Hôtel de Police they had a few more details to go on. Bernadette Hamon had been formally identified by Doctor Padiou, who had also intimated that Doctor Bréhard had recovered a little and was now willing to do all he could to help them. Doc Minet, haggard after a night out of bed, was insistent that the murderer was a man and that he was strong.

'Same rope,' he said. 'Same bruises behind the neck to indicate where his knuckles dug in.'

Prélat, of Fingerprints, had found nothing apart from the message. 'I checked the handbag,' he said. 'The only prints on it are the owner's.'

'What about the window? He must have done it with his finger end. Didn't he leave any dabs?'

'It was done too fast, Patron. You can tell by the way the first stroke of the first letter – the S – runs into it. His finger never stopped. In the same way, it tails off after the 9 at the other end. You don't get dabs from that sort of contact.'

'Nothing round the message?'

'Plenty where people – especially kids – have touched the glass, but nothing that's new. And there's no weapon to check. He took it away with him. He must have been waiting in the darkness and, as she passed, he stepped out with his length of cord and dragged her into the shadows before she could cry out. Then a quick scrawl of a few letters in the dust on the window and he was gone. One minute. That's all it took. In an empty street at night.'

By afternoon they had found Alice Magueri's husband. He was a tall man who worked as a labourer, a man with strong shoulders and big, knotted hands. He had been born Gaspare Magueri just over the border to an Italian father and a French mother and had arrived in France soon afterwards when his father had taken advantage of his marriage to obtain employment in Nice. He had taken out naturalisation papers soon afterwards and the explanation for the slip of paper bearing the name and address came from the fact that Magueri and his wife had separated and he'd failed to keep up her maintenance payments. He had walked out on her three years before and was now living with a woman in the industrial area and she had recently found his address and intended bringing him before the courts.

'I'd have taken the kids, too,' he said. 'But they preferred to stay with her. She'd have had my daughter at the game before long if this hadn't happened.'

It sounded like the usual sad story but Pel wasn't convinced. 'Why did the children prefer to be with her?' he asked. 'Did you beat them?'

'No. Never. I swear on my mother's grave – '

'Did you drink?'

'A little.'

'A lot?'

'Well, sometimes.'

'And when you were drunk did you knock your wife about?'

'Well – I have done.'

'Kids?'

'I have done.'

'What about money? Did you keep them short of money?'

'Never.'

'You like to drink and a labourer doesn't earn that much money. *Did* you keep them short?'

'Well – a bit. Sometimes.'

'So it's no wonder the kids favoured their mother. It was probably thanks to you that she went on the streets and, indirectly, because of that, that she's dead.'

Magueri's jaw hung open. It was clear Pel's logic was beyond him.

47

'Know the Boulevard de Strasbourg-Ecole St. Dominique area?' Pel asked.

Magueri frowned. 'That's up near the university, isn't it?'

'You tell me.'

'Yes, it is. I worked round there once. Near the Military Hospital.'

'November 9th mean anything to you?'

Magueri frowned again. 'That's soon, isn't it?'

'Yes, it is. You anything on your diary for that date?'

'I don't keep a diary.'

'Did you kill your wife?'

Magueri looked indignant. 'Why would I do that?'

'To avoid paying maintenance,' Darcy said. 'It must be difficult keeping two women on one wage. They can be expensive.'

'It wasn't me!'

'Where were you last night?'

'Here.'

'On your own?'

'My wife – well, the woman I'm living with – she works nights. She's a cleaner at Métaux de Bourgogne in the Industrial Zone. She takes the car to get there so I have to stay at home.'

'Anybody come to keep you company?'

'Here?'

'Why not? It's just possible there might be someone else who likes you enough to want to share your company.'

Magueri gave them a sour look. 'I was on my own,' he said.

When the news stories appeared, they came up to all Pel's expectations. *France Soir* had deep headlines: THIRD MURDER. ANOTHER GIRL STRANGLED. *France Dimanche* had: IS IT A LUNATIC? THIRD GIRL MURDERED. *Le Bien Public*, as always, was more restrained: ANOTHER GIRL FOUND DEAD. TWO IN TWO DAYS. Cadet Martin had drawn a circle round them all.

Well, it wasn't too bad. There was a lot of speculation and a lot of digging up of background. Alice Magueri was described as a hard-working housewife parted from her husband –

48

perhaps it wasn't all that far from the truth – and there was a picture of Magueri himself and an interview in which he claimed he still loved his wife. Doubtless *that* was a figment of the imagination of some hard-working journalist a little short on facts. *France Dimanche* carried pictures of 'the heartbroken Doctor Bréhard' and *France Soir* one of Wolfgang Schwendermann, his spectacles gleaming in the light of a flash bulb, looking as if her were blind, clutching his copy of Racine and apparently putting out his hand to ward off the intrusive cameraman. Finally Hélin, all beard and hair and dirty shirt and described as the 'fiancé of Marguerite de Wibaux', had co-operated with a fanciful story of an engagement and a deathless love that had been going on for months – for which he'd doubtless made sure he'd been paid.

Though French journalists were free to comment on any crime they were covering – and usually did – they were often deliberately taken into the confidence of the police and each depended very much on the others. But it gave them freedom to speculate and make suggestions, and sometimes they were wildly wide of the mark. For once, though, nobody had stirred up any panic and they had all printed the warning to women to watch where they went and who they went with, and there was no reference to any mutilations.

The telephone was going all next day, with all the usual helpful people swearing they'd seen the murderer – some even claiming to have seen him at his work – and all the spiteful neighbours eager to accuse someone they didn't like. They all had to be investigated but they all turned out to be false alarms. Though the panic had been contained, the Chief was still far from happy as he called a conference of all the officers and experts concerned.

'We don't want another Boston Strangler loose in *this* city,' he said firmly. 'We want him stopped. And fast. He's the same sort.'

He looked at Nadauld for his comments and the Uniformed Branch inspector sat up.

'I've got every spare man on the streets,' he said, knowing what was in the Chief's mind. You didn't catch murderers, who lurked in shadowed doorways or on the bends of stairs, from inside a police car.

Pomereu, of Traffic, offered to set up road blocks but they decided no useful purpose would be served because they wouldn't find bloodstained clothing or hidden murder weapons. And it was clear the strangler had no intention of fleeing from the city so it was pointless looking for anyone trying to escape. All Pomereu could do was warn his men to watch for anything unusual.

Inspector Goriot had set up headquarters in the gymnasium which had been filled with files, typewriters, telephones, card index systems, and a vast map of the city, on which there were three small red spots – one in the Rue Devoin, one in the Rue d'Enfer, and now one in the Rue Constance.

The Chief looked at Pel.

'Though we know there's a connection,' Pel said, 'it's not yet obvious. The women didn't know each other and each one's friends didn't know the others' friends. There are only two links. The method of death. And one other.'

The Chief didn't ask questions. He knew about the mutilations but understood why Pel preferred to keep those to himself. Though Pomereu, Nadauld and Goriot were all experienced Police officers, it was always possible for something to leak out.

While they were at it they covered everything else that had been happening – the break-ins, the burglaries, the threats, the fights and the frauds. None of these stopped for a murder, though it was true they tended to decrease for a while as the Police investigating the major incident appeared in larger numbers in areas where they were not wanted.

But these crimes were dealt with in bulk, as statistics. The hit and run victim at Borgny had been identified as a Madame Bouchoneau who lived in the city but had been on a visit to her daughter. She was sixty-nine and had apparently just left her daughter to catch a bus home. There was no connection with any other crime and she had been identified by a silver necklace from which hung a small silver medallion bearing the words, 'In case of death, please inform a priest.' The village priest had been out at the time and when he had returned later in the evening, an intense young man with a pale anxious face and glasses, he had been too late to administer the last rites. Murmuring the usual: 'May her soul rest in everlasting peace,' he had hurried to the morgue and given his blessing there. Traffic was handling the case, asking for witnesses and telling garages to keep a look-out for a car with damage to the off front wing commensurate with having struck a pedestrian at speed.

The Abrillards' case was also still in the air. They didn't expect to recover much of the money but there was always a hope they might find the stolen silver in an antique shop. Antique dealers had been warned and their association asked to spread the gospel elsewhere and a possible sighting of the thieves had been made in Vortheau, a village just across the Route Nationale 7, where a bar owner thought they'd eaten sandwiches and drunk a beer in his bar on the day of the robbery.

'At least,' Pel said, 'they're probably still around.'

Things didn't change. They simply grew more so. In the days of horsed highwaymen they could look for their criminals more or less in their own districts. Trains had made crime more wide-ranging, and now, with the aid of motorways and the internal combustion engine, a man committing a felony in Paris in the morning could be in Dijon by afternoon and by evening on the south coast and whooping it up in St. Trop'.

7

Pel's conference, which followed the Chief's, covered a narrower field and was concerned only with the murders.

Claudie Darel had provided coffee for anyone who needed it and they all got in each other's way as they tried to find her a chair where she could sit to take notes. Claudie affected everybody like that. Half the Hôtel de Police was in love with her.

'Same as before.' As they got down to the facts, Doc Minet seemed worn down by the tragedy of death. 'Same suffused face. Multiple ecchymoses of the conjunctivae and the skin. Damage to the cartilages of the larynx and the rings of the trachea. Subpleurel haemorrhages on the lungs. Eyes bulging. Face cyanosed and swollen. In every case, the bruising at the back of the neck indicates he used both hands and the damage to the cartilage in the area of the voice box demonstrates the violence and strength of the attack. He's right-handed, if that's any help, judging by the way the flesh has been creased. He held the rope with his left hand and heaved on it with the right. She had no chance. The rope was deep in the flesh of the neck before she knew what was happening and she obviously would be unable to get her fingers under it to relieve the pressure.'

'Same method in both cases?'

'Same method. A length of rope. They were garrotted.' Doc Minet sighed. 'It wasn't difficult because garrotting's easy. You might be interested to know that the very first cops to be put into uniform wore high collars as a preventative, because they were not very popular and in the narrow alleys of those days it wasn't difficult to slip a rope over the head and pull it tight.'

'It seems it isn't now either,' Darcy growled.

Nosjean had talked at length with every one of the occupants of the flats where Marguerite de Wibaux lived and with the neighbours of Bernadette Hamon and Alice Magueri. Nobody knew anything, not even the students who had virtually lived in Marguerite de Wibaux's pocket. Marguerite de Wibaux had gone out without saying where she was going, something that seemed significant because more than likely she could have been with Fred Hélin, while the fact that her flatmate, Annie Joulier, had been with Aduraz seemed to provide a good opportunity for Hélin to expect to get into her room and into her bed, and a good reason for him to be angry if he didn't.

Several sets of fingerprints had been found on her car – Sergent's and every one of the other girls – but these were smudged and old and were largely overprinted by others which had been identified as Hélin's. Annie Joulier, who had shared a room with her, had said she had had several boyfriends but was not promiscuous and had not been with other men since she had met Hélin. Questioned about where Marguerite de Wibaux could have been on the night of the murder, she could only think she had been with him.

The radio had been pounding out rock music and they had had to persuade her to turn it down as she spoke to them.

'She was upset all day,' she had said. 'Fred was standing her up and I think she went to see him. She wanted to get married and he didn't. I think they quarrelled and she drove around in her car. Or sat in it and wondered what she should do. She'd often wondered if she shouldn't finish it between them.'

It was a different version of the affair from Hélin's.

'Perhaps she told him it was over,' Pel suggested, 'and he was furious because she had money and there were doubtless perks he didn't want to lose.'

'Is it enough for murder, though, Patron?' Darcy asked.

It didn't really seem so. And it certainly didn't explain the other two murders which had obviously been done by the same hand.

Normand, the owner of 69, Rue Devoin, and Roussel, the painter who stored his equipment in the outhouse behind the hostel, had both been checked. Normand had been in Switzerland at the time and Roussel had been watching a film on television in the bosom of his family and had not only been indignant to think he might be a suspect but had even gone so far as to complain that the occupants of the hostel had more than once stolen his paint to do up their rooms.

'Not the girls,' he had admitted. 'It's not the sort of thing girls do. But those other types could. Especially that Moussia. I think he picks the lock. I once found a tin of paint upset.'

Since there was a gap of nearly ten centimetres beneath the door, it was, Brochard suggested, just as likely to have been done by a cat chasing a rat.

It was decided to have everybody in the area of the murder questioned and Goriot was preparing a notice to householders, which was to be posted about the city and given to the newspapers.

'Do you know of any man who was missing during the hours between 10 p.m. and one a.m.?' The dates followed. *'Do you know of any such man who can't explain where he was? You are being appealed to because, though this man might be part of your family, he is a danger to the public and even to you. He might kill again. He is in need of treatment and it is your duty to report him for your sake and for his.'*

Goriot had made it sound as if they just wanted to be helpful, not shove anybody behind bars, but there was no other way of appealing to a family or a wife with suspicions.

Turning to the second murder, that of Bernadette Hamon, they discussed Bréhard and Padiou and the other doctors at the hotel; as well as Charier, and the plumber and the metalworker who shared the yard with him; Josset, the man who had allowed Bernadette Hamon to park her car behind his house, and all her neighbours. Only one of them had looked at all dubious and that was Josset, a fat man with thick spectacles and wet red lips who was known to enjoy picking up girls in bars, even to follow them, but there was no proof of any molestation and you couldn't arrest a man because he'd got wet red lips any more than you could because he'd got a wooden leg.

There wasn't much else, and they could see no connection whatsoever between Magueri and Bernadette Hamon or Marguerite de Wibaux, none between Hélin and Bernadette Hamon or Alice Magueri, none between Moussia and Bernadette Hamon and Alice Magueri, none between Josset and Marguerite de Wibaux or Alice Magueri. That was the thing that baffled them. There *had* to be a connection.

They had drawn a blank with the customers at the Bar des Chevaux, though it had been noticed that Josset was a regular there, as was the plumber and also, curiously, Roussel, the painter, whose equipment was stored at the back of the house in the Rue Devoin where Marguerite de Wibaux had lived.

It was only a small point but they were looking for small points which could provide a common denominator and there didn't appear to be any, except that all three women were dead and all three had cuts on their cheeks. Since the murders had all occurred at night, they could reasonably assume the killer had a daytime job which left him free in the evenings.

'He could be a well-adjusted man working at an ordinary job,' Doc Minet said. 'And still be a psychotic pervert suffering from schizophrenia. Unless he's caught, his obsession will drive him to kill again.'

'One last thing,' Pel said, handing round the report on the muttered telephone call to the police on the night of Marguerite de Wibaux's death, and the photographs of the two crude messages written near the bodies of Bernadette Hamon and Alice Magueri. 'Messages. Received on the dates of the murders. "Les Français maudits," "1940" and "Stras-St D Nov 9," which appears to mean the corner of the Boulevard de Strasbourg and St. Dominic's School on November 9th. Do any of them have any meaning for any of you?'

They didn't, of course. Cryptic messages left by criminals rarely did. Or, at least, not by themselves. Together they might sometimes suggest something. But this time Pel was faced with a row of blank expressions and all he could do was arrange with Darcy and Inspector Nadauld to have a watch kept on the front of the Ecole St. Dominique and the Boulevard de Strasbourg up to and beyond the date of November 9th.

Pel was frowning as the conference broke up, wondering what sort of man the killer was. Normally people killed because they were scared – a disturbed burglar, for instance; even sometimes unintentionally, by hitting someone harder than had been intended. Human beings were an unstable lot who reacted violently to stress.

But these murders had not been by burglars. They weren't

for gain, nor did they appear to be for vengeance. Human beings seemed to have few strong emotions these days, apart from occasional cases of someone having been thrown over by a lover. Which led Pel to sex.

'It's a pity there isn't just *one* gender,' he growled. 'It would mean a lot less murders.'

Darcy managed a smile. 'It would also mean a lot less fun,' he pointed out.

Deep in thought, Pel didn't hear him. Most sex murders, he knew, were because one or the other partner in a marriage was unfaithful. The only other type of sex murders were those committed by deranged people who usually preyed on women or children, and these provide the worst crimes and the saddest type of victim. In many cases even *they* could be avoided because sex deviates usually became known early to the police and usually even had a record. But that didn't prevent psychiatrists declaring them cured as they made their decisions by some social dogma or psychiatric rule, when everybody knew that in psychiatry there were no rules.

They were just about to leave the office when Leguyader of the Lab. appeared with a sheaf of papers. He was making a lot of fuss but Leguyader was always a great one for making a fuss, and it took him ten minutes to explain that all the victims had been killed by a method known as thuggee.

'Knotted cord round the throat,' he said. 'Drawn taut from behind. You'll have heard of thuggee, of course.' Leguyader was a great one for airing his knowledge and it was generally believed in the Hôtel de Police that he spent his evenings reading encyclopedias so that he could trot out the next day what he'd learned in the hope that his colleagues would imagine the knowledge had been stored in his head ever since youth.

'Thugs,' he went on,' were roving bands of fanatical murderers and robbers in central and northern India. Their murders had a religious basis with the victims regarded as sacrifices to the goddess Kali. They operated with dacoits, another form of armed robbers. Their suppression was brought about by a Captain Sleeman of the British Bengal Army. Being British, they made him a general.'

'The British like to reward high principles,' Pel said sarcastically. 'And they're great ones for organising things.

Look at the way they don't arm their Police so they can't shoot people in traffic jams.'

Leguyader glared. Pel returned it tit for tat.

'And *we* don't have any interest in India,' he snapped.

'We *did*,' Leguyader reminded him. 'Until 1748 when the British kicked us out.'

'They're well-known for their bossiness,' Pel agreed. He leaned forward. 'Right then, if he's a thug, do we look for an Indian? Because I'm not aware that we have many here. And why does he cut their faces? Is that a sign of thuggee also? What *about* these mutilations, in fact? Doubtless you've had thoughts on those also?'

Leguyader had and he was in no way put out. 'They look like letters,' he said. 'They were done by a sharp instrument.'

'Scalpel?' Pel was thinking of the doctors involved in the case and the people at the Faculté des Médecins who might have known Marguerite de Wibaux.

'Knife, I'd say,' Doc Minet said. 'Small and pointed. And very sharp. It's impossible to be certain, though, and it *could* have been a scalpel.'

'And what are they? Do they have any significance?'

Leguyader pushed his way in again. 'They seem to be a crude letter,' he said. 'An H, or an M or a W. Even perhaps an N. In three cases it could be the initial letter of the Christian name of the victim. M's the thirteenth letter of the Semitic alphabet, twelfth in the Greek alphabet, eleventh in the Etruscan, twelfth in the Latin and the fourteenth in the early Slavonic. It was used by the Romans to mean a thousand.'

Pel glanced at Darcy, who was trying not to laugh. Why was it Leguyader always liked to make such a song and dance?

Leguyader drew a deep breath. 'W,' he went on. 'The twenty-third of the English alphabet. In the French language it's rarely used. My dictionary gives only thirty-nine words which begin with it and most of them were originally English. The Germans have no sound like the English "w" and we use "ou" as a substitute, while the Spanish use "hu". H: Eighth letter of the English, Semitic, Greek, Etruscan and Latin languages. It's never sounded in France and in Italy it's almost disappeared.'

Pel stared at him. 'And this has some significance?' he asked.

'None that I know of,' Leguyader said. 'But then, unlike your department, my department deals with facts, not imagination.'

As the door closed behind him, Darcy grinned.

Pel didn't return his smile. 'I have better things to do,' he said slowly, 'than to listen to puffed-up twaddle of that sort. He behaves like someone out of *France Soir* which, as we all know, is written for not very bright readers.'

Darcy's grin grew wider but Pel's face was set and his eyes were bleak, and Darcy's smile died. 'Don't let it get you down, Patron,' he urged.

Pel was silent for a while. He was used to violent death. It was something every policeman had to face. Road accidents, collapsed buildings, bombs, were all in their way an obscenity against humanity, to say nothing of the sudden disasters to the flesh which, even if the injuries weren't so horrific, produced much the same sort of shock. But the death of a young girl or a child always seemed twice as brutal, and he sometimes wondered what had caused *them*, of all people, to be picked out. God was supposed to be just, merciful and all-seeing and sometimes it didn't make sense that He allowed the innocent to die when there were plenty others who could well be spared.

'Three people are dead,' he said at last. 'None of them old. One of them very young.' He paused and fumbled awkwardly to light a cigarette. 'And unfortunately,' he ended, 'I suspect we haven't finished yet. I think there'll be another one before long.'

8

He was right, of course, It was an instinct that came from many years as a policeman and a knowledge of criminals, perverts and sexual deviates which told him that, once started on a career of this sort, this kind of murderer found it hard to stop.

However, it didn't come for some time and, as the days passed, every one that went by without another killing was accepted gratefully. It almost began to seem, in fact, that the newspapers had dropped the case,because the headlines no longer leapt out and bit you in the leg. But if the city allowed the crimes to fade from its consciousness, Pel didn't. Madame noticed that he was quiet and distracted. Even the projected purchase of a week-end house by a lake and the fishing that went with it seemed to have slipped from his mind.

She didn't complain, merely keeping Madame Routy out of his hair at meal times, hurrying to smooth ruffled feelings if she slipped past Madame's watch and got in his way. When he left in the morning, she made sure it was she, not Madame Routy, who handed him his briefcase at the door and that she was always waiting for him with an apéritif when he returned in the evening. Several times when she addressed him, her remarks went unnoticed. But she made no comment, simply waiting quietly until he was ready to include her in his thoughts again.

He knew it wasn't over, despite the days that were slipping past. The murders had been the result of an obsession, and obsessive murderers could never throw off the grip their obsession had on them. What was worse, in cases such as this there was no step by step advance towards identifying the killer. As often as not, success came purely by chance and from some careless move on the part of the murderer. All they could do was collect every scrap of information available on every possible suspect so that when the killer slipped up they could jab a finger at the name and say: 'That's the one that fits!' So everything had to be filed, cross-indexed, checked and cross-checked, and Inspector Goriot and his staff of helpers – some of them drafted in from outside the city – went over the filed cards again and again, perusing every single report that arrived on their desks, trying to link them with other cards and other reports in the hope that somewhere in one of them there would be that minute detail which would give them a firm lead. So far it hadn't happened.

Fear in the city continued to abate; as the time passed, despite repeated warnings, potential victims even grew bolder and took less care.

They still hadn't found the hit-and-run driver of Borgny; and of the Abrillards' attackers, though Nosjean was still checking antique shops, nothing had been discovered despite another sighting, this time at the other side of the city at St. Seine which meant, if nothing else, that they were still nearby and would probably eventually have another go.

An interview with Doctor Bréhard confirmed that he and Nurse Hamon had been hoping to marry the following year and that he had intended to set up in practice somewhere in the south with her as his wife, receptionist, clerk and general factotum. The date 1940 meant nothing to him. He looked more in control of himself now but he still found it hard to speak of the dead girl. 'I just can't believe it,' he said.

Doctor Padiou came into the room just as they were leaving.

'Ah, les poulets,' he said cheerfully. 'The fuzz. No offence, Chief Inspector. It's just what the students call you. Personally I have a high regard for you. When I had my car stolen last year you got it back in record time. Fancy a coffee?'

Doctor Bréhard was collecting his papers and his stethoscope so Pel said yes, they did fancy a coffee. As Bréhard left the room, they took the cups Padiou offered.

'It's always available,' Padiou said. 'Sometimes you need it, believe me. There's never enough equipment here, but I don't suppose we're any different from anyone else. What do the police suffer from a shortage of? Stout boots?'

'Personal radios,' Darcy growled. 'They spend more time

being repaired than they do on the streets.'

'Bit like our bleepers. Mine's often on the blink. Doesn't make for efficiency.'

Pel drew him back to the subject of Bernadette Hamon. 'How would you describe her?' he asked.

Padiou considered carefully. 'Lively,' he said. 'I think perhaps after her husband died she'd been too much alone and she wasn't the type to live like that so that when she began to come out of her shell she put all she'd got into it. She liked company. She was fun-loving. At the Medical Faculty Ball a month ago she danced with everybody who asked her. Perhaps because René Bréhard isn't much of a dancer and she enjoyed dancing. And if the man she was dancing with was the same sort, she fooled around a little. You know what I mean – made a great show of the dancing. She was quite a mimic. René never minded.'

'How well did *you* know her? Really.'

'Pretty well, I think. We often went around together. I've been a friend of René's ever since he came here. Sometimes we made up a four with another nurse. Had meals together. That sort of thing.' Padiou eyed Pel dubiously. 'I don't know what you're thinking,' he went on, 'but let's get it very clear; she wasn't interested in me. She had eyes only for René.' He frowned and his mood changed. 'It's sad this happened,' he ended. 'They'd have made a good team.'

There were all the usual alarms and excursions but still nothing new so that there was a cautious easing up on duties, and those policemen's wives who were considering divorcing the husbands they rarely saw were placated for a little longer. It was something that happened several times a year. A few wives were never completely placated and marriages fell apart because, after years of living their lives alone, some of them stopped worrying about their husbands and started lashing out at them instead. For the most part, however, they adjusted well to the strains and, like most women, backed their men to the hilt.

Pel was growing frustrated by this time. He had allowed himself no let-up in the hunt for the man they were now beginning to call Le Rôdeur, the Prowler (a whole series of names had cropped up – Fingers and Midnight Mick being among the most popular). For the fiftieth time he studied the messages they'd found.

Les Français maudits – the cursed French. *1940*. And *Stras-St D Nov 9*. They meant something. The Prowler's conscience was trying to tell them something. Suicides and assassins liked people to know of their sufferings, as if there was an element of egotism about them. Suicides and assassins had an exaggerated self-feeling, wanting to explain, wanting people to know it wasn't their fault.

1940? What did that mean? It was a date that was imprinted on the minds of all Frenchmen of the generation of Pel's father. But what could it mean to students? And *Les Français maudits*? The Cursed French. Why? Pel studied the report for a while then he suddenly sat bolt upright.

'Claudie,' he yelled. 'Bring me a list of all the churches in the city.'

She produced it within minutes and they began to tick off those which had clocks which chimed the hours.

'It was one of these the man at the switchboard heard,' Pel pointed. 'It had to be. Check which ones are five minutes slow.'

It took most of the afternoon but she came back with the answer eventually. 'None of them, Patron,' she said. 'It seems that in this city the guardians of our religious institutions are careful to maintain their clockwork in good order.'

Pel frowned. 'It *must* have been a clock,' he said. 'And it must have been a *church* clock. You can't mistake a church chime for a clock on a mantelpiece.'

'Could it have been a radio or a television?'

'Chiming midnight? The man on the desk times the message 12.05. The radio or the television wouldn't be five minutes slow surely?'

'Patron – ' Claudie was smiling '– I think we've forgotten something. There are *some* church clocks which chime twice. Once on the hour and once five minutes later. I stayed at Torcé-en-Vallée last summer on the way to the south coast. It's near Le Mans and the church was outside the hotel and it chimed every quarter of an hour. On the hour, quarter-past, half-past, and quarter-to. And not once – twice! It was an old church and an old clock, and they said the idea dated back to the days when the people in the fields didn't carry watches, and it chimed twice so that if the cattle were making a noise or a harvester was clattering, they'd hear it the second time. And they made it good and loud so it could be heard several fields away. It kept me awake all night.'

Pel pushed the papers aside. 'Find out, Claudie,' he said.

She came up with the answer the following morning. 'Ste. Odile's, Patron. There used to be a glassworks in that area and the sacristan says it was given a double chime to make sure the people got to work on time. And it's only three streets away from the Rue Devoin, and there's a telephone box with a broken window only fifty metres away from Number 69. That message was sent by the Prowler, Patron. After he killed Marguerite de Wibaux. It doesn't tell us much, but it gives an exact time of death.'

Claudie's discovery didn't move them forward very much but it did at least give meaning to the other messages. They knew now that they *were* linked with the bodies near which they were found. The Prowler, as Pel had thought, was trying to explain his actions. If nothing else, the messages went a long way to prove that they were dealing with someone who wasn't wholly sane.

Pel was beginning to wonder by this time what marriage was really like because he hadn't been married long and he didn't seem to be experiencing much of it, which was a pity considering that he had a wife who appeared to enjoy having him around. It had always been Pel's impression that most people found him a pain in the neck so it seemed a bit of a waste that he shouldn't be able to see as much as he wished of someone who didn't. But for some time now all he had seen of his wife were fleeting glimpses in the morning and evening when he arrived home for hurried meals, all the time guiltily conscious of her troubled eyes on him as he came and went.

As he thought about it, he became aware that there was a pain in his chest. It came from indigestion caused by too many snatched meals but, convinced it was an incipient heart attack, he stubbed out his cigarette and rose to examine himself in the mirror in his office. He was just scrutinising his tongue in the firm belief that the wear and tear of police work was killing him when the door opened and Darcy appeared. Though more than likely he'd been working half the night and had been with a girl the other half, he looked as if he'd just returned from a holiday.

'Hello, Patron,' he said. 'Lost something?'

Pel tried to pretend he was endeavouring to extract a straying lash from his eye. It always irritated him to be caught out in one of his imperfections and, in any case, he always felt there was only one person permitted to be funny at that time in the morning – Evariste Clovis Désiré Pel himself.

'You look like a cat that's been locked all night in a dairy,' he growled. 'You're sex mad, of course, we all know that.'

Darcy grinned. 'I know. I don't seem able to fight it off. But I suppose sin needs working at to be successful.'

The sparring soon ended because Pel's ration of humour never lasted long.

'We've found the point of the messages,' he said as he explained what Claudie had discovered. 'If nothing else, it fixes the time of Marguerite de Wibaux's death. The Prowler telephoned us just after he'd done it, while he was still scared and in an emotional state, and probably as he was leaving the place.'

Darcy frowned. '*Why*, Patron?'

'A cry for help? That's what this sort of thing usually amounts to. In the same way that suicides are really begging for assistance and suicide notes are appeals for them to be understood.'

'"Cursed French,"' Darcy mused. 'Surely that indicates he's not a Frenchman. A Frenchman wouldn't say that. So does it mean he was a foreigner? There are plenty around. There are plenty of people who came from Algeria, for instance – native Algerians among them who had to flee from Algeria when they got independence and might have a grudge against us for the mess we made of it. Algerians who feel that the army was too tough. Something like that.'

'There's no reason why it shouldn't be a Frenchman,' Pel argued. 'He could have some obsessive hatred for France. People like that exist. People who've not got the pensions they feel they ought to have. People who dislike the government they've got. People who feel the Police bear down too hard. There are a thousand reasons why a Frenchman should want to curse Frenchmen. Some of them even become traitors and sell secrets. If nothing else, it means we can't ignore the other messages.'

'"1940" then,' Darcy said. 'What's that mean? Some Frenchman who feels he was let down then? A few did. My father's one. He was a prisoner of war for five years after 1940 and when he gets on the subject of the politicians of that period, he froths at the mouth.'

'That sort of thought would make the Prowler a man as old as your father, then,' Pel pointed out. 'Because 1940 can't mean much to anyone much younger.'

'We have a few on our list who aren't all that young, Patron. Charier, for instance. He's old enough to remember 1940. Josset – he must have been a small boy.'

'And "Stras-St D Nov 9?" What's the significance of that? And why does it mean he has to take it out on women?'

Darcy frowned. 'Whatever it means, we're ready for it. I've got Lacocq, Morell and Aimedieu watching in shifts. And Nadauld has his men all over the place. In cars. In houses. In the grounds of the Ecole St. Dominique. We've got the whole area covered.'

'How much longer have we to go?'

'November 9th's the day after tomorrow.'

They were still discussing the possibilities when De Troq' appeared. He had a brown envelope in his hand.

'I've just come from the Faculté des Médecins, Patron,' he said. 'I was checking on Marguerite de Wibaux.'

'And?'

'Not much about her. She had only one boyfriend and that was Hélin. Everybody thought she was mad to go around with him because she was pretty and moneyed and there were several young doctors who'd have been pleased to be seen with her. There was something, though.' He fished into the envelope and produced a photograph. 'While I was there, I spotted this on the notice board. It was taken at the Medical Faculty Ball last month. The newspaper covers the occasion, of course, and so does a photographer who sticks up a selection of prints in case anyone wants one for the mantelpiece or to send home to Mamma. They're numbered and they can order them. They were taken this year by Photogay of the Rue Amiral-Blanchard.'

He placed the picture on Pel's desk. Like all group photographs taken by artificial light, the faces in the foreground were clear and bright, a lot of happy young people with their arms round each other. Those further back where the flash had failed to reach were more blurred and seemed to be in shadow.

'Mostly doctors and their wives and girlfriends,' De Troq' said. 'I had them identified where possible. There are also nurses, of course, because doctors and nurses go together like bread and cheese. There are also medical students of both sexes, staff from the hospitals, and others involved in medicine such as radiographers, dentists, opticians, ambulance people and so on. In addition, all sorts of odds and ends go as guests because the ball's to raise funds for the Home for the Little Children of the Poor and other medical charities. The tickets are sold mainly in medical institutions of one sort or another.'

He passed across a magnifying glass. 'I thought I saw someone I knew,' he said. 'Take a look, Patron.' His finger jabbed. 'About there.'

Pel studied the photograph carefully, knowing perfectly well it would indicate something. De Troq' was no fool and if he produced a photograph there would be something on it of interest to Pel.

'I see the Hamon girl,' he said slowly. 'Arm-in-arm with Bréhard. Alongside is Doctor Padiou.' He looked up. 'Isn't that girl with him Marguerite de Wibaux?'

'It could be, Patron. But you've not seen it all yet. Look just behind Nurse Hamon.'

Pel peered. There was a group of men, all laughing, and as he studied them he suddenly bent closer.

'That's Hélin,' he said sharply. 'He's right behind her. He's saying something to her and she's got her head back as if she's listening.' He straightened up. 'He *did* know her.'

'That's the way it looks, Patron.'

Pel frowned. 'How did he manage to get to an affair like this?' he asked. 'I'd have thought it would be too expensive for a student on a grant.'

'It is, Patron,' De Troq' admitted. 'But some of them go all the same. Medical students especially. A few like Marguerite who have money and can afford it. She paid for Hélin incidentally, not the other way round. And a few girls who are asked by doctors they know.'

'How about Number 69, Rue Devoin? Did any of that lot go?'

'All of them, Patron.'

Pel looked startled. 'I wouldn't have thought they were *that* wealthy, or that the girls all knew doctors.'

'They didn't, Patron.' De Troq' smiled. 'But it's a big affair and it needs a big staff to run it, so the organisers employ a number of students every year to help. Because it's for charity and students are willing to work for less money. Some work in the bar. Some in the buffet. Some merely keep the dining room clear of plates and glasses. The girls work in the cloakrooms. There are perks, of course. Food and drink and, later, a chance to slip into the ballroom.'

'You found all this out?'

'I got it from Annie Joulier. The organisers are aware of what goes on but they turn a blind eye because they need the students' help.'

Pel rubbed his nose thoughtfully. 'What about the boys at Number 69? It's the boys I'm interested in.'

'They were there, too. Marguerite, whose father's well known at the city hospitals, helped them get the jobs. Sergent and Aduraz worked in white coats in the dining room clearing the debris, Schwendermann and Moussia in the car park. They all seem to have enjoyed the evening, though, because there was plenty to drink and they were well fed. They also got paid. Not much, but enough to make it a good evening out.'

'And did they join the dancing, too?'

De Troq' smiled. 'Sergent and Aduraz did. Under their white coats they wore their best trousers, white shirts and bow ties and they had their jackets with them. Schwendermann and Moussia didn't. Perhaps they didn't intend to. Moussia says it's because it was raining and they got wet through but Annie Joulier says he didn't have a good suit and that's just his excuse, and Schwendermann's hardly the type to join in something of that sort. Instead they had a few drinks behind the bar and went up to the balcony to watch the dancing from there.'

Pel nodded with satisfaction at De Troq's efforts. 'But,' he said, 'only Hélin, of those we're interested in, was, as far as you know, in the ballroom by virtue of possessing a ticket. And he was talking to Bernadette Hamon whom he claimed he didn't know.' He looked at Darcy. 'You and I'll go and see him,

Daniel,' he said. 'Early in the morning before he's properly awake. That way he might let something slip.'

He took a packet of cigarettes from his drawer, studied it for a long time as if afraid it might leap up and bite him, then very slowly took one out, put in in his mouth and lit it. Never allow yourself to be in a position of stress when you might feel the need of a cigarette, all the stop-smoking articles said. There was a fat chance of that ever happening to a cop, he thought as he applied a match.

'We now have a possible connection,' he said. 'If he knew the Hamon girl *and* the De Wibaux girl, perhaps he also knew the Magueri woman. I think it calls for a beer at the Bar Transvaal.'

They were just about to leave when Lagé appeared. He was getting close to retirement and because he was slow he was beginning to run to fat. But, though he was slow, Lagé was a willing slogger, always agreeable to helping with other people's work – something Misset was never slow to take advantage of – and he came in now, peeling off his coat in a state of great excitement.

'Boss,' he announced. 'I might have picked him up!'

'Who?'

'The Prowler.'

'Oh?' Pel was startled because Lagé wasn't given to triumphs of this nature. 'Inform me.'

'Type called Henri Guillon. Caught in the early morning mist at the General Hospital outside the resident nurses' block trying to see into their rooms. They knew him. They've seen him before but this time, in view of Le Rôdeur, they thought we ought to know. I took the message.'

Pel looked at De Troq' and Darcy. A moment before they had been thinking they were on the track of the man they were after but now here was Lagé with a new name altogether.

He took a quick drag at his cigarette. 'You're sure of this?' he asked.

'Yes, Patron. I picked him up.'

Well, it *could* happen. A cop stopping a man for a traffic offence could find he had arrested Public Enemy Number One by accident.

'I questioned him and found he went to the same school as Alice Magueri,' Lagé went on. 'And that later he attended a school for retarded children at Hautville. He's below waiting for you.'

They let him stew for a while as they made enquiries about him in Longvic where he lived. It seemed he was well known for making suggestions to women and had long been in the habit of inviting strange girls to go for a walk. One woman they spoke to, blunter than the rest, told them that if they let him go they were failing in their duty because he was obviously the man they were seeking. 'Don't let up on him if he argues,' she said. 'He was always good with his tongue.'

As it happened there was no need to bring pressure to bear. As soon as they started questioning him, Guillon immediately offered the information that he knew Alice Magueri.

'At school,' he said. 'I wanted her even then.'

'You wanted her?' Pel said. 'How?'

'In bed. On the back seat of the car. Anyhow.'

'So what did you do?'

'I asked her. She wouldn't let me.'

'So you killed her?'

'Yes.'

'How?'

'I stabbed her.'

'Where?'

'Chest. Stomach. Everywhere.'

'What sort of knife did you use?'

'It wasn't a knife. It was a bayonet – an old one from the war. It was my father's.'

'How many times did you stab her?'

'It must have been twenty or thirty.'

'Which hand?'

Guillon lifted his hand. 'This one. I'm left-handed. Could you tell?'

'Where was the body?'

'In the Rue Constance.'

'Where exactly?'

'In a shop doorway, wasn't it?'

'You tell me.'

'Yes. Shop doorway. I dragged her there to do it.'

'Why didn't she cry out? Nobody heard her.'

'I stuffed a gag in her mouth.'

'What did you use?'

'My handkerchief.'

'What else?'

'Nothing. Then I had her.

'In the doorway? After you'd stabbed her?'

'Yes, yes.' Guillon gave them the story in intricate and gleeful detail.

'You must have got a lot of blood on you,' Pel observed.

'Yes, I did. All over my trousers and shirt.'

'Where are they now?'

'I burned them. While I was doing it, she tried to cry out. She wasn't dead. I put my hand over her face.'

'I thought you'd gagged her.'

Guillon didn't pause. 'She spat it out.'

'Tell us about this doorway.'

'There was plenty of room. It belonged to an ironmongers's. There were flat irons, electric irons and electric mixers in the window.'

'What happened then?'

'I went for a drink. I needed one.'

'Still covered with blood?'

'No, no. I changed first and had a bath. *Then* I went for a drink.'

'Is that all?'

Guillon gave him a sly look. 'What more do you want?'

'Did you do anything to her cheeks?'

'Only kiss them.'

'Do you have a knife?'

'I told you. I did it with the bayonet.'

Lagé placed an old-fashioned bayonet on the desk. It was blunt and streaked with rust. 'That's it, Patron. It's not been tested for blood or anything.'

'I doubt if it'll show any,' Pel said.

His eyes bright, a feverish look of triumph on his face, Guillon watched him as he sat back and lit another cigarette from the stub of the old one. For once Pel felt it was justified because he felt faintly nauseated.

'For your information,' he said, 'she wasn't stabbed. She was strangled. She hadn't been gagged and there had been no sexual interference. And the shop where you say you did it, is in fact an empty premises. It closed down some time ago. You're telling me a whole load of lies.'

Guillon stared at Pel for a moment, then his eyes filled with tears. 'Holy Mary, Mother of Jesus,' he whispered. 'I did it, I promise you! I did it!'

'Take him away, Lagé,' Pel said. 'You've been troubled for nothing. He's making it up from what he's read in the papers.'

'What do we do with him, Patron?'

'I should think he's a case for the psychiatrists. Better ask Doc Minet. Just take him out of my sight.'

The beer at the Bar Transvaal seemed more than ever desirable – if only to take away the taste of the interview. But, as they reached the door, the telephone went. This time it was Inspector Nadauld, of Uniformed Branch. He sounded agitated.

'I'm in the Cours de Gaulle,' he said. 'One of my men's just reported finding a body on the railway track alongside. It's another girl. She's been strangled.'

9

The Cours de Gaulle was a wide avenue running from the Parc de la Colombière up to the Place Wilson, which was a wide circular open space with an island round which the traffic revolved. It was surrounded on two sides by railway lines and in the centre was the Monument de la Victoire. The avenue had originally been built in 1920 to celebrate the victory over the Germans in 1918 and, because it had wide stretches of grass and bushes on either side and two rows of sycamores, it was popular in summer with young people, especially in the evening when there was plenty of shadow which allowed them to go into clinches without being seen. Pel knew the district well because it backed on to the Rue Martin-de-Noinville where he'd lived until his marriage.

Halfway along, between the Monument de la Victoire and the park, Inspector Nadauld's car was stationed by the curb, and Nadauld was waiting for them on the grass verge. As they braked to a stop, he came forward.

'In here, Chief.'

They followed him under the trees and he led the way into a thick row of closely planted bushes.

'They're all on their way,' he said. 'Doc Minet. The Lab. Photography. Fingerprints. Pomereu's sending a couple of cars. Goriot knows.'

Pushing through the last of the bushes, they found themselves close to the railway line. Standing by a wire fence were three track workers, in dark overalls and fluorescent orange jackets.

'She's alongside the line,' Nadauld said. He indicated one of the railwaymen. 'This is Nicholas Denais. He's the foreman.'

72

Denais gestured. 'We got a call from the yard,' he said. 'The stationmaster at Dampierre picked up a message from the driver of the 8.30 a.m. to Besançon. He'd seen something alongside the up line and thought it ought to be cleared. He thought it was a suicide. You're always getting them, and we're always having to clean up after them.'

Pel said nothing and Denais went on.

'Dampierre informed the city depot and they passed the message to the yard, who passed it on to us. It's a girl. She's been hit by a train.'

Pel glanced quickly at Nadauld. 'I thought you said –'

Nadauld nodded. 'I did. You'd better come and have a look.'

They climbed the wire fence and followed Denais and his men. The body was alongside the track and it was minus its right leg which had been neatly severed and was lying between the rails. The rest of the body had not been touched by the train and, as they bent closer, they saw the suffused face and the ferocious weal round her neck. This time the scratches on her face were deeper, as if they'd been done in a hurry.

Pel looked at Nadauld. 'Know her?'

'No, Chief.'

'Right. We'll wait for Doc Minet and the specialists before we move her.' Pel turned to Denais. 'What's the procedure in a case like this? We'll need to make a search and take photographs.'

'We'd better inform the yard. They'll contact Control who'll push traffic on to the down line until we're clear here. That'll mean it'll be safe.'

As they stood in a group alongside the track they heard the sound of a train approaching and Denais gestured. 'Better get up the bank,' he said.

'What about the body?'

'It's clear. It won't be touched. There must have been several trains past on this stretch since it was reported.'

It was late afternoon before Doc Minet, the photographers, artists and Lab. technicians had finished and the body could be moved.

'Same as the others,' Doc Minet said wearily. 'The train didn't kill her. She was dead already. She was strangled –' he gestured ' – probably up there in the bushes, then thrown over the fence so that she rolled down until she lay on the verge with her leg across the line.' He looked haggardly at Pel. 'You've got another, my friend.'

As the body was lifted to the grass close to the track and the severed leg laid alongside it on a plastic sheet, Pel turned to Darcy.

'See what you can find on her, Daniel.'

Leguyader, who already had his men spread out searching the approaches to the track, gestured up the bank. 'He got her under the trees,' he said. 'Then dragged her through the undergrowth. You can see the marks of her heels and there's one of her shoes in the bushes. She must have lost it en route. Probably he was irritated at the way we always find them within hours of him killing them and wanted to make it more difficult.'

Pel said nothing. Leguyader was noted for a warped sense of humour and there was nothing funny in the corpse of a young girl.

Darcy looked up, his hands full of the dead girl's belongings. 'No handbag, Patron,' he said. 'Preferred to use her pockets. All the usual. Lipstick. Eyeliner. Handkerchief. No cigarettes.'

'I doubt if she smoked,' Doc Minet said. 'Her fingers aren't stained and her teeth aren't smoker's teeth.'

'Identity papers?'

'Here, Patron. Honorine Nauray. Aged twenty. Shop assistant. Address: 3, Impasse Pezzo, Talant. No driving licence. Two used bus tickets. She obviously didn't have a car.'

'Girl shop assistants of her age often don't.' Pel bent over the dead girl and stared at the livid marks on the grey flesh of her cheek. His eyes turned to Darcy. 'Do you think those cuts form an N?' he asked. 'For Nauray?'

'I'd say an H, Patron.'

'For Honorine?'

'Name of God, Patron, the bastard can't know them all – first names as well!'

Pel was silent for a while. 'The one on Alice Magueri could have been an M – just. It could even have been a rough A. The one on Marguerite de Wibaux, could have been – again just – an M. After all we thought at first it might be a W. But in no way could the one on Bernadette Hamon have been a B.'

'Then they must all be Hs.'

'So what's the significance? What does H stand for?'

'Hélin?'

Pel remembered the photograph of the Faculty Ball they'd been looking at not long before. 'Surely he didn't know *this* one as well?'

'*Is* it sure, Patron?' Darcy said. 'He knew De Wibaux and, judging by that photograph, he probably knew Hamon. And who knows where a prostitute plies her business? He probably knew the Magueri woman, too. If you ask me, Hélin's a bit of a stoat, so he might have been one of her customers and, if he was, how do we know he didn't know this girl, too?'

Pel turned to De Troq' who stood behind him. 'Get out to this address. Find out where she worked. Find out who she was with last night.'

As he spoke, they saw Sarrazin climbing the fence. 'Holy Mother of God,' Pel breathed. 'Now the panic will start.'

Sure enough, it did.

First on the scene, Sarrazin scooped the pool and, being a freelance, offered what he'd discovered to those newspapers who had first call on his services, before passing out a few snippets of information to Henriot and the others and leaving them to find out the rest themselves. The following morning it was plastered all over the daily press and the panic really started.

Though they had taken the press into their confidence, they had been careful to keep back a few details such as the facial mutilations, and, because people suspected the police were withholding things, wild rumours of horrors began to circulate that the bodies had been found in obscene positions, that the strangler was a cat burglar who could climb drainpipes, that he was a man of enormous strength who worked so quickly no sound was ever heard from his victims.

There was intense speculation. What kind of man *was* the strangler? How did he manage to get close enough to his victims to kill without being seen? Could it be even that he was a she? And what were the Police doing that they couldn't catch him?

The Police, in fact, were doing everything possible, and they had immediately brought back all the men from other districts whom they'd released as things had quietened down. Now every available man was on the streets to check on anyone who might be out late at night – taxi drivers, barmen, late deliverymen – knowing all the time that it was a pointless exercise because their quarry was probably on the streets for no other reason than that he wished to be. Officers dressed in plain clothes rode on buses, hung around bars, bus stops, the station, and wandered the dark streets, watching passers-by, studying faces, trying to decide if any of them were not what they seemed or were about the streets more than seemed necessary. It led them nowhere.

New suspects were brought in. Some were men whose names had been sent in anonymously, others were pathetic creatures known to be loiterers, peeping toms, alcoholics. A few of them even turned themselves in, feeling they might have been guilty of the murders during a drunken bout or some sort of blackout. And those people who lived on the fringes of the law began to complain that they couldn't get on with their business for the activities of the Police who were involved in a case that didn't concern *them*.

A woman found dead in a motel room south of the city sent the police cars screaming down the motorway, but she turned out to be a foreign tourist with a recently broken marriage who had taken an overdose of sleeping pills. And a girl returning from a cinema felt she was being followed, and, hearing footsteps behind her, had started to run, only to find that the following footsteps also increased their pace. She arrived home in a state of panic and it occupied two policemen for four hours before Claudie Darel noticed the sound of her own heels on the pavement and worked it out that the girl was running from the echo of her own shoes.

Honorine Nauray turned out to be different from the other victims. She was no Alice Magueri, but she was no Marguerite de Wibaux and no Bernadette Hamon either.

'Her parents were expecting her home,' De Troq' reported. 'But when she didn't arrive they decided she was staying with a friend. She seems to have been a bit of a handful. Always out with men – some of them too old for her, they thought – and often claimed to be staying with friends. When she didn't come home, though, they grew worried and her mother was just

76

about to report her missing when I arrived to tell her what had happened to her.'

'Did they know whom she was with?'

'They thought her boyfriend. Name of André Chatry, salesman, 33, Rue Briogne. But I've seen him and he says she stood him up.'

'So why was she out late?'

'The girls in the shop where she worked think she'd got another boyfriend. She'd mentioned meeting a boy in the bus station buffet when she'd gone in for a coffee after work and they'd seen him hanging about outside the shop on one or two occasions. He had books under his arm so they thought he might be a student. They also said she was experienced in sex and boasted of enjoying rousing a man and then refusing him. But there was no alarm at the shop when she didn't come in because she sometimes pretended to be ill to get the day off. She was fooling a lot of people, it seems, because her mother claimed she'd *never* had a day off since she started work. I'm going to the university now. I've got a description of the student. He had red hair so he shouldn't be hard to find.'

This time there had been no message. No scrawled words. No telephoned mutterings. And it left them wondering if the Prowler had got his dates wrong and had killed Honorine Nauray a day or two earlier than he'd intended – on November 7th.

'Perhaps he learned something,' Pel suggested. 'That she was going away. Or something of that sort. Perhaps he'd been watching her and intended to kill her on November 9th but circumstances threw her in his path a little earlier.'

It was a possibility – except for one thing.

'What about Stras-St D?' Darcy asked. 'The Cours de Gaulle's nowhere near the Boulevard de Strasbourg or the Ecole St. Dominique.'

Enquiries showed that Honorine Naurau wasn't in the habit of frequenting the district round the Ecole St. Dominique at all, in fact. Her route from home to her place of work and back again took her nowhere near it and the teachers who ran the school had never heard of her. She had not attended the school and, apart from the possibility that she had a man friend living

77

in that area, they could find no connection between her and the message, and no one in the area had ever heard of her or seen her.

'Which seems to mean,' Darcy said, 'that it has nothing to do with the Boulevard de Strasbourg and the Ecole St. Dominique. For once, friend Prowler just didn't leave his calling card.'

Pel was on the horns of a dilemma. It was necessary for the safety of women living alone to give publicity to the killings, yet publicity always brought sick imitators, like Guillon, and news of spectacular killings could lead to similar killings, so that publicity could do harm even as it helped.

He was still looking for a common denominator, but there appeared to be nothing beyond the fact that all the women they'd found were unmarried or at least living in an unmarried state without a husband.

Normally when a crime was committed, the police looked first for people in the habit of committing similar crimes, because criminals were usually an unimaginative lot who followed a pattern. Some burglars broke only into shops. Others preferred to work round blocks of apartments. And pickpockets didn't go in for burglary any more than burglars went in for picking pockets. But with sex crimes – and, despite the absence of sexual connotations, Pel was convinced the stranglings *were* sexual crimes – there was every kind imaginable and it was no good going to informers because the Prowler must obviously be working alone. And clearly the reason no clues to his identity had been found was because strangling was only too easy. Pressure on the neck arteries that carried blood to the brain brought unconsciousness in a matter of seconds and required no great strength. Strangling was something to which Pel preferred not to give publicity, in case someone tried it on his friends and neighbours.

The new murder had brought the pressmen down from Paris in hordes, as well as the television crews with their cameras and microphones and sound recording boxes. Pel refused to have anything to do with them and told the Chief so, flatly.

The Chief was angry, partly because he didn't like handling the press any more than Pel did, but chiefly because of the new murder and the lack of progress. Commonsense told him it wasn't Pel's fault, but he was being leaned on in his turn by other people and it was always a case, when blame was apportioned, that it was handed on to subordinates, all the way down to the office cat.

'The damned man has the whole city by the balls!' he snarled. 'The whole city and the whole police force! What in God's name are we doing?'

He didn't really have to ask. Pel was working round the clock, as also – with the possible exception of Misset – was his squad. They were already using every technique of detection available, save clairvoyants and people claiming extra-sensory perception whom, while the American Police didn't hesitate to use them, European Police preferred to leave alone.

'For the love of God – ' the Chief's tirade looked like going on all day ' – we have every device known to mankind helping us – '

'Except personal radios,' Pel interrupted quietly.

The Chief stopped dead in mid-flow and his head jerked round. 'Personal radios won't find him!' he snapped.

'They might save somebody's life,' Pel said. 'If some woman's attacked and the cop on the scene can't call in, she could die before help arrived.'

Pel's comment effectively silenced the Chief but what he had said was true. Everything that was available *was* being used and it still brought them nowhere. All police leave had been cancelled once more and every available man was on the streets, though they were finding it hard, despite their uniforms and identity cards, to question women, because apartments and houses remained locked against them due to the fear that was abroad, and they were having to seek the answers through the cracks of barricaded doors. They weren't the only ones either, because meter readers were not being allowed to do their jobs, any more than were telephone repairmen or delivery men. Even shopping hours were affected because street-corner grocers were finding that women were refusing to shop for their evening meal after the light had gone, and the only people who were doing any real business were locksmiths, ironmongers selling bolts, and kennels which could supply watchdogs. Yet all that had been produced was the astonishing and bizarre, and some of the twisted characters they had turned up from under the stones startled them with the things they'd been up to.

10

The stretch of the Boulevard de Strasbourg round the Ecole St Dominique was a quiet area close to the city boundary and close to the university. Opposite the school there was a reservoir, enclosed and covered with a grass mound, and a public garden. Further along the road was the sports ground with pitches, skating rink and running track. Just to the south-east lay the buildings of the university, lying along the hillside like white bones in the wintry sunshine. The Faculty of Medicine and Pharmacy, the Faculty of Sciences, the Faculty of Law, the National School of Applied Agronomic Sciences, the Anti-Cancer Centre. Further north was the Technical College and nearby the military hospital and not far away the Monument des Fusillés, the memorial to those members of the Resistance executed during the Occupation. Sitting in his car, Pel stared hard and long at it. It connected the area somehow with the date 1940, when the Resistance and the shootings had started. And that seemed to indicate that the Prowler was not, as Darcy suggested, a foreigner, but some embittered Frenchman.

As November 8th waned and November 9th arrived, the men stationed about the place waited and watched. But nothing happened. The streets were dead after midnight and remained dead until daylight when the first motor cars began to appear. The first buses followed, then a few cyclists. Eventually the rush increased as students and lecturers arrived at the university. A few military vehicles headed down the slope from the barracks to the north and a military ambulance or two turned into the military hospital.

All day Darcy prowled about the area in his car, waiting for the panic button to be pressed, while Pel sat in his office ready to set things in motion when it was. They were all ready and at the first sign of trouble could be on the spot within minutes. But nothing happened.

The traffic remained the same as all the other days. After the first rush, the volume dropped to normal, then increased a little at lunchtime, dropped again during the afternoon, then as darkness approached, began to build up once more. Darcy's radio was going constantly, receiving reports from the men they had stationed in the area but none of them had anything to report and they all sounded bored. There wasn't much that was duller than watching nothing happening.

'It'll be after dark,' Darcy said. 'So keep your eyes open.'

Still nothing happened so that they began to expect it around midnight. But it had turned colder and it was hard to maintain an interest when your feet were frozen and the wind coming down from the Plateau de Langres seemed to be coming all the way from Russia.

Pel remained in his office until the early hours of the 10th when Darcy arrived, cold, hungry, puzzled and in a bad temper.

'It was nothing, Patron. It didn't have a meaning, after all.'

For safety, they rang round the sub-stations to find out if anything had been reported. But it had been a quiet night, even quieter, it seemed, than normal. There were a few drunks, a fight in the Rue Jean-de-la-Huerta, a man who had blacked his wife's eye for neglecting the children in the Chenove district, a small explosion in the Industrial Zone, and the usual accident reports that had arrived in Traffic. Nothing else.

'I think you should go home, Patron,' Darcy said. He sounded bitter and frustrated. They had provided for an incident and none had occurred.

When Pel appeared later in the morning, Darcy was on the telephone again, as if he'd been there all night. Pel was looking a little like something the cat had dragged in but Darcy was spotless, immaculate and full of energy, though he couldn't possibly have had more than an hour or two of sleep. He was ringing the sub-stations again.

'There's nothing, Patron,' he said. 'It was a hoax. Perhaps the message was on the window long before Alice Magueri was found. Perhaps it just wasn't noticed. After all, nobody goes in and out of an empty shop. Perhaps it means nothing at all. Perhaps "1940" meant nothing either. Perhaps it was there and Charier and those others who used the yard just didn't see it. Perhaps they none of them mean anything.'

'"Les Français maudits" seemed to mean something,' Pel reminded him quietly. 'It meant that the Prowler had just killed Marguerite de Wibaux. And if that meant something, I think these others mean something.'

During the days that followed they were constantly expecting the telephone to ring with the report of an incident in the Boulevard de Strasbourg. But nothing happened and eventually Darcy and Nadauld removed their men.

Honorine Nauray's date turned out to be a student called Paul Doucet, a youngster with a shock of pale auburn hair that looked as if it had been helped along with doses of dye. He was studying agronomy, a large boy with a weak mouth and anxious eyes, whose size was soft fat rather than muscle. Inevitably his radio was going at full blast.

He admitted at once that he'd been with Honorine Nauray the evening she had died but that he'd left her close to midnight.

'You *left* her?' Pel stared at him. 'To find her own way home?'

'Well, yes. I have a room with my aunt in the Rue Lafosse. I come from Lyons but my aunt lives here. And she's a bit strict. She wants to know where I've been all the time. She's always at me. Where were you? Why were you late in? Who's the girl you were with? I had to get back.'

'And for that you left the girl to find her way across the city alone?' Darcy snapped. 'You condemned her to death! Hadn't you heard the appeal we put out saying that girls should be escorted home?'

'Well, yes, but there was my aunt, you see – '

'Wasn't the girl afraid of being left alone?'

'She didn't seem to be.'

'Perhaps she was putting on a brave face. Where had you been?'

'We went to a party. Some friends who had a record player and a couple of bottles of wine. That was all. We sat around, talking and drinking.'

'What was the name of this friend?'

'Mark Bartelott. He has a room of his own in the Clos des Vosges. He's got money.'

'What happened at the party? Where you with Honorine Nauray all the time?'

'Yes. The others were all in twos. There was a bit of swapping about but they mostly stayed with each other. One couple disappeared. I think they went into the bedroom. But perhaps they left. I don't know.'

'Were people having sex?'

'No. Just a lot of laughing and squealing. One or two were quietly in corners where it was dark. That sort of thing.'

'How about you and Honorine?'

'We did a bit of – well, you know.'

'No, I don't. Inform me.'

'We kissed a bit. That sort of thing.'

'And afterwards? On the way home?'

'She pulled me into the bushes in the Cours de Gaulle. And – well – she was keen.'

'And then you left her?'

'It was getting late but she said she'd be all right. She said she was often late about the city.'

It didn't take them long to check with Mark Bartelott that Doucet's story was true. Bartelott was a good-looking youngster who was obviously used to money and to the confidence that went with it. He was English – which made Pel, always a good racist, wonder if France wasn't becoming cluttered up with foreigners – and he also had a title. He was a milord or something but said he didn't bother to use his title, which, Pel thought enviously, was typical of the nobility. They were so sure of themselves they didn't bother with something he personally wouldn't have dreamed of ignoring. He'd even heard that the English had noblemen who'd given up their titles to be able to sit in Parliament, which showed how crazy they must be, because no one with any sense would give up anything to sit with that lot.

Bartelott spoke good French and had neither the uncertain manner of Doucet nor the aggressive hostility of Hélin. Inevitably his radio was going full blast but this time it was Mozart and he had the grace to turn it off at once. Pel, who was a snob at heart, conceded that, if nothing else, at least the well-

83

born knew how to behave. Friendly, helpful and willing to answer questions, Bartelott gave them a list of names of the people who'd been at his party. They were nearly all students, he said, though he knew Doucet least of all.

'So why was *he* invited?' Pel asked quickly.

'I was sorry for him. I gave him a leg up now and again. Gave him a lift in my car. That sort of thing. I'm doing agronomy, too, and you cling together a bit.'

'What is agronomy exactly?' Darcy asked.

'The science of soil management and crop production.' Bartelott smiled. 'In the old days, people like me, who knew they were going to end up running an estate, just learned to be farmers. There's more to it these days. And with the Common Market it's a help to know something about foreign marketing procedures. That's why I'm learning French.'

Pel was impressed. No wonder old families managed to retain their power. They were more intelligent than people gave them credit for.

'Did you know Honorine Nauray?' he asked.

'Is she the girl who was – ?'

'Yes.'

Bartelott pulled a face. 'Well, I'm sorry about that. Doucet said he'd see her home and I expected he would. I didn't know her much. I'd seen her with Doucet once or twice and he'd told me she wasn't a student. As a matter of fact, it soon became obvious. She wasn't very bright. Rather a dim little light, in fact.'

'She worked in a shop.'

Bartelott was unmoved. 'I've met shop assistants who were as bright as a button,' he said briskly. 'All the same, I'm sorry she's dead. Was it the same – ?'

'We think so. Did she talk with anyone else at the party?'

'Of course she did. Everybody did. But mostly she was with Doucet and they were drinking together, listening to music together, pawing each other a bit. But not much. I don't give those sort of parties.'

'Did they leave with the others?'

'Everybody left at the same time. When I give a party, it starts and finishes when I say so. No gatecrashers and no hangers-on afterwards. I'm here to study French and I like to go to bed, even if I also like to enjoy myself.'

Pel found himself wishing he had the aplomb of an English milord and could tell people where they got off. In fact, though he was unaware of it and despite his not very prepossessing appearance, he had it in abundance.

'Did you see them leave?' he asked.

'I not only saw them leave, I went into the street and talked on the pavement with everybody for five minutes. To get a bit of fresh air. You know what a place can get like if everybody smokes.'

'Did anyone take drugs?'

'Not in my place.'

'When you were on the pavement talking to them, did you notice anybody hanging around. Anybody watching from across the street? Anybody sitting in a car? Anything like that?'

Bartelott shrugged. 'I wasn't looking,' he admitted.

Only the students from the university seemed happily indifferent to the fear in the city, going to parties as usual, organising themselves into bands so that every girl was always escorted to her room. Pel's admiration for them – with a few exceptions – was enormous. They were healthy, cheerful and full of vitality, even if not always full of morals, and they at least seemed alive and determined that a killer roaming the streets wasn't going to get them down.

But the students were always different. They were a different breed these days from those who had stormed the barricades in '68. The old militancy had gone and they were disillusioned with ideologies; with the politically active almost all Communist and split into warring groups into the bargain, they received little support and there was little unrest. They had few clubs or organised social life, however, chiefly because they were not joiners of clubs, and unlike the British and the Americans with their attitude of 'togetherness', being French and individual they preferred what could be called 'apartness', and moved in small groups about the bars and cafés of the city. Nevertheless, they still remained an organised community in constant touch with each other, through their hostels, their lectures, their union, their pursuits, and it was easy for them to guard each other. For the rest of the city it was different. Other people were not so well organised and there were still women who had to be out after dark and couldn't easily arrange protection.

Women living alone hurried home from work and locked their doors. Some arranged to stay with relatives because they were terrified that if they went home and fastened themselves in they'd find the Prowler was already inside and that they'd locked themselves in with him. A few reported heavy breathing on the telephone and everybody started eyeing their neighbours with suspicion. Was the Prowler the man next door, alongside them in the bar, in a traffic jam, in a shop, in a bus or in a train?

By this time, thanks to the stories put out by the press that the Prowler was a man of prodigious strength, people were looking askance at anyone who was interested in sport, gymnastics or weight-lifting, and inevitably Noël Moussia started to complain that his friends were refusing to have anything to do with him.

The request to the public to look out for suspects turned up one or two more peeping toms, while a few people – one a city official of apparently impeccable reputation – were found in beds where they had no right to be. An emergency telephone number was announced which could be called at any time of the day or night and a box with a number was established at the post office where suspicions, suggestions, names, could be dropped without the informant being known in any way. It was tantamount to asking every nut in the city to drag out a writing pad and envelope but it was something they had to face.

They had also asked for information on every strangling throughout France for two years back and already the stack of reports was growing tall, while a fresh round-up was made of all sex offenders and a check was made on every man between eighteen and forty released in the last few years from mental institutions.

Meanwhile, the clothing of every single victim was examined again because threads, hairs, dust could all lead to clues. But nothing materialised and Leguyader, never the man to denigrate himself, had to admit it. The killer, whoever he was, had no weapon but a rope and a sharp knife, and since he was never near his victim for more than a matter of seconds he left no trace.

They were getting nowhere fast. But there was nothing unusual in that. In police work there were no happy endings – only loose ends and sudden endings.

The interview with Frederic Hélin, delayed by the urgency of the new murder, had had to be put off again and again as other things cropped up but, as the panic subsided, Pel picked up Darcy and they headed for the room he shared with his post-graduate friends, Jean-Pierre Jenet and Hubert Detoc, on the top floor of a house in the Rue Henri-Gauthier. The building was an almost exact replica – as if it had been designed by the same architect and built by the same builder – as Number 69, Rue Devoin, where Marguerite de Wibaux had lived. It had the same two roofs over the extended ground floor and male and female students sharing roughly the same number of rooms, with, judging by the noise, the same number of record players – all going full blast.

'They'll all be deaf by the time they're forty,' Pel growled.

Jenet and Detoc were at a lecture and Hélin had just climbed out of bed. The radio was on.

'I had a heavy night,' he explained. 'I decided to stay in a bit. I'll catch up.'

'Catch up what?' Darcy asked.

'Studies. That's the point about university. You're supposed to do your studying yourself. Or hadn't you heard?'

It was the usual attitude. The police were the Fuzz. They were fascist bullies, stopping innocent young students from taking drugs and smashing things up with demonstrations. The complaints, of course, came only from those students who *did* take drugs or smashed things up. The ones who lived blameless lives for the most part had no complaints.

'What is it this time?' Hélin's voice was bored and irritated as he gestured at Darcy. 'I've told him. I've told you. Who else do you want me to talk to?'

'You told us,' Darcy said, 'that you didn't know the nurse, Bernadette Hamon.'

'I didn't.'

'Are you sure?'

'Quite sure.'

'Remember the Medical Faculty ball?'

'I went with Marguerite. She got the tickets through her

father. He was a big shot at the hospital until he retired.'

Darcy produced the picture De Troq' had found and indicated the girl alongside Doctor Padiou. 'Isn't that Marguerite de Wibaux?'

Hélin stared at the picture. 'No, it isn't. She wasn't wearing a dress like that. The one she wore was much more classy, because she was a snobbish little bitch who had too much money and liked always to be the best-dressed of the lot.' Turning, he fished in a drawer to produce another picture. It showed Marguerite de Wibaux and several other young people sitting round the table.

'But if she's not on that picture.' he snapped, 'she's on this. Is that proof enough?'

'Who took this?' Pel asked.

'A friend. He had his own camera. He wasn't the official cameraman.' Hélin gestured at the picture Darcy held. 'And she's not on *that* picture because she just happened to be off it. After all, it is a bit difficult to get five hundred people on the same photograph, isn't it?'

'Right,' Darcy agreed. 'But if *she's* not in this picture, *you* are. Talking to Bernadette Hamon.'

'Who's Bernadette Hamon? You asked about her before.'

'Don't you read your papers?' Darcy snapped.

'Not if I can help it. They're all run by capitalist lackeys like the Police.'

'She was murdered,' Pel said. 'Twelve days after Marguerite de Wibaux.'

Hélin scowled and Darcy's finger jabbed at the photograph. 'That's her! You're talking to her.'

'So what?' Hélin shrugged. 'I expect I was talking to her because she was pretty, and because, I suppose, her boyfriend was stupid enough not to be handy. I think we danced together but I'm not sure. And she didn't tell me her name. Next time I'll make a point of asking so I'll be able to give you a list.'

'Don't try to be funny, my friend,' Darcy growled.

Hélin glared at him. 'Then don't come in here accusing me!'

'What about the night she was murdered?' Pel asked. 'The fifteenth. Where were you?'

'Am I supposed to have done that, too?'

'Answer the question.'

88

'Well, I couldn't have been with Marguerite,' Hélin said. 'Because, if you remember, I'd only recently murdered her.'

'*Where were you?*'

Hélin gave a sarcastic grin. 'I'll have to consult my engagement diary,' he said, fishing out a shabby book from his back pocket. 'I keep my dates in this. Also dirty jokes so I can tell them to my friends, invitations to the Elysée Palace to see the President, the days when Brigitte Bardot invites me down. Things like that.' He flicked a few pages, then he looked up and grinned. 'Sorry.' he said. 'I can't oblige. I wasn't with your friend Bernadette Hamon.'

'Proof?'

'I was with a dame.'

'Which dame?' Pel said. 'A student?'

'Much more important. A doctor. One of the lecturers.'

'Which one?'

'A gentleman never mentions a lady's name.'

'This time you'd better.'

'Then it was Martine Sirat. You might have a bit of difficulty checking with her, though, because at the moment she's in the States.'

'Where?'

'She's supposed to be doing a sabbatical at Brown University in Boston. But she doesn't start there until next year and she's spending the time in between touring. She took unpaid leave. A bit suddenly. Overnight, in fact. I think she wanted to get away from me.'

'Why?'

'Because I'm a ravisher of women, didn't you know? She found out about Marguerite.'

'You weren't sleeping with Marguerite de Wibaux. Were you sleeping with Doctor Sirat?'

'Of course I was. I have been for a year. But I was growing bored. I told her so, and there was a row. We were at her apartment. In her bed, as a matter of fact. I walked out and at the end of the week I heard she was ill and in danger of a nervous breakdown. The next week she vanished to the States. Perhaps she'll marry a splendid upright honest American and forget me. I expect that's at the back of her mind. She was an incurable romantic. I'm not.'

II

As they returned to the Hôtel de Police, Nosjean was just leaving.

'The Abrillards' case, Patron,' he said as he passed, heading for his car. 'I've got another sighting. A woman turned up in an antique dealer's with a tankard, offering it for sale. Said it was her uncle's. There was a tankard on that list we put out of what was stolen from the Abrillards and the type in the shop was suspicious. He said he'd just go round the back and check on prices. But when he picked up the telephone he heard the shop door go and he found she'd disappeared.'

'Where was this shop?'

'Chagnay. I'm going down there now.'

Pel frowned. There had been a shop in Chagnay connected with the château gang who had emptied large houses of their treasures. He remembered he'd almost made a fool of himself over a woman there, and that the shop had been run by an attractive girl.*

'Isn't Chagnay the place where – ?'

Nosjean blushed. Nosjean's heart was never very stable and he had recently lost the girl he had expected to marry to a tax inspector, for no better reason than that the tax inspector worked regular hours, and wasn't asked to turn out in all weathers or face mad criminals armed with guns. He was even better paid.

'Yes, Patron,' he said. 'It is.'

'Lehmann, wasn't it?' Pel asked. 'Marie-Josephine Lehmann – known as Mijo.'

'That's right, Patron.'

*See *Pel is Puzzled*.

Pel remembered her well. She looked more like Charlotte Rampling than Charlotte Rampling herself and Nosjean had always had a penchant for girls who looked like Charlotte Rampling. He had met her while checking on the theft of the art treasures. At the time he'd been pursuing a librarian who looked like Charlotte Rampling and it had been a pleasant change to chase an expert on antiques who looked like her instead. She had taken quite a shine to Nosjean, especially when he had cleared the case up, and he had seen a lot of her for a few weeks until, as usual, the affair had faded away, the trouble this time a lawyer's typist who looked like – have a guess! – Charlotte Rampling.

Pel nodded. 'Good luck, mon brave,' he said.

Nosjean blushed again and vanished. For a senior sergeant he blushed easily.

Nosjean hadn't returned by evening. The weather had broken and the smoky mists of autumn had given way to rain and a rising wind. Listening to it beat against the window, Pel sat in his office, studying reports. It was a pleasant office, much better than the one he'd had before his promotion from inspector: more comfortable chair, better carpet – choice of colour for officers at his level – view of the city rather than the railway track, and a bigger desk because there were more reports to read.

He had long since been relieved of all other duties so he could concentrate exclusively on finding the Prowler. He was assuming that he was a local man or at least someone residing in the area, because all the murders had taken place within the city boundary. Though they had tried every police authority in the country, no similar series of crimes or mutilations had been reported in recent years in any other part of France.

Pel's eyes ran down the list of names he had written out in large letters and propped against his reading lamp. Schwendermann, Moussia, Sergent, Aduraz and all the other students. Hélin and his three post-graduate friends. Doctor Bréhard and Doctor Padiou. Josset, who had permitted Bernadette Hamon to park her car on his premises. Charier, who had found her body. Roussel, the painter who stored his equipment at 69, Rue Devoin. Doucet, who said he had allowed Honorine Nauray to return home alone from the centre of the city at midnight.

Magueri, the defecting husband, and Chatry, the stood-up boyfriend. The list was a long one.

Or was the Prowler perhaps *none* of the people they'd interviewed, someone they'd never heard of? Someone who didn't even know his victims? Some stranger from out of town who had chosen them at random simply because he had the urge to kill?

Pel lit a cigarette without even noticing and started leafing through the dossiers they had gathered on everyone concerned with the case. *Did* the Prowler know his victims? It seemed very possible. They had taken a long hard look at rejected suitors, but not with much expectation of success because these days young men and women tended to transfer their affections much more readily than in the past, and it had been found that, on the whole, rejected suitors took a much more philosophical view of the business and usually considered there were plenty more fish in the sea.

In any case, there seemed to be only one of them.

Honorine Nauray had stood up Chatry, the salesman, in favour of Doucet, the student, but they were unable to find any connection between Chatry and Marguerite de Wibaux, Bernadette Hamon or Alice Magueri. And since they were certain they had all been murdered by the same man, it seemed impossible that Chatry could be the Prowler.

Stubbing out the cigarette, Pel worked in silence for a while, his mind busy, then, as he tossed aside another file, Claudie Darel appeared. He looked up startled.

'You still here?'

'Just finishing the reports, Patron. I'm going home now.'

'Don't stop en route.'

As she turned to the door, Darcy appeared. He cocked a thumb at her. 'Home,' he said briskly. 'Time you weren't here.'

As she vanished, he turned to Pel. 'You, too, Patron. I'm here to take the weight off your shoulders so you can think. What's keeping you?'

Pel gestured at the files. 'Marguerite de Wibaux. Bernadette Hamon. Alice Magueri. Honorine Nauray. That's what keeps me. They were young. Perhaps the Nauray girl was a bit stupid. Perhaps the Magueri woman was a tart. Perhaps the De Wibaux girl was a snob. But none of them deserved to die.' He paused.

'There's a pattern, Daniel, and it's in here somewhere. They all occurred around midnight. Why?'

'Why not, Patron? It's the safest time for a type like the Prowler. Dark. Nobody about. It's the obvious time and strangling isn't instantaneous. Sometimes it makes a noise.'

'The Boston Strangler didn't worry about noise. He watched, and went after his victims. He got into their apartments by posing as an electrician or something like that. After all, it's the easiest thing in the world to say you're the concierge's brother and she's sent you up to check the heating. Most women don't argue. They're too trusting.'

'Patron!' Darcy sounded patient. '*Ours* aren't like the Boston thing. *Ours* have all been outside. On the pavement. And on the pavement there's nothing special about midnight – only ghosts and the fact that it's dark.'

Pel nodded. He felt old and tired and defeated. He closed the files and rose. 'I'm going home,' he said.

Darcy offered a packet of Gauloises. 'Before you go, Patron. It'll help get through the evening without having one at home.'

Pel studied the cigarettes. After all the smoking he did, he felt his lungs must be in tatters. But he needed a cigarette and after only a pause he took one and lit it, deciding his nerves came first and that his lungs would have to look after themselves.

He blew out smoke and gestured. 'It's a humiliation every time I light one of these,' he admitted. 'Cowardice. Lack of moral fibre. What sort of person is it who doesn't have the will to give it up? Not much. I think I'm a waste of space.'

He drove home slowly, feeling dyspeptic and tired. Life seemed to have lost some of its flavour. It puzzled him a little because he knew it wasn't the Chief's complaints or even their lack of progress. He'd been involved in police work long enough not to let that sort of thing worry him. These days it wasn't even his car or the traffic jams in the Place Wilson.

And it certainly wasn't his home because he no longer lived in the dog kennel he had called a house in the Rue Martin-de-Noinville. He lived at Leu with a woman he loved whom he looked forward to seeing every single day as he drove his car out of the car park at the Hôtel de Police.

To his surprise, the door of the house was opened not by

Madame Pel but by Madame Routy, who had seen him coming.

'Madame's not back yet,' she said sharply, and he remembered then being told by his wife at breakfast that she had to go to Lyons on business. Immediately, he felt bereft and the thought of being at home with only Madame Routy to look at suddenly seemed so appalling he almost turned round, climbed back into his car and headed back to the office. But then Madame Routy changed it all in a moment.

'Wipe your feet,' she said.

It was something she'd never have dared say if his wife had been around but it was like a revelation and immediately he knew what was wrong. There wasn't enough conflict in his private life. His marriage was happy and there were no harsh words between him and his wife. But he had the sort of personality that thrived on conflict. Writers always insisted that soured relationships were easier to write about than sweetness and light, because contention stirred the blood. His wife had been protecting him too carefully and he responded to Madame Routy's challenge with spirit.

'I've wiped them,' he snapped. 'Twice.'

'Well, just remember I've done this floor.'

'Badly, I suppose.' Pel glared. 'What's for dinner?'

'Casserole.'

'One of your burnt offerings?'

'Madame herself prepared it.'

'And you ruined it?'

'I take my orders from Madame, not you.'

Pel had noticed. While he counted for nothing, Madame Routy would have lain down and let his wife wipe her feet on her chest.

'I could do with a drink,' he said. 'That is if you haven't finished it during the afternoon.'

As she gave him tit-for-tat, he began to feel better. Even Madame Routy seemed to feel better. Perhaps it was because there had been no spirit in their exchanges for some time and, with harsh words producing the adrenalin, they both felt more alive.

He hadn't even had a fight with Judge Brisard for ages, he recalled. He'd have to try to arrange one. Judge Brisard was Pel's bête noire, pompous, hypocritical, clever; and claiming a hot line to God. In the old days Pel had bullied him unmercifully but, with experience, he had begun to fight back and now detested Pel as much as Pel detested him. It made for a comfortable relationship from which each knew what to expect – nothing! – with Pel holding the advantage because he'd discovered that, despite the photograph of his wife and children on his desk and his mealy-mouthed references to marital happiness, Brisard had a woman, the widow of a policeman, in Beaune. It was something to be saved in case he ever became too difficult.

It was late when Darcy left the Hôtel de Police. Just as he was putting on his coat, Nosjean turned up from Chagnay. He looked a little sheepish and Darcy who, like everyone else, knew about Marie-Josephine Lehmann, guessed he'd been taking her out for a meal. He was dead right. He had.

He'd been a little nervous but Mijo Lehmann had not been bitter about Nosjean's neglect of her, and had asked no questions, though Nosjean had guiltily supplied a few answers, claiming that with his work – all those criminals, you know! – he'd not been able to get to Chagnay in months. He had hoped it had convinced her but Mijo Lehmann was more intelligent than he realised and, a good-natured, gregarious girl, had simply been pleased to see him again because Nosjean was good-looking, clever and articulate, even if his heart tended to drift where it shouldn't. Nosjean had enjoyed himself, promised to see her again, and moreover had got a line on his quarry into the bargain.

When the woman with the tankard had bolted from the first antique shop in Chagnay she had tried two days later at the shop where Mijo Lehmann held office and had been persuaded to leave a name and address.

'Florence Remaud,' he told Darcy. 'Rue du Vieux Pont, Chatillon. I'll look her up tomorrow.'

To celebrate what might be a solid lead and the chance to clear something off the book, Darcy and Nosjean went for a drink at the Bar Transvaal and it was late when Darcy climbed into his car to go home. He deliberately drove via the old part of the city, miles out of his way, his eyes alert and flickering about him, because Darcy was the sort of man who never worried about time off.

Stopping at a bar near the Ducal Palace in the vague hope of bumping into Hélin, instead he bumped into Doctor Padiou and they stood talking and drinking for a while, Darcy dropping carefully primed questions at intervals into the conversation. To his surprise he learned that Padiou had known Marguerite de Wibaux ever since they'd been children.

It came out quite by chance as they talked. Suddenly it seemed that Padiou knew a great deal about her and, since they had so far not associated him with her, Darcy probed.

When it finally emerged, Padiou made no attempt to hide the fact. 'I was born in Belgium, too,' he said.

'So you're a Belgian, in fact?'

'Technically, yes. But only because my father happened to be working on that side of the border at the time and he and my mother were living there. Later he practised medicine in Mezières like Marguerite's father, and we ended up in the same village. Her parents had money. My parents had money. It was inevitable we should know each other.'

'Have you seen much of her here?' Darcy asked. 'Since she arrived at the university?'

'Occasionally. But not much socially. I wasn't interested in her.'

'Why didn't you tell us this before?'

Padiou smiled. 'Simple. You didn't ask and I always understood it was wiser to volunteer nothing in case it got you into trouble.'

Darcy glared. It might be worth looking more closely into Padiou, he decided. He was a likeable young man who had always been helpful, but there was just a possibility that his likeableness was put on, and the fact that he had hidden his association with Marguerite de Wibaux might well be because he preferred to keep it quiet rather than that he was attempting to stay out of trouble. Even at best, it could be regarded as obstructionism and Article 63 of the Penal Code, which related to non-assistance to a person in danger, might well be stretched to fit this case, because holding back facts could be regarded as endangering the woman the Prowler had selected as his next victim.

Leaving in a sour mood, Darcy reflected that however much

they claimed to support the Police, people always seemed to have the wrong idea about them. Assuming they existed for no other reason than to harass them, they never appeared to notice that they protected them from thieves, muggers, terrorists and various other kinds of wrongdoers, or that while they were snug in their beds or the arms of their beloveds, the Police were braving not only guns, knives and bombs but also the bitter weather and the rain that could come down off the Plateau de Langres into the city as if it came direct from Siberia. Perhaps the trouble lay with the few bent policemen who gave the organisation a bad name, and with the media who loved to make much of them when they appeared. After all, thanks to the Police, a few people ended up behind bars, a few frauds were halted in their tracks, a few young girls were saved from – Darcy's thoughts stopped dead.

But not all! There were four women in this city – *his* city – who hadn't been saved and the fact that Padiou had known Marguerite de Wibaux most of her life but hadn't admitted it rather changed the complexion of their attitude to him.

It was after midnight as he drove home through the Rue de Rouen district. The streets were deserted and everything was silent, the flat-fronted houses dark. Every now and then he stopped and waited. He wasn't sure why. Just that it seemed a good idea. On one occasion, he heard a group arguing in an upper room. It sounded like an Italian street riot. The window was open and their voices came out, loud, clear and apparently very angry, as if they were about to snatch up knives and attack each other. He waited for a scream of anguish but it turned out that they were merely discussing where to go on holiday the following August.

Ten minutes later he was watching the last customers drift from a bar, eyeing them as they vanished into the dark and the landlord hauled down the metal-slatted shutters with a roar like a bomb going off. Setting the car in motion again, he drove slowly away. Then, as he stopped at the end of the Rue des Fosses to join the main road, he suddenly heard the clatter of heels and there was something about the noise that indicated urgency – and fear.

Pulling the car across the road, he waited and, sure enough, a woman appeared round the corner, running as fast as she could. She looked young, with good legs and long white-blonde hair floating out behind her. Putting the car into gear, he drove after her as she vanished round a corner. Her head turned and, seeing him following, she ran faster, casting terrified looks over her shoulder all the time. Catching her up, he slammed the car in front of her, the front wheels mounting the pavement to block her path. Half-fainting, she backed against the wall, her eyes large and frightened.

'No,' she gasped. 'No!'

Darcy had scrambled from the car.

'No,' she begged. 'No, please!'

'I'm a police officer,' he said, whipping out his identity card with its red, white and blue strip. 'What's the trouble?'

She seemed to sag against the wall, almost melting into its contours. 'Oh, thank God,' she said. 'I wasn't sure. Are you certain you're a policeman?'

'Well, I've been told so. Darcy's the name. Inspector Darcy. You can telephone the Hôtel de Police if you're doubtful. Why were you running?'

In the reflected glow from the headlights he could see she was pretty and scared.

'This man – '

'Which man?'

'He tried to grab me. He got his hands on my neck. He came out of a dark passage. I thought at first he was a drunk. Then I realised he didn't smell like a drunk. I kicked his shins. He let go and I ran. I thought he was following me.'

'Where was this?'

'Back there. Near the corner by the garage.'

'Get into the car,' Darcy snapped.

'You sure – ?'

'Get into the car! Let's see if we can find him. Show me where it happened.'

She seemed uncertain of him but she got into the car. Darcy swung it round with screeching tyres and they headed back down the Rue des Fosses.

'Round here,' she said.

Darcy swung the car into the next street. It was empty except for a prowling cat, the shadows from the street lamps dark against the old brickwork.

'Where did it happen?'

She indicated an alley and he stopped the car alongside it and took a torch from the glove pocket.

'Stay here,' he said. 'Lock the doors and don't open them to anyone.'

Heading down the alley, he found himself in a yard. There were one or two small outbuildings but they all seemed to be locked and empty. The torch flashed over stacked planks and old motor tyres. Standing on the planks to look over the wall, he found he was staring into the yard at the back of the garage. There were several locked cars there, with one or two wrecks that looked as if they'd been hauled in by a breakdown truck. Turning, he shone the torch on the building behind him and realised at once that it was empty. He tried the doors but they were all locked and the sound of his hammering fist echoed hollowly in empty rooms.

Returning slowly to the car, he found the girl peering nervously through the window, her face framed by the pale blonde hair.

'No one there,' he said, climbing inside as she unlocked the door. 'You're sure this is the place?'

'Certain.'

Driving into the next street, they found the garage locked and dark, its front guarded by a wire mesh gate that looked as if it might keep out small children and dogs but not much else. Darcy was on top of it in a second.

'If a cop comes,' he said. 'Tell him I'm in here. The name's Darcy. He'll know me.'

He prowled round the garage premises but there was no sign of anyone. It was clear the attacker had been as clever as usual and checked his escape route ahead. Returning to the car again, he climbed in, lit a cigarette and offered one to the girl. She accepted it with trembling fingers.

'What the hell were you doing alone on the street at this time of night?' he asked. 'Surely you've seen the warnings in the newspapers?'

Her hand moved in a helpless gesture. 'My mother telephoned that she'd had a fall. She lives round the next corner. I've just put her to bed. I had to come. She thought she'd

99

broken her arm. She hadn't. It was only bruised. I'll get the doctor to her tomorrow.'

'Where do you live?'

'Rue St. Brieuc. Round the corner from the Rue des Fosses.'

'Name?'

'Monique Letexier.'

'Mademoiselle?'

'Madame.'

'Where's your husband? Why didn't he come with you?'

'He's not here. He's in Marseilles. He's a sales representative. He's away most of the time.' She looked nervously at Darcy. 'I'll have to come and see her in the morning. And again in the evening. To make sure she's all right. Feed her. Help her to bath. That sort of thing. What shall I do?'

'Get a taxi,' Darcy said briskly. 'Or get one of the neighbours you can trust to walk with you. If I get the chance I'll come myself. Now let's get you home. I've radioed in so there'll be prowl cars on the streets.'

The Rue St. Brieuc contained a few old houses which had been gutted and rebuilt. They were modern-looking with brightly-coloured doorways and brass knockers, good properties surrounded by the old part of the town.

'I like living here,' she explained as Darcy stopped the car and looked curiously about him. 'I was born here and grew up here. Would you like to come in and have a coffee or something?'

Darcy didn't argue. He never did where a pretty girl was concerned. Inside, she offered him a whisky instead. 'I think I'd rather have a drink,' she admitted. 'Wouldn't you?'

He agreed that it was a good idea. 'Did you see this type's face?' he asked.

'No. He was behind me.'

'Is there anything you can remember about the incident?'

'When I kicked him, he said "Oh" or "Ah". Something like that.'

'Which was it?'

'Does it matter?'

'It might'.

'I think it was "Ah".'

'Anything else?'

'He called me a whore.'

'How?'

'How?' She looked puzzled.

'What exactly did he say?'

'Just the word "Whore!"'

'Why should he say that?'

She studied Darcy with steady eyes.

'Why do you ask?'

Darcy's eyes were equally steady. 'Because there've been four murders in this city recently and one of them *was* a whore. At least she sold herself for money.'

'Well, I don't.'

'Then why would he think you did?'

'I don't know. Perhaps because there *are* one or two round this district. It isn't the best area in the city, you know. One or two hang around the Bar de la Renaissance in the Rue Hauts Pavés. Perhaps he thought I was one. Because it was midnight and I was alone.'

'Anybody round that area know you?'

'Most people do. Somebody must have seen me at times going to my mother's. I visit her regularly.'

'We'll go through the place with a fine-toothed comb tomorrow.' Darcy frowned. 'You say he called you a whore. Is that all he said?'

She tried to recall the incident, frowning at her fingers on her glass. 'He said this "Oh" or "Ah" or whatever it was. Then he said something else – one word – and then "Whore". That's all.'

'What was this other word?'

'I don't know. I didn't recognise it. Perhaps I didn't hear him properly.'

'Keep thinking. If you remember or can think what it might be telephone me at the Hôtel de Police. It might be important. Are you alone here?'

'Yes.'

'When does your husband come home?'

'He's supposed to come every week-end but he doesn't always manage it. In fact – ' she paused ' – he hasn't managed it for some time. There are always excuses. I think he's got another woman down there somewhere. In fact, I'm sure he has.'

The old old story. Staring at Monique Letexier with her ivory hair, Darcy decided her husband must be mad.

'What about you?' he asked. 'What do you do?'

'What do you mean? What do I do?'

'Do you have friends, too. Men friends.'

She uttered a sound which was a cross between a sigh and a protest. 'No, I don't. But men look at me. Probably it's my hair. It's natural, though. I don't bleach it. But it catches their eyes. They try to make passes.'

'Do they succeed?'

'What's that supposed to mean?'

'Do they come home with you?'

'No, they don't. I get rid of them'

He decided she had a great deal more self-control than most women in a similar position.

'What about tonight?' he asked. 'Anything you remember about this man who grabbed you? Did you see his hands for instance?'

'No. I just felt them.'

'Did he seem tall?'

'How would I know? He was behind me.'

'He'd have to be close to you to grab you by the throat. You'd feel him. Did he *feel* short, for instance? If he were shorter than you, his forearms would be resting on your shoulders.'

She thought about it and saw the point of the question. 'He was taller than that.'

'Very tall?'

'I'd say he was normal size.'

'Hair? Did you see any hair? If he had long hair you might.'

'No. Nothing.'

'Clothes? Flapping coat? Scarf?'

'No.'

'Smell?'

'Smell?'

'If he were an old tramp who's living rough he'd smell a bit strong, wouldn't he?'

'Yes, I suppose so. No, he smelled of nothing special.'

'Cigarettes? Cigarette smokers have it on their clothes and on their hands.'

'No.'

'Perfume?'

'Perfume? In Heavens's name – !'

'Murderers have been caught by their perfume,' Darcy pointed out. 'Raymond Lepage in Paris two years ago. He was a queer and almost bathed in the stuff. A woman recognised it and the cops got him.'

She shook her head. 'No perfume.'

'Soap?'

'No soap. I'm sorry, there's nothing I can add. I didn't see him. I only felt him.'

'Don't worry. It all helps. It means we don't have to search for drop-outs and drug-takers. He's obviously somebody who looks as normal as I do.'

She gave him a shaky smile. 'I hope you're not him.'

Darcy didn't think it funny. 'Voice?' he asked.

'He said this "Ah". Well, it wasn't just "Ah". It was different.'

'In what way?'

'I don't know. It just was.'

'What about his feet? Did you hear him come up behind you?'

'No. He must have been wearing rubber-soled shoes.'

'What about a knife? Did you see a knife?'

'He tried to strangle me.'

'He also – ' Darcy remembered their decision to keep the mutilations quiet and changed step. 'There's just one more point. Don't talk about this.'

'To no one? I'd like to talk to someone.'

'Try the Police. Me.' Darcy smiled his toothy smile. 'I'll be available.'

'What about my mother? Suppose I have to get someone to go with me when I see her? She'll wonder why.'

'Spin her a yarn. Tell her you're scared. There've been plenty of warnings in the papers.'

She gave him a twisted smile. 'I was relying on being able to tell a few friends. A woman likes to gossip and this is the best bit of gossip I've had for a long time. Why can't I?'

'The press. You'll get hordes of them on your doorstep. They've turned up in the city in dozens. Besides, we want to keep this as dark as we can.'

'To beat the press boys?'

'To beat the type who's doing it. He won't know whether you saw him or not. Whether you heard what he said or not. So he'll be scared. This is the first time he's failed. Or at least it's the first time we know about. He'll be worried sick. He might even have another go.'

'At me?'

'It's possible, if he thinks you might be able to identify him. But don't worry. We'll be watching you. There'll be someone keeping an eye on you all the time from now on. And *I'll* be keeping an eye on *him* to make sure he *is* watching you.' Darcy rose to his feet. 'It's late. I'd better be off. Lock the door after me. And don't open it to anyone.'

She gave him a worried look. 'Don't go,' she begged. 'You've made me scared. Have another drink.'

It occurred to Darcy that she was not only scared but interested, especially if her husband were indifferent. He was a handsome man and he'd experienced it before. He sat down again.

'What do you do with yourself?' he asked.

'I'm a teacher,' she explained, pouring him another drink. 'At an infants' school. Teaching reading, writing, drawing, how to sit still, how to behave.'

As Darcy finished his second drink and rose again, her eyes were beseeching.

'Do you have to go?'

'This time, yes.' Darcy smiled, showing all his splendid white teeth. 'But I'll be back. There's a lot to look into round here.' He glanced at her admiringly. 'More than you'd think.'

12

If nothing else, the attack on Monique Letexier proved that Le Rôdeur was still with them. But this time he hadn't used the cord he'd used on the other girls. 'If he had,' Darcy said, 'she wouldn't be here.'

They assumed he'd dropped it and, sure enough, Brochard found it – a length of rope knotted at the ends, near the pile of planks Darcy had noticed. Leguyader and the Lab. boys started to go over it but nobody had much hope of their efforts producing an identity, because it looked like nothing else but a piece of old clothes line and there were thousands of those in the city.

Monique Letexier's mother, her arm blue with bruises, confirmed the time of her daughter's visit in response to her telephone call, and the owner of the Bar de la Renaissance admitted that women, whom he knew were not all they ought to be, sometimes used his premises to pick up men.'

'There's nothing I can do about it,' he admitted. 'They talk together. He buys her a drink. They talk some more. I don't hear because I don't listen. They go off together. How do I know what they're up to?'

While they were talking, Aimedieu was checking the yard where they'd found the cord. Like all the other yards they'd investigated in that part of the city, it was drab and decaying and the buildings surrounding it were locked and the windows nailed up.

'Condemned.' The speaker was a short stout individual in green greasy overalls.

Aimedieu turned. 'Who're you?'

The short man stared back at him aggressively. 'Come to

105

that,' he said, 'who're you?'

Aimedieu produced his identity card. 'Police,' he said.

'What's wrong? I've done nothing.'

'I didn't say you had. We're investigating an attack that was made in the street here last night. On a woman.'

The man's jaw dropped. 'Holy Mother of God,' he said. 'Another of these?' His manner changed abruptly. 'I'm Bouyon. Patrice Bouyon. I have the garage round the corner. I've come for some of my planks.' He indicated the pile Darcy had climbed to look over the wall. 'I got permission to store things here until I can take them to the dump.' He gestured at the houses. 'In there, too. Just old tyres and bent fenders that I have to get rid of. Can I have my planks?'

'No,' Aimedieu said. 'You can't. You'll have to wait until we've finished.'

'How long?'

'Might be several days.'

'In the meantime I go bankrupt?'

Aimedieu noticed that Bouyon looked strong and that his thick wrists ended in strong, meaty fingers.

'Where were you last night around midnight?' he asked.

Bouyon looked startled. 'Where I ought to be. In bed with my old woman. Where else would I be?'

'You might have been here.'

Bouyon's face changed. 'Here, steady on. I don't go in for that sort of thing.'

'Have you proof you were at home and in bed with your wife?'

Bouyon gave Aimedieu a cold look. 'Yes, of course. The old man from next door was in bed with us. We always have him in for an hour or two around midnight.'

Aimedieu didn't smile. 'Have you any children?'

'Six. Teenagers.'

'All at home?'

'All of them. My kids behave themselves. They get a thump round the ear if they don't.'

'With six teenagers in the house then, they'd know if you were home, wouldn't they? You needn't worry.'

'Thank you.' Bouyon looked relieved. 'For nothing.'

Aimedieu turned his attention to the old buildings. 'Ever seen anyone in here?'

'They're locked. I've got the key and nobody goes in but me.'

Aimedieu borrowed Bouyon's bunch of keys. Inside, he found the rooms empty except for a few odd cartons, empty bottles and tins, an old suitcase, and scrap iron and tyres from Bouyon's garage. In the kitchen of one of the houses he saw a rat. But nothing else.

'Nobody had been in, Patron,' he reported to Pel. 'The Prowler hadn't been hanging about there.'

Once again they checked everybody involved, but they were all able to show what they were doing. Darcy himself could vouch for Padiou who couldn't possibly have reached the Rue des Fosses from where Darcy had left him and, somehow, that seemed to rule him out from all the other attacks. Only Moussia seemed uncertain. For once Schwendermann had not heard him banging about in his room below, and Schwendermann had been in his room all evening except to go downstairs about 11.30.p.m. to inform the girls on the bottom floor that he'd be out the following night at a lecture.

'Do you always tell people when you're going out?' Darcy asked.

'Iss usual,' Schwendermann said. 'People call. To borrow books. Or for – how do you say it? For company. We have not much money so our entertainment iss just by talking, you know. So, when we go out, we tell someone in case someone comes and they want to wait. You understand?'

'Do people come late at night?'

Schwendermann smiled. 'Students must not get up early like workers in a factory. Often they study late. Often they talk late. To early hours, you see. I think you must ask the others to prove this.'

Darcy did ask the others to prove it, though he knew it to be true. The late customers in the bars in the city centres were invariably students and on the few occasions when they'd been called to some trouble between them it was invariably after midnight. What Schwendermann said was correct, and the girls in the ground-floor flats confirmed Schwendermann's story with a willingness that left no room for doubt. Sure, he'd called in and he'd been in his room all evening because they'd heard his radio and Annie Joulier and Marina Lorans had been to his room about 9.p.m. to borrow sugar, going together because they were nervous of the dark stairs.

Which left Moussia. Nobody had noticed Moussia, it seemed. Moussia's explanation, offered between contortions on the floor, was that he'd had a hangover. He'd drunk too much wine the night before and decided to have an early night.

'I was asleep,' he said. 'I'm sick of this place. Nobody's friendly. They don't like pieds noirs and I'm thinking of moving in with a Tunisian type called Habib in the Rue Novembre 11.'

There was no way of proving he hadn't been asleep, and certainly he'd been seen the night before in one of the city bars knocking back cheap wine with Habib, but that was no proof that he'd remained in his room the following night.

Which left their other chief suspect, Hélin. But Hélin's friends, Jenet, Detoc and Hayn, were prepared to swear that he'd been with them, so that they ended up exactly where they'd been before. Nowhere.

Lighting a cigarette, Pel sat back to study the reports, searching as he always did for that small thing, that trivial clue that linked one incident to another. As he tossed the last file aside, he realised he had smoked his way through half a pack of cigarettes.

Disgusted with himself, he began to work out what it had cost him, and then what it cost him each week to smoke. It wasn't a large step from that to working out what it cost him monthly and from that to yearly and finally to how much he had wasted during his lifetime. It was an astronomical figure and he decided that if he'd never started he could have been a wealthy man.

For a while he wondered if he could make another attempt to give it up but it wasn't with much of a struggle that he came to the conclusion it was a lost cause. And people with lost causes, he decided, might just as well accept they weren't going to win them. As he drew the first grateful puffs on another cigarette, Leguyader arrived from the Lab., apparently delighted by the fact that he could offer nothing helpful. The two things which pleased Leguyader most were being able to produce a mass of evidence which would clear up a case so he could boast that the Police didn't need detectives while they had the Lab., or none at all, so he could see the mounting anger on Pel's face.

This time it was the anger.

'Perfectly ordinary clothes line,' he explained smugly. 'They're different from ropes because, apart from the cheapest, the strands are woven, not twisted, and the weave shows clearly on the enlarged photographs of the victims' necks. So – ' he smiled cheerfully ' – that won't help you much. You can buy clothes lines at any ironmongers, at the Nouvelles Galéries, at street-corner grocery shops. Most women have one; some have two. People also buy them to tie up suitcases and trunks or cartons of books or crockery when they move house. I'd imagine that are probably 25,000 in this city. There isn't much point in asking.'

'Leave me to do my job in my own way,' Pel growled.

Leguyader rose. 'Far be it for *me* to tell you your job,' he said.

Pel glared. Given half a chance, Leguyader would tell *God* His job.

He stared angrily at the door as it closed behind Leguyader. It would be nice, he thought sourly, if Leguyader's left leg could drop off.

Nosjean was next. 'The Abrillard theft, Patron,' he said. 'I think I've found the woman – probably also the man.'

Pel sighed. Nothing was ever finished neatly in police work and the cases on the list always overlapped so that the slate was never wiped clean. And, despite the fact that he was supposed to be wholly engaged on the Prowler cases, he liked to be available to members of his squad if they wished to see him to ask advice.

'Inform me,' he said.

'Name of Florence Remaud. She lives with her husband, Georges Remaud, at 7, Rue du Vieux Pont, Chatillon. He's an unemployed bricklayer's labourer. The police in Chatillon know him. He's not got a record but there's been a rash of break-ins up there and they've been watching him.'

'Perhaps they didn't watch hard enough.'

Nosjean shrugged. 'They've nothing they can pin on him,' he said, 'but they're pretty certain he pinched a camera from a house in the Rue de Dijon when he was working on a building site nearby. Unfortunately they never found the camera.'

'What about the woman? Does she fit the description of the one who tried to sell the tankard? Smart, fair-haired, slim.'

It was Nosjean's turn to sigh. 'Unfortunately, no, Patron. This one's a brunette and scruffy, and she's hardly slim because she's well and truly pregnant.'

Pel sniffed and pushed his glasses up to his forehead. 'Doesn't mean a thing,' he said. 'This has been going on a long time and she was probably two or three months pregnant when they robbed the Abrillards and it didn't show. She could be five months now. It shows *then*, doesn't it?'

Nosjean allowed himself a thin smile. 'I don't know, Patron. I've never been pregnant. But I think you're about right.'

'And this business of being fair-haired. She could have worn a wig. I think we should get a warrant to search the place.'

At the Chief's conference at noon, it was decided they should have even more men on the streets during the hours of darkness. Pomereu promised extra prowl cars and Nadauld said he could produce another dozen men. There would be complaints about overwork but they'd have to lump it.

'Can we borrow a few more from the districts?' the Chief asked. 'And how about you, Pel? Can you spare anybody?'

Pel offered Misset at once. He'd groan that his feet ached and doubtless go down with flu and it would take some doing to keep him on the job, but they'd have to try, if only to make his life miserable. All the same, Pel had a suspicion that they were wasting their time. Pushing men out on the streets wouldn't help a lot in the long run. All it would do would make the Prowler more cautious, because he'd obviously never attack anyone if there were a cop around. And the best cop in the world couldn't make himself invisible while, if the Prowler hid himself first as he undoubtedly did, then he'd inevitably see the cops before the cops saw him.

That lunchtime he and Darcy tried the Hôtel Centrale again. They'd taken to eating there more often these days and Pel could only put it down to the more gracious life he was living since his marriage. Always brimming with confidence, Darcy had never hesitated to use the place but in his Rue Martin-de-Noinville days, Pel's style of living had gone with the house he'd occupied and he had tended to favour the more prosaic Bar Transvaal.

Gau, the manager, greeted them as if they were old buddies. 'I expect you're being kept busy,' he said cheerfully.

He had meant nothing more than mere conversation but, seeing the look Pel gave him, splintered and sharp as broken glass, he hurried on, anxious to put things right with a little jolly conversation.

'We have a special guest with us at the moment,' he said.

Pel said nothing. The President of France? The Queen of England? The President of the United States? Brigitte Bardot even?

'National lottery winner,' Gau whispered. 'He's staying here. Arrived with an attaché case full of notes. Deposited it in the hotel safe.'

'Locked, I trust,' Pel said in the voice he normally reserved for Judge Brisard and those of his wife's relations he didn't like.

'The safe?' Gau smiled. 'Of course.'

Pel's face didn't change. 'The case I meant,' he said.

Gau decided he was joking and managed a laugh. Fishing behind the reception desk, he produced *Le Bien Public*, the local newspaper. 'MILLION FRANC WINNER IN CITY,' the headline said. 'DECIDING HOW TO SPEND IT. I DO NOT TRUST CHEQUES, HE CLAIMS.'

'So he has it all locked in the attaché case,' Gau explained. He gestured at a small spectacled man sitting in the bar with a large whisky in front of him. 'That's him. Henri Bayetto. He arrived this morning from Lyons. He's here because he wants to start a cellar and he can't make up his mind whether to concentrate on Bordeaux or Burgundy.'

'Bordeaux,' Pel said coldly, 'is a medicine. Burgundy's for the strong.'

They used the quiet to discuss the Prowler. The press so far having discovered nothing about the attack on Monique Letexier, they decided to leave it that way.

'Keep it to ourselves,' Pel suggested. 'Let him wonder what happened? Just watch her. If he doesn't know whether she reported it or not, he might come out for another go.'

When they returned to the Hôtel de Police, Nosjean had obtained the necessary warrant to search the home of Georges and Florence Remaud and was just leaving with Bardolle.

The Remauds were surprised to see him back, because they'd seen him off the premises on the previous occasion with wide smiles as if they'd felt they'd seen the last of him.

'I'm going to protest,' Remaud said. 'It's a gross intrusion on human rights.'

He was a slim, good-looking young man with horn-rimmed spectacles who looked as if he read all the intellectual magazines and belonged to all the correct political parties. He knew his rights and continued to quote them as Nosjean and Bardolle went through the house. They took their time, working carefully to leave no untidiness. There was no sign of the guns that had been used – whether they were genuine or imitation – no sign of stocking masks or the suitcase that had been used to carry the loot away, and no sign of the fair wig they were certain Florence Remaud had worn.

'All chucked in the river, I expect,' Nosjean murmured as they met on the landing.

Towards the end of the second hour, however, Bardolle came up with a tankard in a brown paper bag at the bottom of a cupboard under the stairs.

'Yours?' he asked, holding it up for Remaud to see.

The tankard was heavy-shouldered and looked valuable, but it was of pewter, polished over many years so that it looked like silver.

'It's not very valuable,' Remaud said.

'No,' Bardolle agreed. 'No thief would bother to steal that.'

'That's right.'

'Unless,' Bardolle suggested, 'in his hurry he *thought* it was silver.'

'Are you suggesting – ?'

'Me?' Bardolle was all innocence. 'What could I be suggesting?'

Nosjean turned to Florence Remaud. 'This is the one you tried to sell in Chagnay, isn't it?' he asked. '*Why* did you try to sell it? And why did you leave in a hurry?'

She glanced at her husband and he jumped in quickly with an answer.

'You've only to look at her, haven't you?' he said. 'She's five months pregnant. We need the money.'

'And the hurry?'

'Because she was worried. She'd been on her feet a lot that day and she was feeling pains. She's had one miscarriage and she didn't want another. She came home and I put her to bed.'

They couldn't argue about it so Nosjean tried another angle. 'Mind if we take it with us?'

'Why?'

'Just to check it isn't silver.'

'You can see it isn't silver!'

'Well, shall we say we *think* it isn't silver. But it's as well to check, isn't it?'

With Remaud watching warily, Nosjean examined the tankard carefully. Underneath, round the rim in small Roman lettering, there was a name – Edouard Rummus, Lyons.'

'Who's Edouard Rummus?' he asked.

Remaud shrugged. 'The manufacturer, I expect. It'll be on everything they produce.'

'How do you come to have it? Did you buy it? Was it given to you? Or did you find it at the side of the road after it had fallen off a lorry?'

Remaud favoured Nosjean with a glare. 'It was given to me by a type at Corlay. I built them an extension. They gave it to me because they were pleased.'

Nosjean nodded. 'So,' he said, 'if it was given to you by a type at Corlay, why did your wife tell the shop at Chagnay that it was her uncle's?'

As Remaud's head turned, Nosjean caught the glance that passed between him and his wife. Remaud recovered quickly.

'She was mixing it up with another one,' he said 'That one was given to us by her uncle.'

'And that one? Where's that one?'

Remaud didn't bat an eyelash. 'We sold it. For the money.'

Nosjean nodded sagely. 'I thought you might have,' he said.

Remaud was only partly right. The tankard had come from Lyons all right but Edouard Rummus wasn't the name of the manufacturer.

'He's my brother-in-law,' Abrillard said. 'He has a small business in Lyons. Fifteen years ago they celebrated their hundredth anniversary, and they had three dozen of these made to give to their favourite customers.'

'How did *you* come to have it?' Nosjean asked.

Madame Abrillard, her eyes still bruised, looked up. 'They ran out of people to give them to, so they simply gave the ones that were left to their friends. There were only six left by that time. When they'd finished, there was still one left so they took it home and used it themselves. Eventually they gave it to us. Because I'd admired it.'

'You can identify it with certainty as yours?'

'Won't my fingerprints be on it?'

Nosjean smiled. 'Not any more, I should think,' he said. 'Anything else?'

'There's a dent in the side where I dropped it. Near the handle.'

Sure enough the dent was there.

'I used it for flowers,' Madame Abrillard said. 'But I always polished it so that it looked like silver. I think the burglar thought it *was* silver.'

Nosjean smiled 'I think he did, too,' he said.

Though Nosjean was making progress, Pel and Darcy weren't.

Because they were beginning to grow desperate, they pulled in Josset, the man who had allowed Bernadette Hamon to use his land to park her car, and questioned him closely.

He didn't know any of the other victims but he was uneasy and they finally dug out of him that one of his neighbours had once punched him on the nose for molesting his daughter.

'When was this?'

'Five years ago.' Josset's eyes rolled miserably.

'Were the police called?'

'No. He just hit me. He broke my false teeth and my glasses. You shouldn't hit a man with glasses.'

'Men with glasses shouldn't molest people's daughters,' Darcy snapped.

'No.' Josset sighed. 'But it's difficult. I'm a bachelor. And I think I'm different, and she was afriolante – very sexy.'

They plugged at him all afternoon but all they could be certain of was that, although he probably wasn't the Prowler, he could well be a Prowler in years to come.

'Put him on the list of deviates,' Pel said as they released him.

'He'll bear watching.'

With Claudie Darel, looking more like Mireille Mathieu than ever, producing coffee for them or Cadet Martin bringing beer from the Bar Transvaal when they needed something stronger, they went once more through the list, from Wolfgang Schwendermann, who had found the first of the Prowler's victims, right up to Monique Letexier who, but for Darcy's restless prowling, would have been his latest.

They had checked on Doctor Padiou's admission that he'd known Marguerite de Wibaux most of his life and found it true. But it led nowhere and there was nothing in the fact that he'd not mentioned it, beyond what he'd said. Padiou had a light-hearted, indolent manner that made them suspicious but there was nothing they could prove against him.

'Schwendermann knew De Wibaux, too,' Pel said, going slowly down the list. 'So, of course, did the other students – Sergent and Aduraz. Padiou also knew Bernadette Hamon. Doctor Bréhard knew them both, too, because De Wibaux's father occasionally lectured at the hospital and he'd met her through him and through Padiou.'

'None of them seem to have known Magueri, Patron,' Darcy pointed out.

'No.' Pel frowned. 'But Doucet knew Nauray because she was his girlfriend – and he also knew De Wibaux because she was another student.'

'But none of them,' Darcy pointed out, 'knew Monique Letexier. Only *I* knew Monique Letexier.'

'I expect you'll get to know her better, too,' Pel said drily. He took out a cigarette and stared at it as if it might explode in his face. 'Is there no way at all to stop smoking cigarettes?' he asked.

'Only one I know, Patron. Smoke cigars.'

'I tried a pipe once. All it did was set my pocket on fire.' Defiantly, Pel applied a match, dragged the smoke down to his socks, and sat back, feeling guilty but better. He sighed and shifted the files around on his desk for a while.

'There's no pattern, Daniel,' he said. 'And there ought to be. Nothing common to them all.'

'Except that he probably said "Whore" to them all, Patron, as he did to Monique Letexier. That's something we don't know because all but Monique Letexier are dead.'

'It seems to indicate that he thought they were *all* whores. But they weren't.'

'They *were* out and on the streets late at night.'

'But the people we suspect might have killed them don't seem to have been. Not that it means much. Mass murderers never turn out to be among the names on the list. Grenoble will probably pick up some type for interfering with little girls and he'll admit everything.'

'Perhaps,' Darcy went on, 'he doesn't live here at all. Perhaps he's from Langres or Chatillon and just comes in by car when he feels the itch.'

Pel was silent for a moment. 'Letexier,' he said slowly. 'L. An L's different from a W or an H or an M or an N, which is what the others seemed to be marked with – the initial letter of their name. *They* all had three or more strokes. L has only two.'

'M for Monique has more than two, Patron.'

Pel frowned. 'Could it be some sort of witchcraft thing, Daniel? A message or something? A propitiation? A sacrificial mark? There've been black magic murders before now. Ceremonial burnings. Mutilations.'

'Not many inside the city boundary, Patron. Mostly those types come from the mountain or forest villages. Where the people are still only just down from the trees.'

'It can't be ruled out. Is he a nutter who believes in killing as a sacrifice? Do we know anybody who knows anything about it?'

'I don't number any among my friends, Patron, but I'll ask around.'

Pel was still frowning deeply, staring at the smouldering end of his cigarette.

'Something bothering you, Patron?' Darcy asked.

'Yes,' Pel stirred. 'I think next time he might use that knife he has for more than just marking their cheeks. The next one might be rather a messy one.' He sighed. 'You know what it's going to come to in the end, don't you?'

Darcy nodded. 'Yes, Patron. Something to fetch him out from wherever he's hiding. A bait.'

'And you know who that will have to be, don't you?'

Darcy nodded. 'Yes, Patron. Claudie.'

13

Claudie Darel sat opposite Pel. She was small and slight and looked well-scrubbed, a highly efficient and attractive young woman, with straight black hair styled in a bob with a fringe coming down to arching black eyebrows over large brown eyes. As always, Darcy was impressed with how much she looked like Mireille Mathieu. Despite her ability, there was something innocent about Claudie, as not only Darcy had noticed but practically every man in the Hôtel de Police from Cadet Martin, through Nosjean and De Troq', who were both ardently pursuing her – and Misset, who would have liked to pursue her but hadn't a cat in hell's chance – right up to Pel and beyond him to the Chief himself.

She was wearing a neat blue dress and a blue jacket with brass buttons and she was looking brisk and confident. 'I'll do it, Patron,' she said.

'We could get someone from Paris,' Pel offered. 'Someone who's experienced at it.'

'She'll probably be like a house-side and he wouldn't look twice at her.' There was confidence in the words, a certainty that she was attractive to men, yet there was no self-satisfaction, no smugness.

'Besides,' she went on, 'I've done it before. For a molester.'

'This isn't a molester,' Darcy said. 'He's killed four women and there may be others we don't know about yet.'

'I'd still like to do it, Patron.'

'It means walking about the streets. Dark streets. He doesn't operate where there are lights.'

'I'm not afraid of the dark, Patron.'

'Very well,' Pel said. 'We'll have De Troq' following close

behind all the way. He'll be careful, I'm sure.' Despite his worry, Pel managed a smile.

Claudie smiled back. 'I think you should give Jean-Luc Nosjean a go, too, at some point. He'll be jealous as hell if he thinks De Troq's having me all to himself.'

Pel smiled again. Everybody smiled at Claudie, for her freshness, her frankness, her cheek even.

'One of them will be near you all the time. I promise you that.' Pel paused. 'But they can't be near enough to prevent an attack. We can't guarantee that you won't get hurt.'

They couldn't guarantee anything, in fact, he thought. If the Prowler decided for a change to use his knife they wouldn't have a chance.

'You're under no compulsion,' he pointed out. 'De Troq' says he'll do it if necessary. Put on make-up and carry a handbag. He's small. He's done this sort of thing before.'

Claudie smiled. 'De Troq' wasn't after a murderer, Patron. He was after someone who was beating up queers. He didn't have to look feminine, just effeminate, and friend Prowler might know the difference. No, Patron. I'll do it. Can I have a gun with me?'

'Of course. And we'll fix a bleeper to your clothes so we'll know exactly where you are all the time.'

'You'll also,' Darcy said, 'have a radio. Tuned to De Troq' or whoever's watching you so you can let him know if you're being followed.'

Claudie smiled. 'I'll be a walking electronic gadget,' she said cheerfully. 'Son et Lumière. Wired up for sight and sound. When do I start?'

'Tonight. We'll drop you in the Rue de Rouen district and you'll walk around from eleven o'clock until one in the morning which is when he always seems to strike. You'd better go home now and report back here about 10.p.m.'

'I'll be ready, Patron. I'll wear a white coat, so that whoever's following me will be able to see me easily.' Pel nodded approvingly, and she went on cheerfully. '*And* high heels. So that if he can't see me, he'll be able to hear me.'

'Good. Good.'

'I shall also – ' Claudie smiled ' – have on a high-necked sweater in case he tries to use that knife of his to cut my throat, and a pull-on hat with a wad of something thick underneath in case he tries to hit me over the head. Is there anything else?'

Pel beamed at her. 'I think you've thought of everything.' he said.

Glancing at his watch, Pel telephoned his wife and suggested lunch in the city.

'It seems a long time since we met,' he pointed out heavily.

He was warmed by the note in her voice. 'Hôtel Centrale?' she asked at once. 'It's just behind my office.'

There was a panic on when they arrived and the chef, with a good French instinct for theatricality, was in the process of throwing a fit of hysteria.

'It was on the menu,' he was saying in a penetrating whisper to Gau, the manager. 'Sauce poivrade. They were given sauce chasseur. And they didn't even notice.' He slapped his forehead with the heel of his hand. 'I might as well run a hamburger bar. I might just as well serve Americans for whom, as we all know, a meal isn't a meal unless it's between two pieces of bread. I've even heard of them drinking coca-cola with pheasant. One day – *one day!* – someone will call me over and say "This is the wrong sauce".'

Henri Bayetto, the lottery winner, was still sitting in the bar, still with a large whisky in front of him. As far as Pel could tell, he'd been there since the day he'd first seen him.

'He must get through a lot of whisky,' he said as Gau came across to them.

Gau smiled. 'He decided to stay on a little. He likes our city.'

'Satisfied with the service, is he?'

'More than satisfied.'

'Eat a lot?'

'He has a good appetite.'

Pel glanced again at Bayetto. 'Spending much?'

'He likes to eat and drink well.'

'Pay cash?'

'On his bill. He's done a bit of shopping. I recommended a few friends. Suits. A little jewellery for his wife. I sent him to Merciers'. He's looking for antiques now.'

'I hope you've seen his money.'

'I have indeed.' Gau smiled. 'Inside the attaché case. He

showed me. It's full of hundred-franc notes. In packets, fresh from the bank. All neatly stacked.'

They ate their meal in silence. Occasionally Pel was aware of his wife glancing at him but she said nothing until they had finished.

'Are you thinking about the murders?' she asked.

'Yes.'

'You've hardly spoken. I don't think you're really here, are you?'

Pel admitted that his mind had been far away.

'I expect you'll find out who did them in the end,' she said. 'You usually do.'

Mellowed by his lunch, Pel sat at his desk and, taking out a large sheet of paper, began to write names on it and attach them to each other with lines drawn with coloured pencils until it looked a little like a genealogical table. It was his way of trying to set his thoughts in order. Some of the males involved in the case – Schwendermann, Padiou, Bréhard, Hélin, Doucet, knew more than one of the victims. Others like Magueri, the salesman Chatry, and Monique Letexier's husband, who, sure enough, *had* been with another woman at a hotel at Hyères on the Mediterranean coast, knew only one.

Other lines on the chart indicated alibis. Magueri had been at home but, since the woman he lived with was at work, he was alone and, since his wife was on the streets, it was possible that *he*, if no one else, had a grudge against prostitutes. Yet, somehow, it seemed an unlikely premise, because Magueri – who, it had appeared, was hardly moral himself – was not really the type to get worked up about immorality. If the Prowler were anybody on their list, it seemed Hélin or Moussia was still their best bet.

They were really still up against a blank wall, however. The Prowler was anonymous and, Pel suspected, would still be anonymous even when they found him – so ordinary in appearance and behaviour nobody had ever really noticed him.

That afternoon Schwendermann turned up at the Hôtel de Police and asked for Pel. Expecting information, Pel saw him at once, but it turned out to be nothing more than the information that Moussia had left the Rue Devoin and moved in with the

Tunisian student, Habib, in the Rue Novembre 11.

'Why didn't he come himself?'

Schwendermann shrugged. 'I think he iss afraid,' he said in his fussy nosey-parker way. 'He thinks perhaps you watch him.'

'*Why* has he moved?'

'He sleeps out for a long time. How do you say – on and off. Some nights he iss at the Rue Devoin. Other nights he iss with Habib. He leaves late at night.'

'Was there some trouble at the Rue Devoin?'

Schwendermann gestured. 'Iss not popular, I think. The girls do not like him.' He smiled. 'I do not like him much. I think he does not wish to admit he iss not like. Not to himself even, you understand. That iss why I come on his behalf. I am in the city doing my architecture, looking at the old houses. Are many nice old houses here. So – ' Schwendermann shrugged ' – I say I will tell for him.'

It seemed a good idea to have another talk with Moussia and Pel sent Brochard round to bring him in. The Algerian was indignant and tearful by turns.

'I didn't know it was an offence,' he bleated.

'You're expected to report a change of address. You could well be needed.'

'Am I a suspect or something?'

'Everybody in the city's a suspect. And we've enough to do without having to search for you if we need you.'

'Why *should* you need me?'

Pel glared. 'Even if you're not a suspect,' he snapped, 'you could still be a witness. *Why* didn't you inform us?'

Moussia made a defeated gesture. 'Well,' he said, 'Schwendermann likes to mind other people's business and I thought it would be all right.'

It appeared to be just as Schwendermann had suggested. Moussia had been the last of the students in Number 69, Rue Devoin to take up residence there and he had never fitted. Conscious of being frozen out, he had decided to move.

'They're all snobs,' he said. 'Racists, too. Annie Joulier's always poking fun at me. Marguerite, too. After what I did for her as well.'

Pel leaned forward. 'What *did* you do for her?'

Moussia looked at him, then at Darcy then back at Pel. He

licked his lips. 'All sorts of things,' he said. 'Errands. Fetching books from the library. I mended her car. I changed the wheels. That sort of thing. She had too much money, that one.'

As the door closed behind Moussia, Pel looked up at Darcy. 'Daniel,' he said slowly, 'I think we've just heard another good reason why someone should want Marguerite de Wibaux dead.'

When he reached home that night, Madame Routy met him at the door. Very deliberately he wiped his feet for her, making a lot of fuss about it so that she'd not fail to notice. Madame Pel had arrived just ahead of him and, hearing his car, had poured him a small whisky. Because whisky these days cost as much as uranium, it had been Pel's custom before his marriage to save it for important occasions like earthquakes or the end of the world, but she was trying to break him of the habit. As she handed it to him, he caught the warmth in her look. He had always thought of himself as an unlovable individual growing wrinkled and wan before his time because of the pressure of work and the number of cigarettes it forced him to smoke, and to see such affection in his wife's eyes did his heart good. Perhaps, he thought, he might after all be able to struggle on instead of, as he'd often contemplated, giving it all up and going into a monastry or something.

'It's nice to see you again so soon,' he said quietly.

'It's nice to see you, too,' she agreed. 'Though not to see you looking so tired and worried.'

'I like coming home,' he admitted. 'I never used to before. It seems a long time since we sat down together in the evening.'

'Perhaps tonight we can listen to some music.'

Pel's expression faded. 'Not tonight,' he said. 'I have to go out again.'

He was flattered to see the disappointment in her face. 'Do you have to?' she asked.

'I think I do. We're setting up a bait for friend Prowler. We're trying to bring him into the open.'

'What does that mean?'

He drew a deep unhappy breath. 'It means someone has to walk the streets so that he'll attack.'

'A woman?'

'Yes.'

'Who's doing it?'

'Claudie.'

She looked at him in horror. 'Not Claudie,' she said. 'I hope you're going to look after her.'

'That's why I must go in. I can't risk something going wrong.'

'Of course.' He was glad to see she approved. 'I understand. It's surprising how I've learned to understand.' She gestured. 'By the way, we've got a visitor.'

He looked round in alarm. The Chief with a new job? The President of the Republic come to give him the Legion of Honour? One of his relatives? Or, worse still, one of Madame's, on the point of a heart attack or something? Their courtship had been interrupted again and again by the accidents, deaths and similar crises that had occurred among her relations. Despite their wealth, they all seemed to have a gift for dropping dead at the wrong moment.

'You know him well,' Madame said. 'He's in the kitchen having something to eat with Madame Routy.'

'Didier?'

Didier Darras was Madame Routy's nephew and, fortunately, he didn't take after his aunt. In Pel's Rue Martin-de-Noinville days before his marriage, he had been a regular visitor who had brightened Pel's hours because he shared with Pel a hearty dislike of television and his aunt's cooking, and a mutual fondness for boules, fishing and eating out. There had been many times when Pel had lived alone that they had infuriated Aunt Routy by letting her cook one of her disgusting casseroles and then disappearing into the blue so that she had to eat it herself.

Scrubbed spotless, his hair brushed down in damp spikes, his shoes shined until he could see his face in them – to his mother a chief inspector of the Police Judiciaire was akin to royalty – he stood up, wiping his mouth, and they shook hands solemnly. Pel was touched that the boy had troubled to look him up when he now lived so far out of the city.

Didier gestured towards the pantry where Madame Routy was clattering around. 'What's happened?' he asked. 'She's learned to cook. Did *you* make her?'

'Not me, mon vieux. I haven't that much influence. It was

123

Madame Pel.' Pel glanced at his watch. 'It's a long time before dinner. Do you fancy looking round the garden? It has everything. Even a flat drive that's perfect for boules.'

Outside, studying the scenery, Didier grinned. 'I like Madame Pel,' he said. 'She's all right.'

'I'm glad you approve.'

'Nice place you've got here, too. Have you been making a fortune?'

'No,' Pel said, straightfaced. 'It's bribes. Corruption. Hand-outs. That sort of thing. You've heard of it.' He smiled. 'I just happened to marry someone who has a fortune already.'

As they were examining the rockery, the boy turned and looked at Pel. 'I'm thinking of joining the Police,' he said.

'Oh?' Pel was barely listening. 'When?'

'Any time now.'

Pel's head jerked round and he stood staring at the boy, unable to believe he was that old. Yet he was tall and straight and Pel had long since noticed how sturdy he was becoming. He did a few sums in his head. Didier had been about to enter his teens when he'd first met him. And that was how many years ago? Now he must be – Name of God, Pel thought, he was a young man. Which meant that Pel was ageing rapidly. He would soon be reaching retirement, old age and, without doubt, approaching senility. He would very soon – he stopped hurriedly before he had himself dead and buried.

'I'm glad to hear it,' he said. 'I'll give you a strong recommendation. It'll help. Then, before long, I can have you on my squad.' If he hadn't dropped dead in the meantime, he thought with alarm.

'Cadet Martin's about due for normal duties,' he went on. 'You'd have to run the errands, attend to the mail and fetch the beer when we were thirsty. But it would be good experience and stand you in good stead.'

'I'd like that,' Didier said. 'Louise Bray says she'd like me to be in the Police.'

Pel nodded. Didier had been paying court to the girl next door from the day she'd first hit him over the head with her doll. 'A woman's approval's always a good thing to have,' he agreed.

It occurred to him that from now on he'd have to regard Didier as a grown man, not a boy, and there was a moment of awkward silence as he wondered how to continue.

'How did you get here?' he asked.

'Bike. I've got a new one.'

'It was kind of you to come and see us.'

Didier shrugged. 'There wasn't much else to do,' he said. 'Louise has gone to stay with her grandfather.'

The visit, it seemed, had been no more than a last-minute decision to fill in an hour or two, and not, after all, because Didier's heart was breaking at not having seen Pel for some time.

'He lives in Spain,' Didier continued, solemn-faced. 'He bought a flat there. Sitges. Would *you* like to live in Sitges?'

'I'd rather live here.' To Pel anything beyond the borders of France was outer darkness.

'Me, too,' Didier agreed. 'I think the Spanish are a pretty awkward lot, anyway. Cause a lot of trouble down there in the Pyrenees. Not like us.'

Pel smiled. This was French chauvinism at its best. Didier was growing up in the right way. Perhaps he could join Pel's Society of Bigots now he was old enough to appreciate what a bigot was.

'Mind you,' Didier went on, 'I believe they play a sort of boules down there, too.'

'That would undoubtedly make them more bearable. How's the fishing?'

Didier shrugged. 'They're a bit short on rivers, I think,' he said. 'And the ones they have are all too big or too deep. Tidal, I believe. They're a stupid lot, these foreigners.' He grinned, knowing Pel well and teasing a little. 'You just can't trust them, can you? They even speak a different language.'

14

Claudie Darel walked slowly along the Rue des Charbonniers in the old part of the city. It was 11.45 p.m. and her feet were beginning to ache. Normally, she wore heels such as she was wearing now only for special occasions when it was worth having tired feet. High heels didn't go with too much walking.

She had started her lonely patrol an hour before when the bars had begun to empty. Now, close to midnight, the streets were emptying, too, and only an occasional car appeared. One of them had slowed up alongside, the driver with his head out of the window making suggestions, and it had startled him more than a little when she'd snapped at him. 'Push off,' she had said, 'or I'll have you arrested. I'm a police officer.' He had bolted like the proverbial rat up a drainpipe.

She had arrived in the sergeants' room in the Hôtel de Police to find everyone there, all of them ready to take their turn on the streets: Lagé; Misset – complaining as usual about the hours he had to work; Aimedieu with his choirboy's face; Bardolle, looking like an amiable drayhorse; Debray and Brochard, like twins staring out of an old faded photograph; Lacocq; Morell; even Cadet Martin, roped in with the others because on occasions like this nobody was spared. She was grateful for their concern. It helped to reassure her now that she was on her own.

In the silence, listening to her own footsteps, she could imagine the agony of Marguerite de Wibaux, Bernadette Hamon, Alice Magueri and Honorine Nauray as they had realised they were about to die. They had all – even Alice Magueri – been too young to have seen much life and had all been looking forward to a lot more of it. In her heart of hearts she hoped that if anyone caught friend Prowler, it would not be

126

her but somebody like Bardolle, whose fists were as big as sacks of potatoes.

She had done her best to make herself look like a tart. She was wearing too much make-up, her lips a livid slash across a dead-white face, her eyes darkened with eyeliner and eyeshadow, her dark hair twisted on her cheeks into kiss curls. Have I over-done it, she wondered. Do I look like something out of the Twenties? Perhaps I ought to wear garters and rolled stockings and do the Charleston.

Her heels clicked on the road and she wriggled inside her clothes, aware that her brassiere was hauled up too tight to produce a more erotic silhouette. Several men had approached her but most of them had had too much to drink and weren't concerned with chasing anything that was hard to get. She hadn't minded. She knew how to handle drunks and they'd broken up the empty hour a little. In addition, though she tried not to admit it, she was scared, and even with a drunk in the vicinity she had felt safer than she did now when she was alone.

De Troq' was somewhere near at hand but she'd never once seen him and she just hoped he could see her.

She tugged the woollen hat she was wearing over her eye. It made her look a little more saucy but she couldn't see out of one eye half as well as she could out of two. But the hat was padded with dusters and she hoped that if it came to a blow on the head it might absorb a little of the shock. In addition, she had a surprise or two about her just in case. Her gun was in her pocket where she could get at it quickly, and her handbag contained half a brick. It was a trick suggested by De Troq' who had once used it successfully to catch a mugger.

Where *was* the Prowler, she wondered. Had she chosen the wrong district? Or the wrong night? Was he at home with Mamma, playing with the children, or reading the Bible with his wife? Ten to one, he'd turn out to be someone like that. As a cadet she'd once attended a lecture on the varieties of sexual perversions that had left her astonished. She'd learned a lot about the personalities of sex criminals, the symptoms of their illnesses, and the deep compulsions that drove them to violence. Up to then she'd never realised that sex crimes were progressive so that, like drugs, they demanded more and more from the perpetrators; that molesting sometimes led to rape and finally to murder; that you couldn't trust appearances; and that a sexual killer could be a kindly old man who was fond of his dog.

In the shadows nearby, one eye on the white blur that was Claudie's coat, De Troq' yawned. His feet, like Claudie's ached and he wished he could do the job in the big roadster he drove. But there must be no mistake. Nobody must hurt Claudie. Like everybody else in the Hôtel de Police, De Troq' had fallen for Claudie the minute he'd seen her, and he knew that if he allowed any harm to come to her, he could reckon on the contempt of everyone else, very probably a punch on the nose from Jean-Luc Nosjean, and heartbreak from himself.

By this time Claudie had taken to counting her footsteps. It was growing boring and she was beginning to wonder why she'd volunteered for the job. She had arrived in the city from Paris because her father had changed his place of work and she wished to live at home, but she now felt curiously secure in this old city in Burgundy. In Paris, there were too many foreigners, too many types. Even in the Police. Besides, in Paris, there had been no shy Nosjean, no mannered De Troq', two men whose attention made her feel warm and wanted. She was fond of them both, though she had a feeling that when she finally met the man she would marry he wouldn't be a cop. He'd be a type who would stay at home at nights, perhaps a barrister, sitting in front of the fire reading briefs while she attended to the children, and –

Wait!

Because she was always listening, even through her private thoughts, she heard the footsteps behind her in good time. She glanced at her watch. Almost midnight. The Prowler was a little early tonight. He didn't usually strike before midnight. Perhaps he was restless and couldn't sit still.

She quickened her pace to make it harder for anyone to grab her, began to waggle her hips, and pressed the button of the bleeper to warn De Troq'. She hoped it would work. Police bleepers and personal radios always seemed to be on the blink when they were most needed.

The footsteps were close behind now, and she steeled herself, waiting, her grip tightening on her handbag. As the footsteps came up behind her, she sensed somehow that this wasn't the man they were after. The Prowler seemed to move more silently than this, but she was ready for him nevertheless. He was a tall man, and in the light of the street lamp, she saw a face red and pitted with acne. As he reached for her shoulder, she grabbed the wrist, pushed out her hip and heaved, so that he went sailing over her head to land on his back on the pavement with a crash that must have jarred every bone in his body. As he struggled to his feet, she kneed him in the groin and swung the handbag containing the half-brick. It caught him at the side of the jaw with a whack that seemed to lift him off his feet.

She could hear De Troq's feet pounding the pavement. Her attacker heard them, too, and scrambled up to set off in a dazed reeling run into the shadows. As he did so, De Troq' shot past her. For a moment she stood, trembling a little, then set off after him. She found him round the corner, with the attacker backed up against the wall.

'Who is he?' she asked. 'Anybody we know?'

'Soon find out.' De Troq' whipped the man round, wrenched his hands behind his back and slapped on the handcuffs. Swinging him round again to face them, he shoved him against the wall once more.

'Call headquarters,' he said.

While Claudie was speaking on her personal radio, De Troq' glared at the man cowering by the wall.

'Name?'

'Don't hit me!'

'I haven't touched you. Not yet. But I will. Name?'

'Bigeaud. Philippe Bigeaud. I meant no harm. Honest. I just wanted to talk to her.'

Within a quarter of an hour Philippe Bigeaud was at headquarters, and Pel was bending over him as he sat at the table in the interview room. His face was tear-streaked and the acne he suffered from seemed like a raw wound.

'I was lonely,' he was wailing. 'That's all.'

'So why did you grab her?'

'I didn't grab her.'

Darcy appeared, holding a file. 'He's got a record, Patron,' he said quietly. 'Molesting girls. None of them suffered injuries. He just likes to touch them. So far,' he added cryptically. 'He's also been brought in for exposing himself and for indecent behaviour with a child. He's on our list of deviates.'

Pel stared at Bigeaud. He was a sorry specimen with his acne, his long neck and dirty hair.

'Any more?' he asked.

'Worked as a clerk at Plastiques de la France. But they employ a lot of women and they felt it wiser to get rid of him. Father dead. Mother works as a cleaner at the Nouvelles Galéries.'

Pel stared at Bigeaud. 'Marguerite de Wibaux,' he said and Bigeaud stared back at him as if he were a rabbit petrified by a snake. 'When did you last see her?'

'I don't know her.'

'When did you visit her apartment?'

'I don't know her. I've never heard of her.'

'Bernadette Hamon?'

'Who's she?'

'Don't you know?'

'No.'

He didn't know Alice Magueri or Honorine Nauray either. *Or* Monique Letexier. They got nothing out of him and he soon had his head on his arms on the table, sobbing, admitting only to an attempt to molest Claudie.

'That's not the Prowler,' Darcy said in the end. 'He's not the type. You can tell. It's an instinct.'

Pel knew that Darcy was right. It *was* an instinct. All they'd done was save Claudie from molestation – and she'd probably done that herself because Bigeaud had a severe headache and a bruise at the side of his face that was rapidly turning blue.

They left him with one of Nadauld's uniformed men to keep an eye on him and went to the sergeants' room where the others were drinking coffee.

'You all right?' Darcy asked Claudie.

'He didn't touch me,' she said.

'He's not friend Prowler.'

'I didn't think he was.' Claudie shrugged. 'There's always another night.'

'Did you see anything else?'

'Nothing. You'd be surprised how empty streets can be after dark.'

'They used not to be,' Pel said gloomily. 'The place used to be jumping, with the bars full and people standing on corners arguing. Sometimes even fighting. Nowadays everybody stays at home and develops square eyes watching television.'

There was truth in what he said. Television had not only changed a few amateurs into professionals with the details it gave, it had also changed the hours of crime. Criminals, it seemed, also had their favourite programmes and they had pulled in a burglar a few weeks before who had been operating on a different schedule from normal because he liked to watch *Dallas*. 'I wanted to see how it turned out,' he had announced.

'I think we'd better call it a day and have everybody in,' Pel said heavily. 'It's time we went home.'

He was just heading for his office to pick up his coat when the telephone went. Immediately, all the relaxed figures sitting on desks and draped across chairs stiffened.

It was Misset. Misset, of all people!

'There's been another,' he was yelling. 'Near the Bar de la Renaissance, Rue Hauts Pavés. I got there just in time!'

15

Misset was exaggerating a little – but that was Misset all over. He hadn't got there just in time. He hadn't got there at all.

When they arrived, half-expecting to find he had the Prowler in handcuffs, he was standing on the doorstep of the Bar de la Renaissance, trying to look as if he were guarding the place. It was a blank little establishment, done out with plastic surrounds, at the end of a narrow winding street. It had a wide glass front and, with the lights all on, you could see the entire interior from a hundred metres away.

The woman was sitting in a chair drinking brandy. She looked green and her dress was torn near the neck.

'That's her, Patron,' Misset said.

'What about the Prowler?' Pel snapped. 'What happened to him?'

'She said he went down the alleyway there.'

'Then what in God's name are you doing here? Get after him! Go with him, Darcy.'

As they vanished, Pel sat down quietly in front of the shaken woman.

'I'm Chief Inspector Pel,' he said gently.

The landlord appeared. 'This city,' he said loudly, 'isn't safe to live in. I don't know what the Police are doing.'

'The Police,' Pel pointed out crisply, 'are doing their duty. My men were all out on the streets tonight, and we picked up an attacker. Unfortunately, he wasn't the one we wanted. And while we were arresting him, the one we did want was operating here.'

The landlord retired, squashed, and a moment or two later reappeared at Pel's side and sheepishly placed a small brandy in front of him.

'On the house,' he muttered.

Pel leaned towards the woman. 'Can I have your name?'

'Marie-Yvonne You,' she whispered. 'I thought I was dead.'

'Well, you're not, thank God. Where do you live and why were you on the streets alone at this hour?'

'I live at 92, Rue Georges-Caromil. It's just round the corner. I didn't think he'd get me in that distance.'

'It's like wearing a safety belt in a car,' Pel pointed out quietly. 'The time when it matters you're not wearing it.'

'Who wants to wear a seat belt?' the landlord asked. 'It isn't the Gallic temperament to belt up.'

Pel turned, smouldering, his arteries hardening even as you looked at him. 'Would *you* mind belting up?' he snapped. 'And leave me to do my job.'

The landlord backed away as Darcy reappeared. 'Whose bar is it, anyway?' he said to him as he entered.

Darcy looked blank and turned to Pel. 'Nothing, Patron,' he said. 'There's a clear run through the alley to the next street. As usual, he'd planned his retreat. Misset's round there and I've called in all the others to give the place a once-over.'

Pel turned back to Marie-Yvonne You. 'You haven't told me what you were doing on the streets at this hour.'

She gestured at the bar. 'I work here,' she said. 'In the bar. I was going home.'

'*I* could have told him that,' the landlord said loudly. 'If he'd bothered to ask me.'

For a man given to outbursts of bad temper, Pel was being remarkably restrained. 'Couldn't you have got someone to see you home?' he asked. 'A husband, perhaps?'

'I haven't got a husband. I'm divorced.'

'What about our friend over there with the long tongue?'

'He didn't think it necessary. I only live a hundred metres away.'

'Past an open alley end. It's a pity he didn't read his newspaper. All previous attacks have been close to such places. What happened?'

'I helped tidy up here. Lined up the glasses for tomorrow. Then we stacked the chairs on the tables. I don't pull the shutters down or anything like that. I'd just turned the corner when I felt this thing drop over my head. I knew what it was straight away.'

'Go on.'

'I heard him say "Whore", then my legs gave way. I was terrified and I just fell to the ground, and he fell on top of me.'

'Did you see him?'

'No.'

'Nothing?'

'No. I was terrified, I tell you. I thought I was going to be killed.'

'You very nearly were. Did he say anything else?'

'No.'

'Could you recognise his voice if you heard it again?'

'I shouldn't think so.'

'Anything about him you noticed? Tall? Short? Fat? Thin? Anything odd about him? Perfume? Smell of tobacco?'

'I was too terrified to notice and when he fell on top of me I thought that was the end. But I felt him scramble up and heard feet running away and I realised he'd gone. I didn't think of going home. I ran back here.'

'I was just going to pull the shutters down,' the landlord said, 'when she came round the corner, screaming and sobbing. I put her in a chair, called my wife and went to the telephone. I was just going to pick it up when this cop appeared.'

There was a long silence. Pel took out a packet of cigarettes, removed one, stared at it for a while then put it in his mouth and lit it. He drew a deep puff of smoke and looked at Madame You.

'Did you see the cord?'

'No. I just felt it.'

'Or a knife?'

'I thought he strangled them.'

Pel frowned. 'He might have tried stabbing.'

'Holy Mother of God!' She seemed awed. 'No, I saw no knife.'

'He called you a whore. Those were your words. He said that to one other, and one of his victims *was* a whore. We think he feels all women out late on the streets are this type of woman. We think he watched them. Would he have any reason to suspect you of *being* a whore?'

Madame You made a remarkably quick recovery. 'No,' she

snapped in a voice that was suddenly as strident as a football rattle. 'He wouldn't. It's not my fault I'm divorced and have to earn my living. And it's not my fault I have to do it in a bar. I'm a decent woman.'

Pel indicated the glass window of the bar. The lights were fully on and it was obvious that it would be possible from the other side of the street to see everything that went on inside.

'It's a difficult point,' he admitted. 'But I have to clear it up. If he were out there, would he ever see you in here talking to men?'

She looked indignant and well-recovered now. 'I have to talk to men,' she said. 'I wouldn't get far in a job like this if I didn't. If they want to talk, you talk back, even if you'd prefer to spit in their eye.'

'Do these men make suggestions to you?'

'Some of them. Of course they do. Men are all the same. They've only one thing on their minds.'

'Has anyone made such a suggestion to you recently? Someone you didn't know.'

She considered for a moment. 'No,' she admitted.

'The men who come in here: I suppose you know most of them.'

'Yes. They always come in at the same time. One on his way from work. One for a quick one before his evening meal. One because his wife wants help with the kids and he prefers to be out of the way. One or two while they're doing the evening shopping for their wives. They've all got their own special times.'

'Have there been any men in here recently you didn't know?'

She was silent for a moment. 'Well, there's always the odd one. But none I can remember specially.'

'None who made a special set at you? Or kept watching you all the time?'

'No.'

Pel indicated the window, with the notices of football matches and dances pasted to the glass. 'If a man stood across there just down the street, he'd be able to see you. But he'd be in the dark and you wouldn't see him. Did he ever see you leave with a man?'

She looked indignant again then the expression faded and she

135

hesitated. 'Well, he might. After all, there's no reason why I shouldn't. My divorce has gone through.'

'Would he ever see you take one home?'

'No. Never.' She paused. 'Well, hardly ever.'

'You did take men home from here?'

'Once.'

'Perhaps more than once?'

'Perhaps. But I'm not a tart. I want a husband. You don't get them by ignoring men.'

'I appreciate that, Madame. But he had no reason to think you're what he called you?'

'No, he hadn't.'

'Did one of these men ever stay the night?'

She paused and glanced at the landlord who hurriedly looked at the ceiling so that Pel immediately guessed he'd been one of the men himself. 'Well,' she said. 'Once or twice.'

'More than that perhaps?'

'Yes. But there's no reason why not.'

'I'm not questioning your behaviour, Madame. That's not why I'm here. I'm just trying to build up a picture of the man who attacked you to decide if he was the same one who attacked the other women.'

She stared at him. She was sitting upright now and was obviously relishing being the centre of attention the following day when the bar opened. 'And was he?' she asked.

'Yes,' Pel said. 'I think he was.'

'Four,' Darcy said. 'And two misshits. Two in a row, in fact. And no messages. Think he's losing his grip?'

'I doubt it,' Pel said. 'And I think there are no messages because he was in the habit of scrawling them after he'd done his stuff, not before, and on these occasions he was scared enough to bolt. In the case of Monique Letexier, he lost his cord and used his hands and she slipped from his grasp. In the case of the You woman, she startled him by going limp and falling down instead of struggling. It caught him off-balance and, when he fell with her, he decided it was safer to bolt. Next time he'll be more careful.' He frowned. 'If Misset had been a bit swifter off the mark, he might have caught him. Or at least seen him and been able to give us a description. I expect he was standing in the shadows somewhere, having a quick cigarette. Even talking to a woman.'

Darcy grinned. 'You don't suppose it could be Misset, do you?' he asked.

Pel ignored the comment. 'Let's have everybody above the age of eighteen in the Rue de Rouen area checked. There've been three here now – Bernadette Hamon and You and Letexier, with the Rue Devoin where Marguerite de Wibaux was found on the fringe of it. Get on to it. We'll keep everybody on the streets as before. There's only one way this is going to be cracked and that's by catching him at it. Claudie had better share the job with someone else. We'll get a woman from Lyons or Paris. But I suspect he'll lie low for a bit after this. He's probably had a big scare.'

'Big enough to scare him off, Patron?'

Pel frowned. 'Nutters with obsessions don't scare off easily,' he said. 'But they usually have enough brains to lie low when things become too hot.'

Over breakfast next morning, Pel's mind was busy. Madame was discussing the news she'd heard on the radio while he was dragging himself from bed but he hardly heard her. Madame Routy appeared – still miraculously clad in her white overall, so that Pel wondered what Madame did to make sure she wore it. Thumbscrews? A whip? The rack? It had taken him all his time at the Rue Martin-de-Noinville to drag her away from the television.

She moved round the table and slapped down fresh coffee. 'They arrested Paul Horgon in Paris,' she announced. 'It was on the radio.'

Pel looked up over his spectacles. He couldn't remember any Paul Horgon among his suspects.

'He's that actor,' Madame Routy said.

'Which actor?'

Madame Pel looked up and smiled understandingly. 'On the television. He's in that series, *General Hospital*.'

Light dawned. Despite the fact that he watched television only when he couldn't find an excuse not to, Pel knew many of the actors. You had to be a moron not to know them. They occupied more space in the newspapers these days than world statesmen, while the pundits of the chat shows carried more weight than the President of France himself. Inevitably, Madame Routy would know Paul Horgon. Doubtless, she hadn't missed a single beat of his heart since the series started.

'It's shocking,' she said. 'Arresting him like that.'

'Like what?'

'Well, in front of everybody.'

'What did they arrest him for? Surely you know.'

'They say he assaulted a girl. One of the girls in the series.'

'How did he assault her?'

'How – ?'

'With his fists? With an axe? With an iron bar?'

Madame Pel looked up again. 'Sexually,' she said quietly.

Pel gave Madame Routy a disbelieving stare. Doubtless the fans of *General Hospital* were filling the gutters with their tears that the rotten black-hearted flics should dare arrest their hero, while the cries of woe from the producers worrying about viewers' ratings were setting the pigeons whirring into the air. It was amazing how important a man or woman could become merely because they could sit in front of a camera and lay their personality on the line. Even politicians failed these days because they couldn't do that.

'I expect the Police had their reasons for doing it the way they did,' he said. 'And if he's guilty I hope they put him away for a long time.'

'They couldn't!' Madame Routy was shocked. 'The series depends on him!'

Pel stared at her in amazement. 'Name of God, woman,' he said sharply. 'The damned man's only an actor! There've been four murders in this city recently – all women! – and you're mooing like a sick cow about somebody who prances about in front of a television camera who's probably got the potential in him to do the same! You wouldn't have uttered a murmur of protest if he'd been a train driver or a shop assistant – or, for that matter, a policeman!'

Madame Pel, who'd been listening to the exchange with some amusement, decided it had gone far enough and that if Pel wasn't halted in mid-flow he'd probably explode with his indignation. She gestured to Madame Routy to leave and gently chided Pel for his outburst.

'You mustn't talk to her like that,' she insisted quietly.

'But, mon Dieu, to talk about a man as if he had a special dispensation from the Almighty to attack people just because he's a television personality – '

'Pel!'

Pel stopped dead, recognising the iron hand in the velvet glove. He collected himself. 'Geneviève de mon coeur?'

She smiled her quiet smile. 'She's a widow and she has nobody.'

Only me, Pel thought, both of us living with daggers drawn in a perpetual state of vendetta. It made him feel ashamed and he decided, though he knew it wouldn't last, to be nicer to the old trout.

'I was a widow, too, Pel. I know how lonely it can be.'

Pel felt so humble he wondered if he ought to throw himself at her feet. She changed the subject abruptly.

'My cousin wrote that she'd like to come and see us,' she said. 'She'd like to bring the children. They've read about you and they'd like to meet you. She says she'll bring us some plants to get the garden going.'

It did what she'd intended. Madame Routy forgotten, Pel subsided into a rumble of uncertainty. He didn't mind the plants because they didn't run about or make a noise, but he wasn't so sure about the children. Madame worked on him, however, and by the time he rose to go his equanimity had been restored. Madame waved him off as he climbed into his car.

He had avoided lighting a cigarette so far, but now he put one in his mouth and lit it from the car's cigarette lighter. It wasn't, he tried to persuade himself, because he *needed* a cigarette – surely he could overcome that sort of thing – but because this new car of his had this simple device which meant he could light a cigarette without taking both hands off the wheel. He'd paid for it so he might as well use it. No good Burgundian would wish to waste something he'd paid good money for.

One of these days, he decided, he'd buy himself a new suit to go with the new car. Before he'd married, in the days when Madame Routy could never find time between television programmes to press his suits, they had all looked as though he slept in them. Now, with Madame to watch over him and jolly him gently into clothes that suited him, he was in danger of becoming the pride and joy of the Police Judiciaire. Then he remembered that he'd just bought a new car. Perhaps he'd better wait, he decided carefully. Until next year. Or the year after. Or perhaps even the year after that. One of these days, anyway.

He was actually beginning to feel better about things when Nosjean appeared in his office and punctured his balloon at once.

'It's all off, Patron,' he said.

'What's all off?'

'The identity parade I fixed up for Florence Remaud. Judge Brisard says it can't go ahead.'

'Why? They had the tankard.'

'It's because Florence Remaud's pregnant, Patron. What's more, she's making the most of it. They've got Maître Gaborais to represent them, and he and Judge Brisard were talking all yesterday afternoon. Judge Brisard says we'll never be able to line her up. Gaborais would eat us whole. And we'd have the press of half France on our necks. Putting a pregnant woman on an identity parade. Endangering her unborn child.'

'Standing still? That's dangerous?'

'That's the way Judge Brisard says we have to think, Patron, because that's the way Gaborais will argue. There's another thing, too. She's dark. When she was seen by the Abrillards she was fair. Abrillard said so. So did the antique dealer in Chagnay. So did Mijo Lehmann.'

'It was a wig.'

'I know that. You know it, Patron. Doubtless, so do Judge Brisard and Maître Gaborais. But we didn't find a wig and nobody saw her put it on or take it off. When Judge Brisard had them in his office she was as dark as I am and Mijo Lehmann says she wouldn't dare identify a dark pregnant woman as a fair slender woman. Abrillard says the same. We've lost her, Patron. Judge Brisard doesn't think it's worth putting her in court even. Remaud's got to go up before the magistrates on his own.'

Pel shrugged. 'Well,' he said, 'I suspect they'll lie low for a bit after this, anyway. I don't think for a moment they'll give up crime. They'll just try something else, somewhere else. In this job you have to console yourself with the thought that, even if it isn't obvious, like a strong laxative we're probably doing more good than we realise. And there's always our friend, the Prowler.'

16

Indeed there was. By this time, the murderer had picked up a few more nicknames – Les Griffes, Claws; Saise-Gorge, Grab-throat – but, for the moment things were quiet again as Pel had suggested they would be.

Unable to bring Florence Remaud before the magistrates, Brisard had had to concentrate his efforts on Georges Remaud but Maître Gaborais, being on the fly side, advised Remaud to plead not guilty to stealing but guilty to receiving and, because it was his first known offence, he was bound over and with his wife walked out of court past Nosjean and Pel with a large smile on his face.

'It's a wonder they didn't give him a couple of thousand francs from police funds,' Nosjean said bitterly.

He seemed so downcast Pel took him for a drink, and because it was handiest, he chose the Hôtel Centrale. As they pushed through the swing door, they ran into what appeared to be the panic to end all panics. Gau, the manager, the under-manager and two assistant managers, to say nothing of the housekeeper, the receptionist and a few other officials were in a huddle in the entrance hall, all apparently blaming each other.

'A check should have been kept,' Gau was saying in a whisper that was as near to a shriek as it could get.

'But we were instructed to give him all he asked for,' one of the assistant managers protested.

'There should – ' Gau spotted Pel and Nosjean standing in the doorway and shooed everybody away. 'Come in, come in,' he said urgently. He was looking pale. 'You'll have heard what's happened? We just telephoned the Hôtel de Police.'

As they talked, Darcy appeared. 'What's going on?' he asked.

'I got a message that somebody was wanted urgently.'

Gau tried to explain. 'He isn't Henri Bayetto at all,' he said.

'Who isn't?'

'The man who claimed to have won the lottery.'

They were about to sit down when he ushered them out of the hall. 'Under the circumstances,' he said, 'it might be better if it isn't made too public. I'll find a room for you and send in something to drink.'

It turned out to be champagne. 'Just the thing for a fatal illness, an operation, or conducting an enquiry at the Hôtel Centrale,' Darcy grinned.

When Gau reappeared he was carrying a businessman's attaché case with a label on the handle stating it belonged to one, Henri Bayetto.

'From the safe,' he said. 'It's locked.'

'I doubt if that presents a lot of difficulty,' Darcy said, fishing in his pocket and producing a bunch of keys.

'He went out yesterday morning,' Gau went on. 'And he hasn't come back yet. Then an hour ago I received a warning from a friend of mine at the Hôtel de la Poste at Lyons. He said they'd had a man there posing as Henri Bayetto, the lottery winner, and he'd left without paying his bill. He'd deposited an attaché case with them, believed to contain money, but they've just opened it because they heard the same thing had happened in Marseilles, Avignon, Valence and Bourg. It contained nothing but waste paper.'

Darcy had the attaché case open now. It was packed tight with neat bundles, and they found themselves staring at a surface of brand new 100-franc notes.

Gau's face fell. 'It's *not* waste paper,' he said, reaching hurriedly for the case. 'My God, this could destroy us! We'd better return it to the safe at once!'

Pushing his hands away, Pel leaned forward and carefully withdrew one of the 100-franc notes from the rubber band that was holding it to the top of its pile. Underneath was nothing but neatly-cut plain paper. Gau's jaw dropped again.

'It *is* paper!' he whispered.

His eyes swept frantically over the packed wads, trying to calculate if there were enough of the notes topping the piles to pay Bayetto's bill. Darcy guessed what was in his mind and, taking the note Pel had withdrawn, held it up to the light.

'Don't build up too many hopes,' he said. 'Even these are forgeries.'

Gau's jaw clicked down again. 'Name of God!' he breathed in agony. 'Merciers', the jewellers, asked if we could vouch for him and I said we could! So did Demanges', the tailors. He even bought an antique silver cigarette case from a dealer in Ferry-le-Grand.'

'Which, doubtless,' Darcy said dryly, 'he's already sold in St. Seine l'Abbaye to raise some ready cash.'

Gau clutched his throat. 'He's been buying on credit as if there's no tomorrow. They'll sue us.'

It wasn't hard to decide that 'Bayetto', like most people with criminal inclinations, was working to a pattern and was moving across the country from south to north, using big hotels in departmental capitals, and after remarkably few telephone calls from Gau's office he was eventually turned up at the Hôtel du Centre in Chaumont. Only another five minutes were required to contact police headquarters there and half an hour and another bottle of champagne later, a telephone call was received to say that he'd been picked up, that there was another attaché case full of paper in the hotel safe, and that 'Henri Bayetto' was, in fact, one Maurice Jouhandeau, a printer from Nice. He had cut the paper on his firm's guillotine and forged the 100-franc notes himself. He was sick of scratching for money, he said, and had decided to have one good blow-out whatever it cost him. It looked like costing him a stay in jail but, according to the Police in Chaumont, he didn't seem worried. He'd had his blow-out and was prepared to pay the price.

It was only a small incident, really, but the two bottles of champagne had cheered Nosjean up and lightened the day a little at a time when light relief was badly needed.

There was still no sign of the Prowler, however. He had vanished into thin air again. The nightly watch continued nevertheless and Claudie was still doing her patrolling through the dark streets. She had now been joined by a woman officer from Lyons and, though so far they hadn't produced the Prowler, between them they had brought in three molesters, one of whom they'd never heard of and didn't possess a record.

They continued to wait. A man was brought in for shooting his workmate because he worked too hard, and finally they found the driver of the hit-and-run car which had killed the old woman in Borgny weeks before. Despite the lapse of time a suspicious repair shop foreman had remembered Nadauld's instructions and had reported a car brought in for a new headlight. The owner had turned out to be the very priest who had pronounced his blessings over the body of the victim, on whose neck, by an irony, they had found a necklace carrying a medallion bearing the words: 'In case of accident, call a priest'. Hurrying home from a meeting, he had been driving too fast and had failed to see her. Such was his horror and fear, he had not dared to stop and, though knowing perfectly well that his first duty should have been to attend a dying human being for whom he was responsible, he had spent the rest of the evening sitting in his car in the woods near Borgny, praying and trying to pluck up courage to return to his presbytery. The magistrates would inevitably decide that, while he might be forgiven for his panic, he would still have to pay a fine hefty enough to make the next few years of his life pretty spartan.

By this time a lot of people were beginning to think that, like the Remauds, the Prowler had disappeared from the area. If he were operating in someone else's territory, then the ball was out of their court for the moment. If he should turn up in Lyons or Marseilles or Paris or Toulouse or Amiens, they were ready with the details, but nothing happened and slowly they relaxed and the Chief's conferences reverted to normal. Had he, like Jack the Ripper in London, died? Even the press seemed to have forgotten him.

But Pel hadn't. Sitting in his office, like a spider in the centre of its web, he was warily watching, ready to pounce. He had taken to chewing gum in the hope of cutting down his cigarettes. All it did was make his jaw ache.

Because Madame was in Paris at a business conference, Pel had reverted at once to his old habit of taking his breakfast at the Bar Transvaal. Madame Routy's breakfast coffee, magnificent when Madame Pel was home, had at once changed back to something that tasted as if it had been made from iron filings flavoured with shellac, while the croissants had reverted to the day before yesterday's.

It was raining when he arrived in the office and Misset, inevitably, was doing nothing apart from telling funny stories. Misset was always telling funny stories and his victim this time was Aimedieu. Aimedieu was coughing over the first cigarette of the morning while, like a hen picking up corn in a farmyard, he laboriously banged out on a typewriter the words of a report he was making on the previous day's activities.

'Why are the five continents of the world like the five ages of women?' Misset was asking.

'Go on.' Aimedieu sounded as if there had already been other jokes that morning. 'Why?'

Misset held up his thumb. 'Africa: The teenager. Virgin, but unexplored.' He held up his first finger. 'The United States: Twenty to thirty. Technically perfect.' The second finger rose. 'Asia: Thirty to Forty. Remote but mysterious.' The fourth finger. 'Europe: Forty to fifty. Ravaged but still full of charm.' The little finger rose. 'Australia: Sixty onwards. Everybody knows of it but nobody's ever seen it.'

Aimedieu gave him a pained look. 'Heard it,' he said. 'While I was still at school.'

It didn't put Misset off. He laughed a lot at his own jokes. 'Wait a minute,' he said. 'Have you heard the one about – '

Seeing Pel at last, he abruptly began to sort through the papers on Aimedieu's desk as if that were what he'd been doing all the time. As Aimedieu slapped furiously at his hands, he turned away in confusion, picked up a file and pretended to peruse it. Pel wasn't fooled for a minute.

In his office he was met by Cadet Martin with the newspapers, all marked, police cases in red, other items in blue. Claudie appeared soon afterwards, with the mail. Despite her late nights and though everybody who was on the street patrol after dark was given the morning off, she always managed to appear, taking her time off after lunch, which Pel considered a very noble attitude because you hadn't time to go home when you were coming back again in the evening and most people on split duty merely stayed in the office and hoped they'd be noticed for their earnest attitude towards their work.

He picked up the mail. Claudie never opened it these days in case it contained something that might be a threat and would need dusting for fingerprints. And since a letter bomb had been posted to Pel some time before he had insisted on opening the mail himself, with Claudie standing by to make notes if necessary.

He was just on the point of opening the first letter when Darcy appeared. He was brisk, smart, spotlessly clean and looking like one of the better-class film stars from the Thirties. The three of them were still talking when Nosjean himself appeared in the doorway. He looked flushed and excited.

'Patron,' he said. 'It's started again! They've found another body. In a house in the Rue Fructidor. Rue de Rouen district again.'

'Strangled?'

'Not this time, Patron. Knife job.'

Pel tossed down the mail and looked at Darcy. The messy one he'd feared seemed to have arrived.

17

There were already two police cars in the street. Barriers and tapes had been set up and Nadauld was making arrangements to divert traffic.

'This way,' he said, heading down a passage.

Pel followed him, noticing at once that the Prowler had chosen his spot well again. It was once more in the old part of the city, surrounded by crumbling and decaying houses. Near the police cars was a lorry with the name of a demolition firm on its side. Near it a driver and two men waited, looking shaken and bewildered.

In the yard at the back of the houses two policemen, caped against the drizzle, were standing with two more men in overalls.

'Georges Presnau. Gérard Boulanger.' Nadauld made the introductions. 'They found her. Presnau runs a demolition firm and Boulanger's his foreman. They're due to work here but they arrived late because the lorry wouldn't start. They came to the back of the house to have a look-see while their labourers unloaded the equipment. These houses have been locked up for some time, but they found one of the doors forced. She's just inside.'

Presnau jerked a hand at the open door. The room was empty except for a few broken bottles, a carton full of rags, and a broken chair. The floor was uncovered and in the centre, on the bare boards, was the body of a girl. She was large in stature, well-fleshed and heavy, and lay on her back with her head turned away from them. Her dress had ridden up over plump white thighs and she wore a pink raincoat, while near her head was a plastic triangle she had obviously been wearing against the rain. Her hair was matted with blood and when they crossed the room to look at her from the other side they saw her throat had been cut.

Pel's eyes narrowed. 'Nosjean,' he said. 'Get someone on to checking dry cleaners and laundries straight away. And let's have the clothing of everybody so far involved in the case examined for bloodstains. Put Misset on it. He's surely capable of that.'

'Daniel – ' as Nosjean vanished, Pel turned to Darcy ' – have a search made for the weapon. This time there *is* one. Get Bardolle to run it. And let's have everybody we can on it. Everywhere in the yard. Everywhere in the building and the neighbouring buildings. In the street outside.' He bent closer to the body and, though at first they were difficult to spot because of the blood splashes, he saw the same marks of mutilation on the cheeks.

'Same as before,' he said. 'An H or an M or a W or an N. Something with two up-strokes and a straight or crooked cross-stroke.'

The photographers had arrived now and were busy with the routine of lights and flash bulbs. Another man was making a drawing.

Doc Minet appeared, and placed his bag on the floor to bend over the body. 'No need to tell you how this one died,' he said.

'Any attempt to strangle first?' Pel asked. 'Like the others.'

'Well, she wasn't dead when he did that,' Minet indicated the mutilated throat. 'Or there wouldn't be so much blood. I'll tell you later.'

Leguyader's men arrived, chattering to themselves. They were still discussing a football result but they all became silent as they saw Pel. He didn't encourage light-heartedness at the scene of a crime.

Prélat, of Fingerprints, was dusting the plastic triangle but he looked up and shook his head. 'I expect the dabs are hers,' he said.

'Keep at it,' Pel said. As Darcy reappeared he turned to him. 'Press appeared yet?'

'No, Patron. But they will.'

He was right. They arrived within the hour. First Sarrazin, then Henriot, then the others. Pel went into the street to talk to them.

'We have no name yet,' he said. 'You'll be given it as soon as we get it.'

'Is it the same as the others?' Henriot asked.

'At the moment it's impossible to say. It could be, but the method's different so it might not be. Keep it as quiet as you can. We don't want a mass exodus from the city.' Once again, he made no mention of the mutilation of the cheek.

By this time, Darcy had a line of men moving slowly up the street. There were others in the yard, covering every inch of space, another group going over the building itself, another man investigating the contents of the carton.

Doc Minet rose, wiping his hands. 'The wound to the throat is what caused death,' he said. 'There is an indication on her neck of the marks of a cord, which seems to suggest he grabbed her with it. But they're not pronounced enough to suggest anything beyond a grab. She has a broken nose, several displaced teeth and bruises round the mouth. It's my view that he grabbed her and dragged her in here to finish her off, but somehow – perhaps because she's big and was probably strong – she wriggled free. So he hit her in the face with his fist and knocked her unconscious. Then, while she was on the floor, he grabbed her hair, jerked her head back and cut her throat.'

'And the mark on her cheek?'

'Done after she was dead. It looks like an H.' Doc Minet looked at Pel, an old man suddenly weary of his job. 'It's another one, isn't it?' he said.

18

This time there was no message. The surroundings where the body had been found suggested there might have been one – scrawled or scratched on the crumbling plaster, on an old door, in the dust on the floor. But, though they searched the whole area, they found nothing. It puzzled Pel because he felt there ought to be one.

Then the letter arrived. It came in the afternoon post. It was the envelope which first attracted Pel's attention. It was cheap, the sort that could be bought in any supermarket, and the address was written in a red felt-tip pen. The sheet inside was part of a notice about old age pensioners receiving an increase in their weekly emoluments and the message had been written on the back – like the address on the envelope, in blunt computer lettering. Finding an excuse to send Claudie from the room, Pel quietly handed it to Darcy.

'*I am back,*' it read. '*Do not forget your Friend. This City needs a Clean-up. And Evildoers must face the Musik and on their Faces have the Brand for all Men to see. You think I have been on Holiday. I have not. I am on the Streets all the Time. French Morals are the blackest. 1940 was the start. Your friend, the Prowler.*'

'There's nothing wrong with French morals that I've ever noticed,' Darcy said, frowning. 'And what's this about 1940?' He studied the message again. 'It's genuine, Patron. He knows about the mark on their faces and nobody else but us does. Not a word of it's appeared in the media.'

Pel nodded and Darcy continued. 'He's spelled "Musik" phonetically with a "k", so he must be somebody like Magueri or Josset – that type – and we can rule out the students and the

151

people at the hospitals and the Faculté des Médicins. Whatever else, they know how to spell.' He studied the message again. 'And what's so special about 1940? We all know what happened then, God help us. It's printed on our hearts. But what's the significance to *him*? There's one thing, Patron, this also seems to rule out the students because if you asked them half of them wouldn't *know* what happened in 1940. They're too young. Even their fathers would still have been in short trousers then.'

They took the message along to the Chief, who was older and had, in fact, been a youth at the time. The date had a lot of significance to him, but nothing that connected it to the Prowler. They also brought in Judge Polverari, who had been a young soldier in 1940, and even Judge Brisard, and they discussed the message for a long time.

'Does it go to the press?' the Chief asked.

'I should say not,' Pel said. 'We don't know yet what it means – and it might not mean anything. It might just be part of his obsession and of no special significance. But it'll be as well to keep it to ourselves. It'll just be one more detail that might trap him into a confession when we get him.'

They discussed for a while just who should be informed about the message and in the end decided to let it go no further. Pel was in favour of showing it to trusted members of his squad but Judge Brisard felt it should not be shown and the Chief backed him up.

'Too much's leaked from this headquarters to the press,' he said. 'I think we should keep this one to ourselves. It's a long message and we might find it has a real meaning.'

Back in his own office, Pel studied the message again. 'It's a taunt,' he said. 'He thinks we can't catch him.'

'We can't,' Darcy pointed out flatly.

'We will, Daniel. We will.' Pel reached for his cigarettes, lit one, drew the smoke down and pushed his spectacles up on to his forehead. 'You'd better let Fingerprints have this to see what they can make of it. Nothing I expect. These days every eleven-year-old boy who watches television knows you mustn't leave fingerprints. In the meantime, we'd better start a check on post offices. One of them's lost that sheet from its wall and someone might have noticed who took it. The felt-tipped pen won't get us anywhere. They can be bought in packets of ten at a time at the Nouvelles Galéries. You'd better handle this yourself, Daniel. If the Chief wants it kept quiet, you can't put anyone else on it. But it might be worth while finding out who handled these notices at the central post office, who sent them to sub-post offices and, when they arrived, who stuck them up on the wall. It might give us a lead.'

Pel didn't get home that night at all, so he was glad his wife was in Paris at her conference. He managed eventually to contact her at her hotel.

'I've been trying to get hold of you,' she pointed out. 'Madame Routy said you were probably enjoying yourself in the city.'

'She would,' Pel said. 'I've been busy. There's been another.'

There was a long silence then her answer came quietly. 'I saw it on the television. Is it the same as the others?'

'This time it's worse.'

'Oh!' There was another silence. When she spoke again her voice was worried. 'People here are talking about the murders. They're saying unpleasant things about the police. They say there must be incompetence.'

'I suppose they're bound to.'

'They commented on it because your name's in the paper and it's the same as mine. They don't know you're my husband, of course.' The voice became angry. 'They don't know . . .'

'Geneviève!'

She stopped dead. 'Yes?'

'This sort of thing always happens. The police are always accused of incompetence at times like these. Sometimes, I suppose, they are incompetent. But most of the time they're giving it everything they've got. Don't let them upset you.'

There was another silence. When her voice came again it had a different, stronger note to it. 'Yes, Pel. I'll do as you say.' She paused. 'Will it cause a lot of trouble, this new one?'

'Yes,' Pel admitted. 'It's started a bit of a panic already.'

It had indeed. The big boys from the Paris newspapers, who had gone back to the capital after milking the story dry had come screaming back down the motorway and, instead of the informal chat they liked to have with the local boys, they'd had to lay on a big press conference. Pel left it to Darcy who was careful to hand out nothing more than they wanted to give.

'Name: Gilbertine Guégan. Aged twenty-one, 19, Rue Joliet.'

'Married?' someone asked.

'Married. But separated.'

'Same as the others, Inspector?'

'Same as the others,' Darcy said. It was an outrageous lie because it wasn't, but she was dead like the others so it was fair enough.

'Any suspects?'

'We have our leads but they all have to be followed up.'

The usual stuff. All the delicate tightrope-stepping round awkward questions. All the clinging to the points they wanted kept secret – especially the message and the facial mutilations. But the press were satisfied and went howling back to their hotels, in search of telephones.

Gilbertine Guégan was known to the police. She had a record for shoplifting which went back to the days when she was only fifteen, had married at seventeen because she was pregnant and had promptly abandoned both husband and child to go on the streets. It might have been a reason for murdering her, but neither her husband nor his parents, who looked after the child, were types who might have gone in for killing. And, since they were all together and at the time of the murder in the company of a neighbour, they were out of the running straight away.

Was it one of Gilbertine Guégan's clients? Somebody she'd swindled? Somebody she'd stolen from? It was always a possibility. But commonsense told them she was dead for exactly the same reason as Alice Magueri – because she was a prostitute. But that asked the question, why the others? To a certain extent Marie-Yvonne You, who had escaped, also fitted the bill. Even Honorine Nauray might have been described as of doubtful morals. But why Marguerite de Wibaux and Bernadette Hamon? And why Monique Letexier, who had also escaped? They could have been attacked for that reason only if the Prowler had spotted them out alone late at night and jumped to the conclusion that they were on the game, too. It seemed to indicate some sort of perverted obsession connected with an unbalanced moral outlook, but in a city with a population of 350,000, where did you look? Leaving out all the children, old people and women, you still had at least 70,000 males who could have done it. They could search them all, check their clothing, ask them if they had a red felt-tipped pen or had stolen a notice from a post office, but it was hardly practical. The solution would have to come from somewhere else and Pel, as usual, suspected they already had the vital clue and hadn't noticed it.

'I want every man called in,' he said. 'We're going to check every male in the city.'

Darcy looked startled. 'It'll take until Christmas, Patron.'

'Then let it. And let's try spreading a rumour that we're going to make an arrest. Perhaps someone knows something but daren't give the information, and it might loosen a few tongues. In the meantime, let's check again – everyone we know who's been connected with the victims. *Everyone*.'

The Chief's conference was a grim affair. By this time the case was involving the Police at all levels – from village cops right up to the Ministry in Paris, because trendy politicians with an axe to grind were asking why the forces of law and order were so ineffectual. With the suggestions of inefficiency, pressure was also being put on the Chief to call in men from the capital; and even police officers from other authorities, on the telephone about cases that had nothing to do with the Prowler, were finding it hard to avoid making snide remarks. In the bars all the old jokes about the Police were being handed round, while the suspicion in the air set wives against husbands and neighbours against neighbours. In Mornay-la-Comtesse, the Police had to turn out for a minor riot caused by a hasty word in a bar, while in Dome a husband was charged with assaulting his wife because, after accusing him of going with another woman, she had raised his blood pressure to boiling point by suggesting he might even be the Prowler.

His temper barely under control, the Chief delivered a lecture which, though he was well aware it was unfair, verged on the accusatory. But the comments from outside were beginning to get under his skin by this time and he was lashing out in all directions without much thought for whom he hit.

Pel's conference, which followed, was no different. It had

started all over again, the questioning, the lists of names, the checking and the rechecking. Nobody had produced any information about bloodstains and all their suspects seemed to have alibis. Somewhere among them, Pel knew, one of them was false but so far they hadn't found it. Nosjean had checked the suggestion of witchcraft and come up with nothing. There were a lot of people who knew a lot about it but none who knew what an H or an M or an N or a W might mean.

The list of suspects was as long as your arm and included every possibility – even people like Bigeaud, the molester of women, and the owner of the Bar de la Renaissance, who by this time had admitted sleeping with Marie-Yvonne You. And it could still be someone they'd not even heard of, someone who was a stranger, a foreigner even. France was full of visitors, tourists, leftovers from other people's revolutions, and people who preferred France simply because she was France.

And 1940? What did it mean? Looking down the list of names that had come to the surface since the first murder, Pel had to admit that it couldn't possibly mean much to many of them.

For hours he sat with a dictionary. The most likely letter cut on the victims' faces appeared to be an H and it had to have some significance. But what? To the Prowler, it seemed to represent vengeance. But for what? And what had 1940 to do with it? Not one of the victims could by the remotest stretch of imagination be blamed in any way for what had happened then. Could the marks perhaps have been an M – for Moussia, who was an oddity if ever there were one? Or even a crude J – for Josset? Could it be an H for Hélin who, they had established, went with prostitutes? He had admitted knowing Alice Magueri and finally Marie-Yvonne You, and, though he denied knowing the Gúegan girl, there was a chance he was lying about it as he'd originally lied about Alice Magueri. At that moment in the absence of Judge Polverari, sick in bed with flu, he was being questioned by Judge Brisard who was trying to trip him up over Marguerite de Wibaux.

But if it were Hélin, why? What had he to do with 1940? The De Wibaux girl wasn't a prostitute – quite the contrary, as Hélin had good reason to know – which meant that if the women had been killed, as they believed, because they'd been assumed to be on the streets, then Marguerite de Wibaux must have been killed *only* because she'd been seen with Hélin, who was known to go with prostitutes and she'd therefore been assumed by the killer to be also of loose morals. But that implied that Hélin didn't do it because *he* knew very well that Marguerite de Wibaux *wasn't* of loose morals. They were going round in circles.

'Didn't the Parisians brand women who went with the Germans?' Pel asked. 'In the Liberation in 1944. They stripped them and marked their foreheads with swastikas. Could *that* account for "1940"?'

'Others as well as the Parisians went in for branding scarlet women,' Darcy said dryly. 'Didn't the Protestants do it in America?'

'We haven't many Americans here,' Pel said. 'They prefer Paris or St. Trop'.'

Nevertheless, Brochard was delegated to find out more about it because nothing, however small, could be missed. Meanwhile, the check on the male inhabitants of the Rue de Rouen district was still going on, though nothing so far had emerged.

'It will,' Darcy said with certainty. 'You'll see, Patron. It'll come up eventually. Out of the ground when we're least expecting it – like the mighty Wurlitzer.'

They had discarded almost at once the idea that the new killing was a copycat murder. And the search for the weapon had turned up nothing, so they could only assume that the knife which had ended Gilbertine Guégan's life was still in the killer's pocket, waiting for his next victim.

The printed sheet which had carried on its rear surface the message from the Prowler had been missed from seven post offices in the city alone. But no one had noticed it disappear and none of the people involved in the issuing of the sheet could possibly be involved, while not one of the men on their books could be proved to have owned a red felt-tipped pen or clothing which carried bloodstains. Only Hélin, in fact had objected to having his clothing examined and they could even put that down to the monumental chip on his shoulder and his hostility to the Police. Nothing had been found at dry cleaners or laundries and there were no fingerprints on the message.

There was one point that both Darcy and Pel noticed, however. For the first time they had a victim with two names which began with a letter with a curve in it. In every other case, one or both of the names had had initial letters which could be formed with straight slashes of a knife and might be mistaken for an H.

'Unless,' Darcy said, 'it's a crude G. After all, carving your initials on dead flesh in a hurry can't be easy.'

The pressure was kept up, and several public-spirited men put up a reward for information. Immediately, the Hôtel de Police was swamped with telephone calls from people eager to claim it. Someone had seen a man covered with blood in Aignay. Nobody else in Aignay had, however. Hotel registers were examined. Every pervert in the city was checked again. The usual hoaxers who thought it funny to burden the already over-burdened Police with false alarms, the clairvoyants who saw bodies in coal sheds, wood sheds, forests and cornfields, all had to be checked and all were proved to be false. Every postbag brought letters on all sorts of paper. Most of the anonymous ones turned out to have been sent by malicious neighbours.

Madame returned from Paris, full of gentleness as she saw the strain in Pel's face. Madame Routy got a mouthful that staggered her when she attempted to tell him to wipe his feet. When Leguyader tried to be funny, he, too, was slammed down with a speed that startled him. And while Darcy's teams continued with their enquiries, while the city's inhabitants locked their doors at night, while Claudie Darel and the woman from Lyons trudged their lonely patrols, watched by the rest of the squad, Pel and Darcy – now with Nosjean to help – went again and again through the reports.

'"Ah", Patron,' Nosjean said, looking up.

Pel looked up. '"Ah"?'

'Monique Letexier. She said he said "Ah". But that somehow it was different from the way most people say "Ah". Does it mean anything?'

'What *might* it mean? How many ways can you say "Ah"?'

Nosjean shook his head. 'I don't know, Patron,' he admitted. 'I don't know. And this letter he carves on their cheeks. Now that we've had Gilbertine Guégan, it doesn't seem to stand for their names any longer.'

'That was a doubtful starter from the beginning,' Darcy said. 'How could he know their names before he killed them? They came from different parts of the city and he doesn't seem to have chatted them up first.' He tossed down the papers he was going through and rose to his feet. 'I'm going to have another talk with the Letexier girl, and the You woman,' he said. 'You never know. They might have remembered something important.'

But he didn't sound very hopeful.

19

When Pel called on Doc Minet for his report on Gilbertine Guégan, the old man was tired and dispirited. As he pushed the folder across he sighed and opened a packet of cigarettes.

'I thought you'd given up,' Pel said.

Doc Minet shrugged. 'I've started again. This sort of thing *makes* you.' He managed a twisted smile. 'I had an aunt once who *always* had a cigarette in her mouth, even when she was preparing meals. I never saw her knock the ash off so I can only think it fell in the food. But she must have stirred it in well because nobody was ever ill. Perhaps it's less dangerous than people would have us believe.'

Pel closed the folder and leaned forward. 'What makes an obsessive murderer?' he asked abruptly.

Minet shrugged. 'I'm not a psychiatrist.'

'Surely you know?'

'Yes, I suppose I do.' Minet shrugged. 'Usually they're people who never grow out of boyhood ideas. They can be perfectly normal in other ways, though. Charming. Warm. Kind. Unobtrusive. Law-abiding. Usually over-serious, mind you, or resentful, and hot-tempered over imagined grievances. That sort of thing.'

'Go on. Anything else?'

'Politically vehement but also usually politically naïve. Unstable. Self-centred. Often in a depressed state. Unbalanced opinions. And tricky. Very tricky.'

'How?'

'They can seem simple and kind but that's because they're also cunning and can put on an act.'

Pel paused. 'What causes them to become like this?'

'Hereditary genes as a rule. It's there in the blood. Usually there's a trace of it in one of the parents, but it can miss a child, of course, and appear in the grandchild so that its parents, knowing nothing of their own parents' aberrations, are startled to discover their child's an oddity. It usually lies dormant through the early years, then starts because of something traumatic that's happened, or even for no clear reason at all. But not always. Perhaps it's just that he had problems with his relations with women. In some people the sex drive's strong enough, if no other outlet's available, to drive them to rape.'

'There's been no rape.'

Minet gestured. 'Perhaps he's incapable. Perhaps he suffers from frustration and works out his frustration in this way. Perhaps he's a homosexual even, working out a grievance against women. How do we know? Despite what the psychiatrists say, we still don't know a lot about the workings of the mind. The psychiatric boys *think* they know but, in my opinion, half the time *they* need as much study themselves as the people who lie on their benches.'

The old man sighed. 'And it's true to say,' he went on, 'that many people with psychiatric problems would probably never have had them if they hadn't first been told about them or read about them somewhere in a book. Psychiatry's like gardening: plant the seed and it can take hold and multiply until a perfectly normal human being can discover he has problems he'd never dreamed about. And if that's what psychiatry does, then it has little real value, and a psychiatrist's no better judge of a man's state of mind than anyone else. Especially since patients in mental homes soon learn how to handle them. Anyone who wants a quick release is usually bright enough to learn to give the answers that will expedite it. Because they can't break out, they soon realise they can get out by convincing the people in charge of them that they're safe. There's far too much written and said these days about mental illness and people can grow infatuated with their symptons. Perhaps when I retire I'll spend my time writing about it.'

'Are you going to retire?'

'I'm getting to that age.'

Pel hesitated because the old man seemed weary. 'Do you have a list of city psychiatrists?'

Minet heaved himself from his chair and took down a book from a shelf. 'If you're looking for a list of oddballs,' he said, 'you might also try the social workers and the university Social and Psychological Department. Everybody knows that every generation's in a worse psychological mess than the one before it and I dare bet there are more psychiatric cases at the university than there are anywhere else.'

It was a sweeping statement. On the strength of it, Pel decided, Doc Minet ought to be admitted with Didier as an honorary member of the Society of Bigots. It would be nice to have some company.

Climbing into his car, he headed for the Department of Social Service. The director was a thin-faced man who looked as though he were in need of help himself.

'We have a number of people on our books suffering from obsessive emotions,' he admitted. 'None of them are likely to be murderers, though.'

'I'll be the judge of that,' Pel said. 'I'd like a list.'

'You can't go along and question these people, you know. They're often on a knife edge. They'd be upset for days. It would take my people all their time to get them straight again.'

'Which would you rather have?' Pel asked acidly. 'One or two of your customers upset for a bit and your workers a touch overworked, or another woman dead in the city?'

The director gave him a shocked look but he agreed to get out a list for him.

The psychiatrists in private practice took roughly the same view but it didn't stop Pel getting his lists. It was surprising what Pel, who was far from prepossessing, could do when he chose to. Most of the psychiatrists were tall, handsome, languid men noted for their calmness and charm, while Pel was short, indifferent-looking and eccentric, and because of his temper, bigotry and obsessions, might easily have been considered as a case by any one of them. But before he'd finished, he'd bullied them all into dipping into their files.

Finally, he went to the university and called on the resident psychiatrist there. He was a young doctor called Mahé who was refreshingly cheerful and didn't seem to take his job too seriously. He appeared, in fact, to feel it was just a more cushy way of making a living than working a practice or patrolling the wards of a hospital.

'Of course modern students are susceptible to strains,' he admitted. 'More than ever before. Modern life *causes* strain and it's increased for students by the fact that they have to pass their examinations. Sometimes exam results are the only way of getting a job and for a lot of them these days there won't *be* a job even then, degree or no degree. That doesn't help. They're a funny lot, anyway. They believe in nothing these days. *Je m'en foute* – I don't give a fuck: that's their favourite expression, and they all seem to want to avoid the adult rat race that comes after university. When you ask them their ambition they say it's to be put in a satellite circling the earth.' Mahé grinned. 'Most of it's show-off, of course, and because they're young, but you have to face it, most of them are struggling on grants and they don't see a lot of dolce vita.'

'Are they all the same?'

'Name of God, no! A few, with wealthy or indulgent parents, have a wonderful time dashing about in cars, but even some of those fall into what you might call depressing company.'

Like Marguerite de Wibaux, Pel thought.

'Some of them sail through it, though. They come here determined to have a good time and they make sure they have it. And they're sometimes the ones who get good results, because they don't exhaust themselves with their studies. Even a few of the bright ones decide that educational slavery's not what going to university's about – which it isn't, of course – so they do their own thing. They don't have the clubs and societies here like they do in some countries – and the club centre doesn't amount to much more than a few rooms with a bar, a ping-pong table, a notice board with an appeal for digs or free lifts to Paris, and a record player for the *surboums* on Saturday nights. But if they're level-headed, they manage to enjoy life and have a wonderful time and end up with good second-class degrees. *They*'re often the ones who get the best jobs and turn out to be the best, most-balanced citizens.'

Doctor Mahé smiled. 'But there are, of course, the clever ones who come up hoping for a first-class degree because they feel they ought to have one, or because their parents are pushing them, and sometimes they ruin their health getting them. Sometimes, even, they *don't* get them, because they work too hard and pass their peak before the examination. Finally, there are the other two classes – the geniuses, to whom nothing's any trouble, and those who've just scraped into university and find it all too much for them. A few fall in love. A few fall out of love. A few get into debt. A few fall ill. A few change their minds. There are dozens of permutations.'

'Do you have any names?'

Mahé gave him the names without a murmur and Pel ran his finger down the list. There wasn't one he recognised. He offered his own list but Mahé shrugged.

'Moussia,' he said. 'I know him. Everybody seems to know him. A show-off. A boaster. Compulsive chaser of girls. Insecure childhood, I'd say, and it makes him aggressively self-assertive, but, as far as I know, nothing more.' He glanced again at the list. 'The others – ' he shrugged ' – I don't know them and they've not asked to see me. With one exception.'

'Oh? Who?'

'Hélin.'

Pel sat up. Judge Brisard had subjected Hélin to hours of questioning in which, so Pel had heard, thanks to Hélin's quick brain, Brisard had come off considerably the worse. But he'd had to let him go in the end because, like the Police, he'd been able to find no real reason to hold him, and his alibis had been too tight. Perhaps Mahé knew of things which so far had eluded the Police.

'What's his background?' he asked.

Mahé smiled. 'Unusual,' he said. 'He was under supervision as a young teenager. Always in trouble with the Police or his school. I don't know the details but eventually he pulled himself together and began to do well at school. He'd left it almost too late, though, and he had to flog himself to death to get into university. But he's clever and he made it.' Mahé paused. 'Unfortunately, it changed him into a cynical young man with a house-sized chip on his shoulder. If he could only get a good job and – ' Mahé smiled ' – a decent girl who had some influence on him, he could become a useful citizen.'

'So far, though,' Pel said, 'that hasn't happened, has it?'

Mahé shrugged. 'Unfortunately,' he agreed, 'no.'

'What caused all this rebelliousness? There must have been a reason. Was it a broken home?'

Mahé's shoulders moved. 'Well, yes and no. His grandfather came from a wealthy family who'd always provided soldiers for the Belgian army. But he threw up his profession and, because he'd been trained for nothing else, was never able to make anything of his life. He drifted from one place to another, and his son, Hélin's father, suffered accordingly. He married very young but left his wife and child and simply disappeared. The third generation – the child – Hélin – sank low enough, as I said, to get involved with the Police. It's a miracle, in fact, that he pulled himself out of it and, though he'll never be anybody's favourite man, I suppose, at least, he won't end up as a drain on society. His qualifications are good and they'll be better still when he's finished his exams. He'll get a good job.'

Pel frowned. There seemed to be something missing. 'Hélin going wrong I can understand,' he said. 'His father going wrong I can understand also. But what about his grandfather, who seems to have started the rot? If his family had always been soldiers, why did *he* throw it all up? A mix-up of genes that produced a weakling?'

Mahé smiled. 'Much simpler than that, I suspect, though I suppose you're partly right. Like a lot of Belgian soldiers after the collapse of Belgium he found himself swept along with the defeated regiments and ended up in Paris. As far as I can make out, he was embittered by the surrender. I think it was too much for him and, instead of joining the Resistance like the tougher-minded types, he just packed it all in. I suppose, to be surrounded by several thousand other troops who felt they'd been betrayed, must have been a soul-shaking experience. But then, it was for a lot of people in 1940, wasn't it?'

20

1940.

It seemed an enormous stroke of luck. Did they at last have the meaning of '*1940*'? Did they, in fact, have the meaning of *all* the messages? Did '*Stras-St D Nov 9*' refer not to their own city but to Paris. It had to, because nothing had been reported from the Boulevard de Strasbourg and the Ecole St. Dominique? Not even now. They had almost willed something to happen but nothing had.

Snatching a street guide to the capital from his shelf, Pel opened it hurriedly, flipping the pages over in such haste he crumpled them. Eventually, he found himself looking at the streets of the Tenth Arrondissement, the Buttes Chaumont, the Gare de l'Est and the Porte St. Denis. He ran his finger across the page and, yelling for Darcy, indicated what he'd found.

'Boulevard de Strasbourg-Boulevard St. Denis,' he said. 'They meet near the Porte St. Denis. That message about Stras-St D Nov 9 had nothing to do with the Boulevard de Strasbourg and the Ecole St. Dominique in this city. I can't think why it didn't occur to us before because half the cities in Eastern France that are big enough to have one have a Boulevard de Strasbourg. It was the Boulevard de Strasbourg and the Boulevard St. Denis in Paris in 1940 that it referred to.'

Darcy looked puzzled. 'So what happened there on November 9th, 1940?'

It didn't take long to find out. Nothing.

Puzzled, because they'd been expecting a street riot, some sort of battle, a shooting at least, they checked with the library and the history department at the university, even finally with the archives of the Paris police at the Quai des Orfèvres who dug out their files and examined them for them. They all came up with the same answer. And they had it in detail. Nothing.

By November 9th, 1940, the occupation of the capital was complete but there were no incidents because the occupying troops were behaving well, appearing as benefactors come to rid France of corrupt politicians rather than as conquerors, and all that was seen of the enemy were fresh-faced polite young soldiers armed with nothing more dangerous than cameras.

The archivist was an elderly inspector who had taken part as a young policeman in the famous battle of the Préfecture against the Occupying Forces in 1944, the first organised resistance in the capital against the enemy, and he remembered everything vividly. 'It was all propaganda in 1940, of course,' he said. 'To make the Occupation straightforward and easy. The Gestapo came later.'

There had, of course, been a few scuffles and a few arrests of embittered Parisians, but nothing very spectacular and even those demonstrations had been directed more against the politicians who had brought about the débâcle than against the enemy.

'And on November 9th?' Pel asked.

'Nothing of any note whatsoever. Certainly not at the corner of the Boulevard de Strasbourg and the Boul' St. Denis.'

It left them flattened and disappointed. They had expected something – if not of earth-shaking importance at least of sufficient moment to have been noticed.

'So if it wasn't anything of national importance,' Pel said, 'it must have been of importance to some individual.'

'To the grandfather,' Darcy said.

They both knew whose grandfather he was thinking of but Hélin had an alibi for every killing and they still couldn't see how they could connect him to all of them. Nevertheless, it set Pel thinking, and he realised that so far they had only half the picture. They had reports on everybody connected with the case but they had come from French Police files only and, remembering what Didier had said about not trusting foreigners, he laboriously began to check the background of every single male whose name had cropped up in the course of their enquiry, right back to childhood. Everybody. Even the men who had stumbled on the body of Gilbertine Guégan, one of whom had turned out to have been born a Czech. Since there were several other foreigners or people like Moussia whose parents had been foreigners until they had acquired French nationality, he invoked the International Radio Link for police enquiries. It involved several countries and it took time, but the answers slowly began to come back. It worried him that there was so much to go through and that he had to leave a lot of the reading to Nosjean, because he knew the Prowler was more than likely already watching his next victim.

Some of the replies had to come a long way. Padiou's came from Belgium, Aduraz's from a town in Spain Pel had never heard of. Schwendermann's came from Siegen. Bartelott's came from Scotland Yard and as Pel studied it and saw his high-powered connections his eyebrows shot up. If they had to arrest Bartelott, he felt, it would probably result in war. Chatry was an Alsatian. Doucet, the boy who had abandoned Honorine Nauray in the Cours de Gaulle, was illegitimate, had never had any basic roots and had moved from one home to another all his life. Doctor Bréhard had also come from a broken home and had even been the victim of a tug-of-war between his parents, shuttling between Grenoble and Paris, once even to the United States. The most striking report of the lot was Hélin's. He had been involved in a series of breakings and enterings in Belgium with an older man, and, at the age of fifteen, had finally been surprised with him by a policeman while on a roof. His companion had shot the policeman dead and been shot in his turn by the policeman's partner, and Hélin had watched him fall thirty feet to be impaled on a set of railings in the street below. It was at this point that he had dropped his criminal activities and settled down to work.

Pel sat studying the reports for a long time, his face thoughtful. Some of the replies he'd received hadn't supplied everything he sought, and his requests had had to be repeated so that he was still waiting for their completion. Lighting a cigarette, he began to wonder why he'd ever bothered to get married because these days he hardly ever saw his wife. Doubtless, he thought gloomily, any day now she'd be asking him for her release.

He pushed the piles of papers on his desk around for a while.

The thing they needed was there somewhere, he felt certain. He had never believed in flashes of deduction. Police work wasn't like that and the answers were always in the documents. Tomorrow he'd get De Troq' or Nosjean to go through Goriot's collection. While he was a good organiser, Goriot had never been noted for inspiration.

He rubbed his eyes and stubbed out his cigarette. He had lost count of the number he had smoked that morning and his inside must be like the ashpan under a fireplace.

While Pel was ploughing through the reports Darcy was prowling the city streets. Darcy liked to prowl the city occasionally, to get what he called the 'feel of the place'.

At lunchtime, suspecting Pel might have gone to the Bar Transvaal, he was on the point of heading there for a drink when he decided instead to try the Bar du Destin. As he turned away from the zinc with his beer, he saw Schwendermann peering myopically through his thick spectacles at a book. He looked up in surprise as Darcy appeared alongside him and, jumping to his feet, he jarred the table and just managed to catch his coffee before it slid to the floor.

'A long way from the university,' Darcy commented.

Schwendermann smiled. 'Yes, sir. I am watching the architecture of the city. I have acquired many old books and it is interesting to see what iss done to buildings. Sometimes the end is chopped off or rebuilt. Mit others, it iss removed – vervollständigen – completely. And sometimes – ' Schwendermann's eyes lit up ' – sometimes you can even see where the old buildings were even after they have gone.'

'Very interesting,' Darcy said in a tone as flat as a smack across the chops.

'How does your investigation go, sir? You have found the guilty one perhaps?'

'Not yet.'

'You have not arrested Hélin?'

Darcy was silent for a moment. 'Should we have?' he asked.

'That iss up to you, sir. But have you not asked him? Where he iss when Marguerite iss murdered.'

Darcy sipped at his drink. 'Where is he supposed to have been?' he asked.

'He iss not where he said, I think, sir.'

'You've heard something?'

'At a lecture, sir. I hear his friend Hayn talking mit him. They think I don't know but I have very acute listening. He say to Hayn he must keep his mouth shut.'

'About what?'

'Sir, I don't know. But I think it iss to do with where he iss the night Marguerite iss killed.'

'He was with his friends. They said so.'

'But Hayn *iss* his friend and Hayn iss told to keep his mouth shut. I have wondered if I should tell you.'

When Schwendermann had gone, Darcy stared at his beer for some time before deciding to look up Hélin.

The house in the Rue Henri-Gauthier where Hélin and his friends lived looked exactly the same as Number 69, Rue Devoin even to lay-out, decoration and furnishing; spartan, bare, practical, and with little of value that could be damaged. It also seemed as full of music and the noise of young people arguing and, because no one heard him above the racket, no one appeared as he climbed the stairs to the room Hélin shared with his friends, Jenet and Detoc. It was empty. But Hayn, who occupied a separate room, was in and he stood up uncertainly as Darcy entered.

The radio was going and Darcy strode across to it and switched it off.

'Hé!' Hayn came to life at once. 'What's going on?'

'Police,' Darcy said.

'I guessed that much. From your manners. Where's your pal?'

'Which pal?'

'Everybody knows the Police go round in pairs. So that if one can read perhaps the other will be able to write.'

Darcy said nothing, balancing on his toes, his big hands hanging at his sides. He gave Hayn the sort of look the chairman of a charitable organisation might have given an obstreperous pauper. He was an easy-going man who liked to think he could keep an open mind, a mind as open, in fact, as the gates of Heaven were open to sinners; but there was one thing that annoyed him, and that was clever people like Hayn sneering at the Police.

'That was a foolish thing to say, my friend,' he said slowly. 'Being rude puts you in bad straight away. You've heard of the traffic cop who used to warn motorists not to get him into a bad temper because it gave him indigestion and that made it tough for the people he came up against. I'm the same. I'm a malicious type who bears grudges.'

Hayn suddenly looked nervous. 'What do you want?'

'Where's Hélin?'

'If he's not in his room, he's out.'

'How do you know? Did you hear him go?'

Hayn jeered. 'You must be joking.' He held up his hand. 'Listen!' As he became silent the sound of all the radios in the building came flooding in together. 'You think you'd hear anything with that lot going?'

'So!' Darcy gestured. 'If he's out, where is he?'

'How do I know? Getting drunk with the others, I expect. Or with a bit of fluff. He'll be needing a bit of light relief after all that questioning. He was there hours before they let him go. Why do you want him?'

When Darcy explained, Hayn looked shifty. 'You can't pin Marguerite's death on him,' he said. 'He was with us. All night.'

'You sure?'

'You calling me a liar?'

Darcy smiled. With his strong white teeth, he looked as though, if he couldn't subdue Hayn in any other way, he could at least bite him. 'You ever been in jail?' he asked.

'What's that got to do with it?'

'We have an excellent one here. Number 72, Rue d'Auxonne, we call it. It has other names. Some of them not very complimentary because it's not all that comfortable.' Darcy pushed at a pile of clothes and books on a chair so that they fell to the floor. 'But they do at least make you keep the place cleaner than this pigstye.'

'What are you getting at?'

'You could find yourself in there, my friend. Under Section 60 or 63 of the Penal Code. One deals with accessories to crime, the other with non-assistance to a person in danger. I'm sure we could make one of them fit and they can carry heavy sentences. You fancy that?'

Hayn began to look worried and Darcy pressed. 'Now, think again. Where was Hélin the night Marguerite de Wibaux was murdered?'

'With us.'

'Would you be prepared to swear that in court? You'd better be, because perjury can carry a heavy sentence, too.'

Hayn hesitated and tried to evade giving an answer, which seemed to suggest he had a reason for evading it and Darcy leaned harder. In the end, he admitted that Hélin had *not* been with him and the other two on the night of Marguerite de Wibaux's death.

'He left just before it must have happened,' he said.

'Where did he go?'

'I don't know. I think he went to see that lecturer he was rolling – Doctor Sirat.'

'But he wasn't with *you*?'

'No.'

It was late afternoon and Pel was deep in the reports again when Darcy appeared.

'Chief,' he said. 'Hélin. Those pals of his who said he was with them the night Marguerite de Wibaux was murdered were lying. Schwendermann put me on to it. He heard Hélin talking. At some lecture. I saw Hayn and he admitted it. He said Hélin left them about half an hour before the De Wibaux girl was killed.'

'What about Hélin? What does *he* say?'

'I didn't see him. He wasn't in. I've arranged to have him picked up. Hayn said he thought he was with that woman he mentioned at the time – the one who went to the States – Doctor Sirat. And he could have been. But if he was, why didn't he mention it when we talked about it?'

'Keeping her name out of it?'

'He didn't keep her name out of it when we were wondering if he'd done for Bernadette Hamon. And we know there could be a connection with those messages. "*Paris*." "*1940*." His grandfather was there. We know that. Perhaps he was involved in some sort of incident on the Boulevard de Strasbourg on November 9th that year. Nothing big enough to be reported but something that was important enough to him. Something that would make his grandson want to call us the cursed French. A fight with a Frenchman? Perhaps a wounding? Something like that. Hélin's a Belgian, Patron, and there was a lot of bitterness in those days and a lot of blame being bandied around – us, the Belgians, the Dutch, the British.'

Pel pushed aside the files he'd been studying. 'There may be something in it,' he agreed. 'It might be worth looking into. I think we should bring him in and let Judge Brisard have another go at him. Find him, Daniel. Wherever he is.'

They were still discussing it when Nosjean appeared. He was excited. 'Chief, we might have a lead!'

Pel stared at Darcy. After weeks of nothing, they were suddenly being swamped by leads.

'We've just got one.'

Nosjean looked blank and they explained. Nosjean brushed Darcy's story aside.

'This is a better one, Patron,' he said. 'I've turned up a brooch.'

'I'm not interested in brooches,' Pel snapped.

'You'll be interested in this one, Patron. I found it in an antique shop in Ferry-le-Grand. You remember I was enquiring at all the antique dealers over the Abrillards' belongings. This type – a guy called Treville – was very helpful, and when I heard about Bayetto buying an antique cigar case over there I wondered if it was from him. It was, and I thought I'd return the favour by telling him to contact the police in Chaumont in case they'd found it among Bayetto's belongings. They had, and Treville was so pleased he promptly came back with some more information – that he'd found this brooch among things he'd recently acquired. It came in while he'd been off ill for a day or two and his assistant hadn't noticed anything special about it. Treville spotted it as soon as he returned to work.'

Pel glared. 'For God's sake, Nosjean, come to the point! And that business is over, anyway! Remaud's free! Let it ride!'

'Patron – ' Nosjean was not to be put off ' – it's nothing to do with Remaud. Take a look at it.'

He fished in an envelope he was carrying and laid the brooch on the table. It bore a single zircon in an old-fashioned setting and appeared to be of no great value. Pel lifted his eyes to look at

Nosjean.

'Look on the back, Patron.'

Turning it over, Pel saw that across the centre of the mounting was a set of initials.

'M. de W.,' he said slowly. His head jerked up. 'Marguerite de Wibaux!'

Nosjean grinned. 'I insisted on taking it away,' he said. 'Treville's not a bad sort and he's always co-operated. All he asked was that we keep his name out of the paper. He doesn't want people to think he receives stolen goods.'

'We'll have no option if it leads to the killer,' Pel observed. 'It'll have to come out in court. Did he remember who brought it in?'

'Yes, Patron. It was a student. Strong-looking and dark-skinned. He thought he was Algerian or Tunisian or something like that.'

21

'Moussia.' Pel frowned, his thoughts whirring. 'Strong. Ath-
letic. Insecure childhood. Aggressive self-assertion. Claims to
know how to get girls but in fact unpopular with them.
Resentful, perhaps, because he thought none of them wanted
him. Does his family have some connection with the Boulevard
de Strasbourg area in Paris in 1940?'

'His father joined the North African troops, Patron,' Darcy
pointed out. 'He said so. He fought in Italy. He was Algerian
and in those days before independence Algeria was part of
Metropolitan France. He *could* have been in Paris on a visit and
been caught there by the Occupation. And he *could* have got
back to North Africa because the rules weren't strict in those
days and you could get from the Occupied to the Unoccupied
Zone without too much trouble. A lot of people bolted to
Algeria. Perhaps he did.'

Moussia was indignant and frightened at the same time. 'Why
have I been brought in?' he demanded.

'To answer a few questions,' Pel said. 'Does the year 1940
have any significance for you?'

Moussia looked bewildered. '1940? Why should it? That was
the year of the Occupation, wasn't it? Why should it have any
significance for me? I wasn't even born.'

'What about your father? Where was he?'

'As far as I know in Algiers, which was where he lived. It was
where my mother lived, too. But I don't know. And I can't ask
him because they separated and I think he's dead now. I'm not
even sure of that.'

'Did you know your father well?'

'Not much. I wasn't very old when they split up.'

'Did he ever talk about Paris?'

'Only to say that he thought Paris had let the Algerians down. That was after independence, though. He considered himself a Frenchman and he had to take the first ship to Marseilles before he got himself shot.'

'Was he in Paris in 1940?'

'I shouldn't think so. He'd only be about sixteen and he didn't come from the sort of family that could afford to send him to Paris. Why? What's it to do with anything?'

Pel looked at Darcy and Nosjean. Moussia caught the glance and licked his lips nervously.

'Will I be able to go now?' he said. 'Is that all?'

'Not quite.' Pel had been sitting with his hand over the brooch Nosjean had brought in. Now he removed it and pushed the brooch forward. 'Do you recognise that?'

Moussia's face fell and his dark skin went grey. He nodded silently.

'It was recovered from the antique dealer in Ferry-le-Grand. They say it was handed in by a man answering to your description. Was it you?'

Moussia nodded again.

'Whose is it?'

'It was my mother's.'

'What was her name? Before she married?'

Moussia hesitated. 'Michelline de – de Walbecque.'

'You don't seem very sure.'

'Yes. Yes, I am.'

'De Walbecque's the name of one of the professors at the university,' Nosjean said in a flat voice. 'I spoke to him only recently. On the Prowler case.'

'Well – ' Moussia's head turned nervously from one to the other ' – well, that's what it is.'

'Check with the university, Nosjean,' Pel said. 'They'll have the parents' names.'

'They won't have mine!' Moussia's voice rose. 'Because they come from Algeria.'

They sat in silence as Nosjean left the room, Moussia fidgeting constantly with the windcheater he was wearing. Nosjean returned within minutes.

'Father: Amin Abda Moussia,' he said. 'Mother: Noëlle Besnier.'

Pel pushed the brooch across the desk again. 'It says "M. de W." on the back,' he pointed out. 'That doesn't go with Noëlle Besnier or Noëlle Moussia either. Would you like to think again?'

Moussia's mouth opened and shut without a sound emerging.

'How did it come into your possession?'

'I bought it.'

'Where from?'

'A shop in Dole.'

'Name?'

'I forget.'

'Describe it.'

'I – I can't.'

'When?'

'Two months ago.'

'Why?'

'For a girl I know.'

'Which girl?'

'She lives in Marseilles.'

'Name?'

'Monique Coudrais.'

'Why buy a girl with the initials M.C. a ring carrying the initials M. de W.?'

'It was second-hand and cheap and I could afford it. I was going to have them taken off.'

'If you bought it for this girl in Marseilles why did you sell it in Ferry?'

'She threw me over.'

'So why not keep it for the next one? You told us you have no trouble getting girls.'

'I decided I didn't like it after all.'

Pel leaned forward. 'Come on. That brooch belonged to Marguerite de Wibaux, didn't it? Are you trying to persuade us that a brooch in your possession carrying the initials of a girl who was strangled, a girl who lived in the same group of flats as you, a girl who knew you, who'd been to parties you attended – that it didn't belong to her?'

'It didn't! It didn't!'

'Then who *did* it belong to?'

'An aunt of hers.'

'What!'

Pel sat bolt upright and he saw Darcy and Nosjean exchange glances. 'You'd better tell us the truth,' he said.

Moussia was shaking with fear. 'The initials stand for Marie de Wibaux. That's her aunt. Her father's sister. She's a spinster. She gave it to Marguerite but Marguerite hated it because it was old-fashioned and decided to sell it and say she'd lost it. It was insured so she actually got money for it from the insurance company. A guy came to see her about it. She said it was worth five hundred francs and they paid up. Other people do that sort of thing, don't they? – pretend they've lost something and then claim the insurance.'

'I've no doubt. Go on.'

'Well, she gave it to me to look after because she was afraid the type from the insurance company would want to search her room to make sure she wasn't telling lies.'

'Which she *was* doing.'

'Yes.' Moussia gestured tiredly. 'As a matter of fact he arrived early and very nearly caught us with the damn thing on the table. I nipped out the back way.'

'Which back way? There is no back way. The door's screwed up tight.'

'Not that way. Through the window on the landing.'

Pel had become very still. 'This is something we haven't yet heard about,' he said. 'Inform me.'

'Well, it was easy. I'd done it before. I was once set on by a gang of kids who wanted to do me over.'

'Why did they want to do you over?'

'They were town kids. They don't like students much. They resent us having grants.' Moussia's dark face split in a nervous smile. 'They forget we're the élite of the next generation. There'd been a slanging match in a bar and they were waiting and tried to grab me as I was coming home. I dashed into Number 69. When they didn't find me they kicked the front door in.'

'You hid?'

'Not likely. They'd have found me. I nipped upstairs and

slipped out of the landing window alongside Sergent's room. The ground floor sticks out a bit further than the others so there's a roof. I dropped down to it and then to the ground.'

'Didn't it make a noise? Didn't it disturb the girls in the flat below?'

Moussia sighed. 'Next day Annie Joulier said she thought she heard burglars but as nothing was missing nobody enquired any further. We got the door fixed and that was that.'

'Did you return the same way?'

'Not possible. You'd have to climb up to the lower roof – and that's too high. Then from there you'd have to climb up to the landing window by Sergent's room. And that's impossible, too.'

'You can't get in that way?'

'Not unless you're a gymnast.'

'Which you are.'

'No, I'm not. I'm a weight-lifter. You'd have to be a cat burglar. Or two and and a half metres high, which I'm not. I waited in the yard at the back of the house until they'd gone then I slipped in through the front door.'

Pel glanced at Darcy and Nosjean, then changed the subject abruptly. 'Let's get back to the brooch,' he said.

'Yes – well – ' Moussia gestured ' – in the end, when Marguerite got the money for it from the insurance, she decided she'd better get rid of it for safety. Because she was scared to do it herself, I'd had it valued for her at the shop in Ferry-le-Grand. The guy said it was worth about five hundred and fifty francs.

'That's a lot of money for a student!'

Moussia shook his head. 'Not to her. Her family's rich. I said she oughtn't to be seen selling it and I'd get rid of it for her. I told her I'd been offered four hundred and fifty. She was quite happy. After all, her family had plenty of money and she'd just got five hundred from the insurance company. She agreed to give me fifty if I got rid of it. For safety I took it to Ferry again and the guy gave me the five hundred and fifty. I kept the extra hundred.'

'*And* the fifty she promised?'

'She gave it to me.'

'She didn't do very well out of it, did she?'

Moussia's head moved silently from right to left and back

again. 'She wasn't being very honest either,' he said. 'And she had all the money she wanted. I didn't. And it didn't stop her treating me like dirt later.'

There was a long silence then Pel leaned forward. 'Is this why you didn't wish to admit to having the brooch?'

Moussia drew a deep breath. 'Yes. I also thought if you found I'd had it you'd think I'd done her in.'

'We did. We still do.'

'I didn't! I swear!'

Pel sat back in his chair. 'You'd better stay here for the time being,' he said. 'Check with her family, Nosjean. Find out if she had an aunt with a brooch like this.'

As Nosjean left the room, Moussia turned to Pel. 'Are you going to arrest me?' he asked. 'For false pretences.'

Pel sat very still. 'It might even be for murder,' he said.

As Moussia was taken away, Darcy looked at Pel. 'Think he's the Prowler, Patron? He's known to pester girls.'

'Not pester them, Daniel. Follow them.'

'What's the difference? He also knows how to get out of that house in the Rue Devoin without being seen.'

'Out. But not in.'

'He probably knows a way in, too, that he's not telling us about. With a rope or something. What do we charge him with?'

'Not false pretences. Not yet. Not with five murders on our hands. Let him stew. See Judge Brisard. He ought to be able to deal with it. In the meantime, I think you and I should have another look at that house.'

Several of the students – Sergent, Schwendermann and two of the girls – were in their rooms as they searched Number 69, Rue Devoin. The room that had been occupied by Marguerite de Wibaux was still unoccupied but her belongings were still there. Pel switched on the radio.

'Go upstairs, Daniel,' he said. 'Then come down.'

When Darcy reappeared, Pel looked up. 'Well, go on,' he said.

'I've been.'

'I didn't hear you above the radio.'

As they talked, Annie Joulier came tearing into the hall,

yelling at the top of her voice that Moussia had been arrested. How she'd found out it was hard to tell but there was an immediate uproar and a gabble of voices, then all the girls shot out of the house to spread the news.

'Do we stop them, Patron?' Darcy asked.

Pel shook his head. 'Let them go. It's true enough and it'll keep the press out of our hair.'

They continued to prowl round the building, searching in the broom cupboard, and finally in the yard at the back. It was a dank, shadowed sort of place away from the sun during the day and the street lights at night. By the outhouse built into the rear wall where the painter kept his equipment, Pel stopped. 'That lock doesn't seem a very good one, Daniel. Will it come open?'

Darcy had it open within minutes. Inside they stared at the tins of paint, the cans of turpentine, the brushes soaking in water and white spirit, the paint-stained rags, the stepladders and cleaned-out pots.

'Patron – ' Darcy's head turned ' – those steps. Moussia said you couldn't get back into the building without being seen. But if you knew that lock could be picked, you could. Easily. Especially after dark.'

Hoisting himself to the top of the wall, he peered over. 'Empty yard here,' he said. 'Looks derelict. He could easily climb down and nip over here and return the same way. There are bricks stacked on the other side.'

'How does he get back in the house?'

'The steps, Patron. He could get on to that lower roof over the ground floor.'

'He has to get in a floor higher. How does he manage that? There was no rope in his room.'

Darcy frowned. 'There must be *some* way. Perhaps he had it hidden somewhere. Perhaps we should go through that place again. Perhaps he has it in one of those suitcases in the kitchen. Having got back in, he sits tight until early next morning when he goes out – who's to worry about anybody going *out* in the morning? – puts the steps away, relocks the shed and comes in through the front door as if he's been out for nothing more interesting than to buy a morning paper.' Darcy paused. 'And, Patron, he didn't have to do any climbing to kill Gilbertine Guégan. He wasn't here. He was lodging with that pal of his,

Habib, at Rue Novembre 11. Still – ' Darcy pulled a face ' – leaving those steps out all night where they could be found – he was taking a risk, Patron.'

Pel's expression didn't change. 'Murderers do take risks,' he said. 'Let's go back and see what Judge Brisard's made of him.'

22

Judge Brisard had made nothing of Moussia. In his usual pompous manner, he had told the policeman who had brought Moussia to his office to wait outside the door. Judge Brisard was a large, strong man despite his broad hips and plump behind, and was confident, as he always was, that he could handle his witnesses. Unfortunately Moussia was strong, too, and as Judge Brisard had leaned back in his chair, full of self-satisfaction, to deliver the lecture with which he usually prefaced his interrogations, Moussia had celebrated the policeman's departure by pushing him – and his chair – over backwards, breaking the chair and knocking Brisard unconscious. He had then climbed through the window of Brisard's private washroom and disappeared. The Police were unconcerned about the black eye and the lump on his head that Judge Brisard had acquired, only that his self-importance had allowed their prisoner to escape. But what they had to say about him was nothing compared with what Pel had to say.

'He should be cut into strips and fed to the pigs,' he breathed.

Pink with fury, he sat at his desk and lit a cigarette to try to control his temper, while Darcy used the telephone to tear lumps off everybody within reach. In addition to false pretences and suspicion of murder, Moussia was now wanted on charges of assault and battery, evading arrest, and assailing the majesty of the law in the person of Judge Brisard.

Several cigarettes later, Pel had calmed down enough to remember that it was about time for Claudie to go out on the streets and that if Moussia were about she could well be in great danger. Collecting Darcy, still red-faced from shouting down the telephone, he headed for the sergeants' room. Claudie was standing in the middle of a group of men, ready to leave.

'Even with that lot on your face,' Misset was saying, indicating her make-up, 'you're an improvement on my wife. And not half as fierce The way she goes on at me, I need police protection.'

When they saw Pel they broke up quickly, Misset's face suddenly so blank it looked as if it had belonged to someone else who'd just walked away and left it.

They watched Claudie depart. Darcy went with her to check the placing of his men. Still angry, Pel returned to his own office, hoping to take his mind off what had happened by absorbing himself in the pile of paper on his desk. The reports were still coming in from abroad, some for the second time because the first ones had not been complete enough to satisfy him. De Troq', who was in the next room going through the local files, watched him heading for his office but wisely kept silent.

Around ten-thirty the two of them slipped out to the Bar Transvaal for a drink. Because he was tired and was still angry, Pel had a whisky and, in a rush of blood to the head, because he wasn't normally so generous, he offered De Troq' one. It shocked him when he accepted because De Troq' didn't normally drink the hard stuff and he hadn't expected him to say yes.

When they returned to the Hôtel de Police there was a message from the police sub-station as Chenove to say they'd had a sighting of Hélin.

'What was he up to?' Pel asked.

'We think he's been with a girl who lives here. Her parents are away for a few days and the house's empty except for the girl, and we think he was taking advantage of the fact.'

It sounded typical of Hélin.

'Where is he now?'

'He's disappeared. A neighbour reported the sound of violent quarrelling and when we went out to investigate we found the girl in tears with a black eye and no sign of her boyfriend. But she gave us his name. It was Hélin. They'd had an argument and he'd walked out on her. We've got everybody out looking for him. We'll find him.'

'Unless he's already back here!'

Replacing the telephone, Pel arranged for a warning to be sent out to Claudie and the men on the streets that Hélin was somewhere about the city. They still had no real proof against him but Pel wasn't taking any chances.

Returning to his office, he put on his spectacles and began to shuffle the files round to find those for Hélin and Moussia. Several new reports had come in and, picking up the top one, he read the name on the cover and idly scanned the first few lines. For a few moments he stared at them, then abruptly he sat up, adjusted his spectacles, crushed out his cigarette, lit another without noticing and continued to read, by this time totally absorbed. When he'd finished, he laid down his spectacles, stubbed out his cigarette without having drawn on it at all, and sat back, breathing deeply. Turning the file over, he stared at the name again, and, lifting his head, shouted at the next door room. 'De Troq'!'

As he looked up, he saw De Troq' standing in the doorway. 'I was just on my way to see *you*, Patron.'

Pel lit yet another cigarette, crushed it out after one puff and indicated the folders in front of him.

'It's here,' he said in an awed voice. 'Every bit of it.'

De Troq' looked startled and waved a sheet of paper he held. 'It's here, too, Patron. In this. It's not conclusive but I dare bet I'm right enough to bring him in and lean on him.'

They exchanged the name they'd settled on and stared at each other, aware that they'd both reached the same conclusion, but for entirely different reasons.

'It was in the reports that came in from outside,' Pel said. 'An attack on a prostitute. Someone tried to strangle her but she was strong and escaped. The police had their suspicions but our friend was staying with an aunt out of town at the time. At least, he was *supposed* to be staying with her but they think, in fact, that he'd quarrelled with her because she was always chivvying him about his behaviour and that he'd returned home. But they could never prove it because his aunt swore he *was* with her and his mother swore he *hadn't* returned home. Those two women must have known it could have been him. But they kept quiet, and thanks to them five women are dead. He was seventeen at the time. He's now grown into a man and his obsession's grown with him.'

As Pel stopped, he suddenly became aware of the time and glanced at his watch. 'Eleven-ten,' he said. 'Let's go and pick him up.'

'If he's not already out there on the streets, Patron.'

Pel gave De Troq' a quick glance. 'Is Darcy back yet?'

'Not yet, Patron. He's due any moment.'

'Right. Get your car. I'll leave a message for him to say where we are and to get Claudie back inside.'

As De Troq' shot off down the corridor, Pel headed for Darcy's office where Cadet Martin was dozing near the radio, waiting for Darcy to return and take over. He sat up with a jerk as Pel appeared.

'Claudie,' Pel snapped. 'Have you heard from her?'

'Not for some time, Patron.'

'Call her. Tell her to come in at once. We've got the Prowler. There's no need for her to take any more risks.' Pel tossed the file he'd been studying on to the desk. 'Give that to Inspector Darcy as soon as he arrives. That's our boy. Tell him I'm going over there now to pick him up. I'll be in touch.'

As Martin scooped up the file and reached for the microphone in one move, Pel headed for the door. De Troq' was waiting in the street with his big roadster.

They drove in silence. When they arrived at their destination, several radios and record players were going. They went upstairs. Bangs on the door brought no reply from inside, only the sound of a door opening elsewhere in the building and a blast of music coming up the stairs with a girl's voice demanding to know what was going on.

'Where is he?' De Troq' shouted.

'He's not gone out, so he must be in his room.'

Pel gestured at the door. 'Break it down, De Troq'.'

The crash brought another yell from below. 'Hey! You can't go breaking into people's rooms!'

'I think we can,' Pel said. 'We're the Police.'

De Troq' was already inside the room, with Pel hot on his heels. The room was empty and the first thing they noticed was that the bed had been pulled to the window and stripped of its coverings. The sheets, dark blue in colour, had been knotted together, tied to a bed leg and hung out of the window.

They stopped dead, staring at each other, then De Troq'

started sniffing about like a tracker dog. He nosed through drawers and, lifting the lid of the iron stove, picked up a poker and eventually came up with the charred fragments of a jersey.

'He's been burning clothes, Patron,' he said. 'Only one reason why a penniless student would burn clothes. They had blood on them.'

Pel had stopped in front of a large white-painted cupboard that looked like a wardrobe. 'Open it, De Troq',' he said.

De Troq' had it open within seconds. Pinned inside the door was a group of smudgy photographs of unclothed girls. They might have shocked people in 1908 but they were unlikely to inspire much enthusiasm in anyone normal in the present relaxed moral climate. They were all too fat by modern standards, with drooping bosoms and thick thighs. But, one and all, they were naked.

De Troq' passed over a book he'd dug from the back of the cupboard. It was a life of Toulouse-Lautrec in photographs, some of which showed the dwarf painter standing in his studio with groups of naked models who could well have been harlots. There were other books of a similar nature and a group of biographies.

'*Der Marquis de Sade und seine Zeit*.' De Troq' read the names aloud. 'German. *Sade, Mon Prochain*; French. *The Life And Ideas of the Marquis de Sade*; English. He's got one by Von Sacher-Masoch, too, Patron. The type who invented masochism – *Gelizische Geschichten*. And one on the same subject in English by an American author. There are others, too. All languages. All perversions. He believed in getting to know his subject.'

Reaching into the cupboard again, he fished out three large notebooks written in spidery scrawls. The writing was different in each case.

'Can you read them?' Pel asked.

'Yes, Patron. They're diaries.' De Troq' was silent for some minutes. Then he said: 'This one belongs to a soldier who was in Paris in 1940. His grandfather, I think. It concerns the women he went with. It goes into some detail, too.'

'He must have found it among his possessions when he died. And this one?'

'I think it must be his father's. Seems to be much the same, judging by the subject and the dates. Women again. But different women, different places, different times. But roughly the same content.' De Troq' read briefly then picked up the third notebook. 'This one's the grandson's – our boy. There's not much in it but he has some strong things to say about prostitutes.'

'I'm not surprised.'

'His grandfather caught syphilis from a woman in Paris during the war. There's even a date, Patron. He's underlined it in red and put a big ring round it.' As he pointed, they bent over the notebook. 'November 9th., 1940. He spent a lot of time in hospital. He even gives the place where the old boy picked her up.' De Troq's head lifted. 'The corner of the Boulevard de Strasbourg and the Boul' St. Denis.'

'Go on,' Pel snapped. 'What else?'

Moving impatiently about the room, he waited as De Troq' rapidly scanned the handwritten pages.

'It seems to have wrecked the family home,' De Troq' said. 'His wife left him and took the family with her. One of the children was a son, our man's father, the writer – ' De Troq' tapped the second notebook ' – of this. It was obliging of our man to summarise it all in *his* notebook. It makes it a lot easier to grasp. It seems this son wasn't much better than his father because he was also later caught with a woman. Seven years ago. He lost his job because of it.'

'Naturally.'

De Troq' was turning the pages of the third notebook. '*He* committed suicide. It left his wife and son – our boy, the writer of this book – penniless. There's your motive, Patron. Women ruined two generations of his family.' De Troq' flicked over a few pages and looked up again to meet Pel's eyes.

'It's all here, Patron,' he went on.' Set out neatly – so he could study it when he felt like it, I suppose – as plain as if it were daubed on a wall. It's even got De Wibaux's name here. His grandfather was at it and so was his father. I'd say that, thanks to his mother and that aunt of his, he grew up believing that all women but those two had loose morals.'

Pel was staring about him. 'So where is he now?' He gestured at the diary De Troq' was holding. 'Does that thing indicate how he operates?'

'There are some references to his movements, Patron.'

'Dates?'

'Yes, Patron.'

De Troq' spread the notebook on the table and they studied it together. The dead women were all there and easily identifiable either by name or description or by some name he'd given them. 'Marguerite de Wibaux.' 'Bar des Chevaux' – the place where Bernadette Hamon had been in the habit of taking a quick cup of coffee late at night on her return from the hospital. 'Alice Magueri.' That name was in full, as if she'd picked him up and even told him her name. 'Doucet's woman' – obviously the only way he'd known Honorine Nauray. 'Blondie' – the name he'd given to Monique Letexier. 'Woman, Bar de la Renaissance,' by which he clearly meant Marie-Yvonne You. Obviously he hung about outside late-night bars watching for what he considered immoral behaviour. Finally, 'Gilbertine Guégan.' Then there were three names they'd not so far come across. 'Daisy Amaad.' 'Louise-Marie Pienaar.' 'Sylvestrine Boch.'

'I think those three are prostitutes, Patron,' De Troq' said. 'I know two of them. Daisy Amaad works near the Ducal Palace. I brought her in once for an assault on another girl – this one, Louise-Marie Pienaar. She said she was stealing her clients. He obviously talked to them, because he knew their names.'

Alongside the names or descriptions of Marguerite de Wibaux, Bernadette Hamon, Alice Mageuri, Honorine Nauray and Gilbertine Guégan was the letter H, a date, and a cross like the cross at the head of a grave. The identities of Monique Letexier and Marie-Yvonne You had been cut across with a single line. Against the remaining names were question marks.

'These must be women he's marked down for later, Patron.'

'Is there anything to say where he is now?'

The tension was electric as De Troq' hurriedly turned pages. So much so, they barely noticed the beat of the music that seemed to fill every corner of the building. Then, at the end of the notebook, De Troq' came up with another list. There were four names on it, three of them the new ones they'd already noticed – Daisy Aamad, Louise-Marie Pienaar and Silvestrine Boch. But to this list had been added another in different ink, framed at each side by a question mark. Alongside it was that day's date. The name was Mireille Mathieu.

They stared at each other. This was the name of a girl the killer obviously didn't know so that, like Monique Letexier, he'd had to give her a nickname. And there was only one person they knew of other than Mireille Mathieu herself who looked like Mireille Mathieu.

'Claudie,' Pel said. 'Thank God she's been brought safely inside.'

When they left the building, through the group of curious students waiting outside, a light drizzle was making the streets wet and the car headlights were reflected on the black asphalt. With Claudie safely withdrawn, the urgency had gone out of their chase because they knew enough about the Prowler now to know he planned his killings, and when he didn't find her where he expected he'd return home. As De Troq' drove, Pel spoke into the radio.

Darcy, by this time back at the Hôtel de Police and in touch with the men on the streets, sat up in his chair as he heard Pel's voice.

'Patron,' he said. 'I've been trying to find you.' He sounded anxious. 'Have you picked him up?'

'We're looking for him now.'

'Patron – !'

'We've taken a man off the beat to watch the place for when he returns. Get Nosjean over there. He's out now but they can pull him in when he comes back. Is Claudie safely in?'

'*No*, Patron – '

'What!'

'No, Patron – '

'Then, in the name of God, get her in! He's looking for her! Tell her to come in as fast as she can before he finds her!'

'Patron!' Pel was just about to put down the microphone when Darcy's voice came back, loud and alarmed. 'We can't contact her! We've lost touch with her! So has Nosjean!'

23

Pel was sitting bolt upright in his seat. 'You mean you've lost her?' he yelled.

'You know what these damned radios are like, Patron!' Darcy sounded desperate. 'They never work when you want them to. She may just be somewhere the buildings are too close, but she's been off for a good ten minutes now and Nosjean's doing his nut because he's lost her in the dark. We've been trying to reach her ever since you left.'

'In the name of God, Daniel,' Pel snapped, and you could almost feel the sudden tension in the car. 'If anything happens to that girl somebody will pay for it! Get everybody on his toes! Everybody! We're heading for the Rue de Rouen district!'

The streets were dark and empty of traffic. People in the Rue de Rouen area mostly didn't have cars but those who did had parked them in the streets, empty lots and backyards, and were preparing for bed or watching the late film on television.

De Troq' crouched over the wheel of the car as they moved past the alley ends. The headlights caught the stare of a cat, then it slunk down a passage and vanished. A solitary old man trudged home from a bar, his coat flapping in the breeze. There was nothing else.

'Where is she?' Pel kept saying. 'Where is she, De Troq'?'

'Hold on, Patron,' De Troq' begged. 'We'll find her. She'll be all right. I'm sure she will. Nosjean's probably picked her up again. Nosjean wouldn't let anything happen to her. I know he wouldn't. *I* wouldn't.' He spoke with such earnestness Pel glanced quickly at him.

'Besides,' De Troq' said, though this time he didn't sound so certain, 'Claudie can look after herself. Remember how she handled that Bigeaud type. Straight over her shoulder. All he got out of it was a set of strained balls. And she's still got my half-brick in her handbag.'

'It won't be much good,' Pel grated, 'if he grabs her from behind.'

'He won't, Patron! He won't!'

But Pel knew De Troq' was only trying to convince himself and was as scared as he was himself.

They turned into the Rue des Fosses. It was deserted, as if nobody wanted to share it with the darkness and the drizzle. A drunk emerged from an alleyway and leaned against the wall, staring dazedly as they passed.

'Patron!' It was Darcy's voice. 'We've picked her up! She's somewhere near the Rue de Panama. But she's been without cover for half an hour. Nosjean's on his way as fast as he can and we have cars closing in.'

De Troq' jammed his foot down on the accelerator and, as they swung into the Rue de Panama at last, he slowed and they rolled down the windows. The street was winding so they couldn't see along the whole of its length. But it seemed empty. There wasn't even a prowling cat. Like all the other places where the attacks had occurred there were empty houses and few lights.

The place was silent, then they heard the faint sound of a train down in the yards near the industrial area of the city, coming quite distinctly across the silent night. For a while they sat still, the car in the shadows with its lights off, listening.

'Can you hear her heels?'

The train sounded again then, faintly, over it, they heard a cry nearby.

'Down there!' Pel snapped.

They leapt from the car and started to run. For a moment, Pel thought they'd made a mistake then, in the shadows, he saw a girl fighting with a man. She had her hands to her throat and was bent backwards as he pulled at her. He was tall and heavy and his hands were behind her head.

De Troq' shouted and a white face turned towards them. As the man released the girl and swung away she slid to the pavement at his feet. De Troq' literally dived over her.

The running man staggered as De Troq' crashed into him to

send him reeling, then Pel had reached him, too. A foot kicked out at Pel's legs and he went to his knees, but he had his arms tightly round the man's ankles and De Troq' swung a fist. The struggling stopped just long enough for De Troq' to roll the man on to his face and wrench an arm up behind his back, his other hand on the back of his head, grinding his face hard down into the wet pavement.

As Pel struggled to his feet, Nosjean arrived at the gallop.

'Patron, is she all right?'

'No thanks to you if she is,' Pel snapped, knowing even as he spoke that it wasn't Nosjean's fault but that of the unreliable personal radios they carried. As he bent over her, Claudie stirred. 'Thank God,' he breathed.

The cord, a length of clothes line knotted at each end, was still across her throat, the free ends hanging down her back, and there was a livid weal along her neck. Otherwise, she wasn't much harmed, though she was shuddering from shock.

'Have we got him?' she said.

'We've got him.'

'Well, perhaps it was worth it. But I wouldn't like to go through that again.'

A police car rounded the corner and stopped near them with a squeal of brakes. Almost immediately another arrived from the opposite direction. 'Get her home, Nosjean,' Pel said. 'Fast as you can. And make sure she has someone to stay with her.'

As they pushed her into one of the cars and it set off towards the centre of the city, Pel turned towards De Troq'.

'Let's have a look at him,' he said.

De Troq' heaved the man to his feet, slammed handcuffs on his wrists, and pushed him against the wall. A pair of spectacles, crooked on his nose, caught the glint of light from the headlamps of De Troq's car.

'Schwendermann,' Pel said quietly.

Schwendermann seemed as shocked as Claudie, standing with his back against the wall, his face grimy from the dirt of the damp pavement. De Troq' fished in his pocket and produced a small flick knife. As he pressed the button in the handle, the blade shot out, glinting in the light.

'What was it for?' Pel snarled at the sagging figure by the wall. 'What was that mark you put on their faces?'

Schwendermann's mouth opened and he gagged on his words before he managed to get it out.

'*Hure,*' he said. '*Hure. Alles. Immer. Dieselbe.*'

'What's he say?' Pel demanded. 'You speak the language.'

'"Whore",' De Troq' said. '"All. Always the same." *Hure*. That's what he was carving on their faces, Patron. H. For *Hure*. It's the German word for "Whore" and the word Monique Letexier heard him say – the one she didn't understand. We forgot the Germans were in Paris in 1940, too.'

'His grandfather *and* his father,' Pel said in a wondering voice. 'Especially his father, who was a pastor in the church. No wonder it tipped the balance between sanity and insanity.'

'I wondered more than once if he was the one,' De Troq' admitted.

'Why in God's name didn't you say so?'

'Because there was nothing to back it up, Patron. I couldn't find anything any more than anyone else could. Not until tonight. The report from the Siegen Police just confirmed what I thought.'

Pel frowned. 'But *you* didn't see the report from Siegen.'

De Troq' expression was faintly smug. 'No, Patron. But I speak German fluently. The "Ah!", Patron. A strange "ah". It wasn't "ah"; it was "ach", as the Germans pronounce it. And that note he sent you was solid German construction from beginning to end. The inverted verb. The capital letters for the nouns. The spelling of "music" with a K. You'd kept that note to yourself. I hadn't seen it before tonight. As soon as I did it stuck out like a sore thumb.'

Schwendermann was gagging again and they began to push him towards the second police car.

'The girls,' he managed to say. 'They take off their clothes. There is no goodness. Never. Nowhere.'

'It must have been that party that started it off,' Pel said slowly as the car drew away, with Schwendermann huddled between two policemen in the rear seat. 'The one we heard about. Where Moussia spiked Marguerite's drink and she started stripping. That and his mother – his aunt, too! – always going on at him. They were constantly drumming the evil of loose women into him and he was taking revenge on them.'

De Troq' frowned. 'Probably a bit of sexual frustration, too, Patron. Resentment because none of the girls showed any interest in him.'

Pel drew a deep breath. 'He'd been in the habit of hanging about outside bars and places where prostitutes gathered. Marking them down. He even thought Bernadette Hamon was one because he saw her go into the Bar des Chevaux late at night. Perhaps also because he saw her enjoying herself at the Faculty Ball. She was only fooling about but he thought *she* was wicked, too.' He sighed. 'Name of God, he was clever! Doc Minet said they were. He knew the stairs creaked so he went out of the window. And he knew the way out because I expect Moussia had boasted about it. Moussia didn't think you could get back in but our friend found a way. With dark sheets. So they wouldn't be seen at night. And he was never out long because he knew the streets too well; he even had old maps showing every alley and short cut. With a batch of records on the record player he could be out for three hours or more and, with the sound of the floorboards creaking before he left and after he returned, no wonder Moussia thought he was up there all the time.'

'He was taking a big risk all the same, Patron.'

Pel drew a deep breath. 'Was he? He picked his times. The night he killed Marguerite de Wibaux there wasn't anyone to hear him on that lower roof because Annie Joulier had gone up to Aduraz's room at the other side of the house. And, after that, when she'd moved into the room with the other girls and Moussia had moved to the Rue Novembre 11, there wasn't *anyone at all* on his side of the house!'

The lights were still on when Pel turned his car into the drive and halted it outside the garage.

He was still shaken by the narrowness of Claudie's escape. But for something Didier Darras had said – just a few words that had clicked in his mind at the time – 'These foreigners. You can never trust them' – he might never have called for the foreign reports that had finally thrown up the attack on the prostitute so long before in Siegen. Perhaps there was more in his Society of Bigots idea than he'd realised.

As he entered the hall, the lights came on and he saw Madame on the stairs. She was just about to make some comment about the lateness of the hour when she saw his face and her expression filled with concern.

'I'm all right,' he said. 'Just tired.'

'Something happened. I can tell.'

'Yes. The Prowler almost got Claudie.' Her hand went to her throat and, as he reached out to touch her, she put her arms round him. 'But it's all right. We arrived in time. We've got him. It's over.'

If you have enjoyed this book and would like to receive details of other Walker mystery titles, please write to:

Mystery Editor
Walker and Company
720 Fifth Avenue
New York, NY 10019